"Darling—Marty." She touched a lipstick to her mouth. "How did that—uh—matter turn out in Chicago? I know you couldn't write me about it, and I was a little worried."

I blinked and came out of my trance. I said that certainly I remembered. "Well, that worked out pretty well, darling. The cops had a guy on ice for a couple of other mur—matters. He was indubitably guilty of them, understand? So they braced him on that one, and he obligingly confessed."

"Oh, how sweet of him! But of course, he had nothing to lose, did he?"

"Well, he was really a very nice guy," I said. "It's hard to repay a favor like that, but I did the little that I could. Always took him cigarettes or some little gift."

She turned her head for a moment, gave me a fondly tender smile. "That's like you, Marty! You were always so thoughtful."

"It was nothing," I said. "I was only glad that I could make his last days a little happier."

FIREWORKS:
THE LOST WRITINGS

Also by Jim Thompson

Now and On Earth • Heed the Thunder
Nothing More Than Murder
Cropper's Cabin • The Killer Inside Me
The Alcoholics • Bad Boy* • The Criminal
Recoil • Savage Night • A Swell-Looking Babe
The Ripoff* • The Golden Gizmo*
A Hell of a Woman • The Nothing Man*
Roughneck* • After Dark, My Sweet
Wild Town • The Getaway • The Transgressors
The Grifters • Pop. 1280 • Texas by the Tail
Ironside (novelization of TV series) • South of Heaven
The Undefeated (novelization of screenplay)
Nothing But a Man (novelization of screenplay)
Child of Rage • King Blood • The Kill-Off*

*Published by
THE MYSTERIOUS PRESS

FIRE-WORKS:
THE LOST WRITINGS

JIM THOMPSON
EDITED & INTRODUCED BY
ROBERT POLITO & MICHAEL McCAULEY

THE MYSTERIOUS PRESS

New York • London • Tokyo • Sweden

MYSTERIOUS PRESS EDITION

This Mysterious Press Edition is published by arrangement with Donald
I. Fine, Inc., 128 East 36th Street, New York, N.Y. 10016

Cover illustration by Stephen Peringer

![logo] Mysterious Press books are published in association with
Warner Books, Inc.
666 Fifth Avenue
New York, N.Y. 10103
![logo] A Warner Communications Company

Printed in the United States of America

First Mysterious Press Printing: August, 1989

10 9 8 7 6 5 4 3 2 1

Acknowledgments

This project could not have been completed without the generous assistance of Alberta Thompson, Pat Miller and Sharon Reed, or the steady guidance of Blaine Campbell; and to each of them we express our deepest gratitude.

We also wish to thank John Ferguson and *The Boston Phoenix*, Phyllis Jacobson, Rachel King, Tom and Margaret McCauley, Dennis McMillan, Maria Pagan, Sheri Saperstein, Wellesley College, and the staffs of the Library of Congress, Widener Library and the Special Collections Department of UCLA Library.

Kristine Harris and Sue Jacobson lived with *Fireworks* longer than they care to remember, enduring much with wit, forbearance and understanding; our debts can only begin to be repaid on the dedication page of this book.

Contents

Introduction
Jim Thompson: Lost Writer

by Robert Polito

A nd I hit her in the guts as hard as I could.
  My fist went back against her spine, and the flesh closed around it to the wrist. I jerked back on it, I had to jerk, and she flopped forward from the waist, like she was hinged.

Her hat fell off, and her head went clear down and touched the floor. And then she toppled over, completely over, like a kid turning a somersault. She lay on her back, eyes bulging, rolling her head from side to side . . .

There was a funny sound like she was trying to laugh.

And then I saw the puddle spreading out under her.

I sat down and tried to read the paper. I tried to keep my eyes on it. But the light wasn't very good, not good enough to read by, and she kept moving around. It looked like she couldn't lie still.

Once I felt something touch my boot, and I looked down and it was her hand. It was moving back and forth across the toe of my boot. It moved up along the ankle and the leg, and somehow I was afraid to move away. And then her fingers were at the top, clutching down inside; and I al-

1

*most couldn't move. I stood up and tried to jerk away, and
the fingers held on.*

I dragged her two-three feet before I could break away.

At the outermost edge of American literature, in a
swamp previously inhabited only by Hubert Selby and
William Burroughs, Jim Thompson awaits reclamation.
Buried under the shabbiest conventions of pulp fiction—
all but three of the twenty-nine books he published between
1942 and 1973 were paperback originals—and picking at
the banality with offhand brilliance, his novels pursue the
most debased imaginative materials as doggedly as do
Amy Stanton's fingers in Lou Ford's recital of her murder
in *The Killer Inside Me*. Reading one of them is like being
trapped in a bomb shelter with a chatty maniac who also
happens to be the air-raid warden.

Take Ford, the deputy sheriff of Central City. He's a
closeted intellectual who winds down with Krafft-Ebing's
Psychopathia Sexualis. His public life—his "act," as he
styles it—is a dumb show in which he mimics a stereoty-
pical Texas lawman. Cunningly "in character," he needles
incessantly, taking secret vengeances with hectoring plati-
tudes and cornball routines. "Polite, intelligent: guys like
that were my meat. . . . Striking at people that way is almost as good as the other, the real way." As Ford presses
on, his account proliferates with instances of "the real
way," in a deadpan spiral of horror—every killing de-
mands a sequel, each preceding from the sadism that in-
fects his sexual relationships. But for all the casual
savagery here (the beatings, the shotguns fired into open
mouths, the bodies that smash like pumpkins—"Hard, then
everything giving away at once"), the central grotesquery
in *The Killer Inside Me* is Lou Ford's crafty voice. With
his ingratiating mix of good cheer and hard-boiled idioms,
alternatingly swaggering and shrinking but always self-re-
garding and observant, Ford cakewalks through his story
like a shrewd con man. As he juggles his double life, put-

ting on himself and the reader as he'd earlier toyed with his victims and laughed at his pursuers, you never entirely disbelieve him—even though it's certain he's given himself away, and likely that he's a callous killer posing as a psychopath. Neither do you ever wholly part company with Thompson's rock-ribbed sympathy for Ford, even after the inevitable occurs—"All I can do is wait until I split"—and, in one of the strangest and ugliest endings in fiction, he and his world explodes in our faces.

Thompson's boldest writing about criminals—*The Killer Inside Me*, *Pop. 1280*, *A Hell of a Woman*, *The Kill-Off*, *Savage Night*, *The Getaway*, *The Grifters*, and *After Dark, My Sweet*—is fueled by a lurid intelligence that bulldozes distinctions between sensational and serious culture. Like Weegee's photographs of spectacles and disasters, or Andy Warhol's canvases of car wrecks, race riots, and electric chairs, his novels revel in their own slippery, contradictory status. Too persistent and obsessive to be cast off as kitsch or camp, they have a sour comedy that mocks grim pretension. As a result, Thompson's novels are more plausible and sassier than either nonfiction chronicles of the mass murderers his monsters spookily parallel (the wise-cracking cannibal Ed Gein or Ted Bundy, the smooth, boy-next-door mutant) or such celebrated descents into psychopathology as Cormac McCarthy's *Child of God* and Norman Mailer's *The Executioner's Song*.

Although he worked in a variety of pop and pulp genres —Westerns (*Wild Town* and *The Transgressors*), rural soap operas in the manner of Erskine Caldwell (*Cropper's Cabin*), melodramatic thrillers (*The Golden Gizmo*), snappy, anecdotal autobiographies (*Bad Boy* and *Roughneck*), historical fiction (*South of Heaven*), and novelizations (at least two of which, *Nothing But a Man* and *Ironside*, offer passages as splenetic as his original novels)—Thompson's most characteristic performances mark him as the blackest beast of what is coming to be known as American *serie noir*. His books are unimaginable without the precedent of the crime writers who published in the *Black Mask* of the '20s and '30s. The voyeuristic sadism that distinguishes the sleuthing of Race Williams in Carrol John Daly's stories, the surreal, stylizied violence in Paul Cain's *Fast One*—these anticipate the cruel habits of his heroes. The laconic, detached rhythms and acrid wit of Hammett and Chandler—not to mention their more squalid settings (Poisonville in *Red Harvest*, or the sun-and-hang-over-blinded LA of *The Long Goodbye*)—also have obvious analogies in Thompson, though the focus of those better-known writers is always on the detective. Closer in spirit is Horace McCoy's first-person account of a raging gangster, *Kiss Tomorrow Goodbye*. And closer still (though he scorned the *Black Mask* crowd) are the compact masterpieces of James M. Cain, *The Postman Always Rings Twice* and *Double Indemnity*, especially their headlong narration and bitches' brew of doom and compulsion.

Placing Thompson in this sequence is a complicated matter. It's true that nowhere in his novels does Thompson allude to a world beyond that of the pulps. But he detonates the cliches of the tradition he's inherited—not (as an important writer might be expected to do) by seeking to transcend them, but rather by sinking into them so deeply that they are turned on their heads. Thus the string-of-firecracker witticisms that in Hammett or Chandler are emblems of the detective hero's masterly ease and stoicism become for Thompson's characters evidence of mental imbalance. Not only are the jokes more bitter and twisted (in *A Hell of a Woman* Dolly Dillon boasts, "some of the deals I've worked were as raw as a tack-factory whore"), but often they possess a lunatic literalness (Lou Ford titillates the unsuspecting fiancé of a woman he's just left in a bloody heap by wisecracking, "I'd bet money that she's all stretched out waiting for you").

Similarly, the "neutral" style that the crime writers learned from Hemingway—which lives on the surface in tight, worked-over language, so that every perception is immediate and concrete, and character is reduced to external reaction—here betokens rampant schizophrenia. Like Lou Ford (who in the end is probing his own motives, as though he were watching a movie—he even confesses, a la Bundy, to a lawyer "hypothetically"), Sheriff Nick Corey in *Pop. 1280* slowly mutates from a servile, bantering lout into a demonic schizo. His tired, self-loathing babble, with its seemingly random religious wrinkles, after a few giddy turns of the screw tightens into the conviction that he's the scourge of God. Corey is chillingly distanced from the consequences of his mission, which among other bits of butchery includes tricking one of his girlfriends into shooting his wife. Eventually his pity becomes his terror, just as he emerges as Judas to his own Christ ("The fella that gets betrayed and the one that does the betrayin' all in one man!").

Thompson's most formally dazzling staging of these issues is *A Hell of a Woman*. Dolly Dillon, ostensibly not a psycho but an avaricious blockhead with a few kinks (violence and misogyny), precipitously unravels; and as he dissolves so does his narrative. First he begins to talk to himself, in increasingly disembodied and sniveling rages, casting long episodes in the second person. Then abruptly the novel splinters, and Dillon confronts us with whole chapters in an alternative pulp mode—part Horatio Alger, part frothing nonsense—entitled "Through Thick and Thin: The True Story of a Man's Fight Against High Odds and Low Women," which breezily whitewashes his guilt and blunders. In the final pages he rends utterly, and the book has two conclusions in alternating lines of roman and italic type, each as hideous and rank as the other.

Where Thompson does not exaggerate the tough-guy voice of the noir authors, stretching their stagy, willed cool until the mask cracks, he nudges it toward numbness, automatism, walking death. Dolly Dillon says of himself, "I was like a mechanical man with the batteries run down"; Nick Corey suggests more generally, "So ain't we all relatively inanimate, George?" Indeed, the logic of the endings to *The Killer Inside Me*, and *A Hell of a Woman* requires that we believe that the narrators have been speaking from the grave. This might be dismissed as an awkwardness of the genre (in McCoy's *Kiss Tomorrow Goodbye*, Ralph Cotter describes his own fatal shooting) were not Thompson's characters so dubious about their vital signs. In *Nothing More Than Murder* Joe Wilmot insists, "They can't hang me. I'm already dead. I've been dead a long time." To Nick Corey the houses of Pottsville are indistinguishable from caskets: "Just pine-board walls locking in emptiness." An aptly clipped fable Tom Carver coughs up to a prison doctor in *Cropper's Cabin* circles the netherworld these zombies drift through:

It's—well, it's kind of like this, doc. Like a story I read one time about a man. He got to where he couldn't see, not really see, you know. He had eyes, but somehow they didn't tell his mind anything. And his ears were the same way. And his mouth. Somehow he couldn't find any words to come out of it; and he couldn't taste anything. And all over his body, doc, he was kind of numb. He couldn't feel anything. And he knew there was something wrong—he knew what was wrong. But there wasn't a thing he could do about it, him or anyone else. Not a thing, and it was a waste of time to try. Because he was dead.

In *The Getaway* this drift is nailed down to a tangible locale when, in perhaps Thompson's nerviest conceit, a cross-country escape to Mexico culminates in a three-stage descent into Hell. More audacious versions of Lou Ford's sly jokes, each sequence turns on tidy, gruesome objectifications of crime-novel commonplaces. Cornered after botching a routine bank heist, Doc McCoy and his wife hole up, as it were, in a pair of coffin-sized underwater caves for forty-eight hours—and for nine pages as fitfully claustrophobic as anything in Beckett. Next they're forced to hide in a room dug out of a mound of dung (everything they've touched having turned to shit); naked, wiping away sweat with their soiled clothes, they wait for the heat to go

off. Then comes the final getaway to the dominion of El
Rey and the "happy decent life" Thompson's people are
always killing for, here a Swiftian paradise of eternal
blankness: "You tell yourself it is a bad dream. You tell
yourself you have died—you, not the others—and have
waked up in hell. But you know better. You know better.
There is an end to dreams and there is no end to this. And
when people die they are dead—as who should know better than you? . . . They call him the devil, and accuse him
of thinking he is God. And El Rey will nod to either
charge. 'But is there a difference, senor? Where the difference between punishment and reward when one gets only
what he asks for?' "

Even the feral desire and the spider-and-the-fly sex that,
especially in Cain, triggers madness and destruction are
flattened out by Thompson into hollow, smirking carica-
tures of passion. Although his misogynists typically rant
that the traps they find themselves in were baited by raven-
ous, castrating vixens, never has the convention of the
deadly woman seemed less femme and more purely fatale
—or more gratuitous. Whereas Walter Huff in *Double Indemnity* and Frank Chambers in *The Postman Always
Rings Twice* lay out their obsessions like big cats pacing
off the dimensions of their cages, the unfortunates in
Thompson's novels aren't quite sure what's pulling them
down. As Dolly Dillon writes of his siren, "And it wasn't a
pretty picture, by any means; she was about as far from
being a raving beauty as I was. But something about it kind
of got me. I tripped over a crack, and almost went sprawling." Or Joe Wilmot: "If there was ever a woman you
wouldn't look at twice she was it . . . She looked like a sack
of bran that couldn't decide which way it was going to
fall . . . And then I was kissing her like I'd been waiting all
my life to do just that." And in their creeping delusions
they are always mixing up the women in their lives. "Yeah,
it must have been Doris—or was it Ellen?" slurs Dillon.
"Three goddamned tramps in a row . . . or maybe it was
four or five, but it doesn't matter. It was like they were all

the same person." Actual sex is infrequent, and approached as one might the removal of a tick—disagreeable, if necessary, and inseparable from acts of extinction.

Thompson's fiction is as slithery and treacherous as any of his cheerful killers. With so much in motion—the spinning shards of *noir* formulas, the furtive, often insane narrators—there's no comfortable place to sit. Moreover, Thompson never directs his stories toward retribution or redemption. His variations on familiar *Black Mask* routines serve the same function as his characters' homy jests and impersonations; he trots them out to camouflage what Lou Ford calls "the sickness." And the underlying ooze and slime is so pervasive that this disease seems as basic to the creation of the universe as hydrogen. Remarkably, their nods to hard-boiled conventions do not so much toughen Thompson's novels as humanize them—they're all we have to hang onto in the ferocious downdraft. All else is a wasted, sucking nihilism that's as unsparing as the most lacerating rock and roll—The Velvet Underground's "Sister Ray," say, or "White Light/White Heat"—and as final as a snuff film.

Robert Polito
New York City, 1989

Prologue

A Road and a Memory

I can still see that homely, grass-grown trail
   That clung so closely to the shambling fence:
Sand-swept, ruts filled with every gale;
   A helpless prey to all the elements.
A shower would make those soft black tracks a mire
   That sucked at wagon wheels and made the horses sweat;
The sun would turn them into flinty fire
   That burnt and tore each unshod foot they met.
In winter, with the grass and sand-burs dead,
   I walked the bellying center of the trail
And filled the gopher holes that might have led
   To broken legs when moon and stars should fail.

Each morning found me plodding down that road to school.
   The evening sun was low on my return.
And every roadward thing construed itself into a tool
   To make my hot resentment deeper burn.
Those tortuous ruts were like two treacherous bars
   So spaced to show an eye-deceiving gape

9

So while one ever struggled for the stars
   They hugged too close for actual escape.

Escape: tell me the meaning of the word:
   Produce the man who's touched a star, for me.
Escape is something for a bird;
   A star is good to hang upon a tree.
Not long, however, lags the flesh behind the mind.
   I left the road, the ruts, the holes, the dust.
And sought a symbol of another kind
   To mark reward for labor, right and just.
. . . and twenty years have trickled through my hand.
   The hand is soft; it's white, preserved and clean.
As unlined, vacant as the wind-brushed sand;
   As meaningless, as—mean.
The road? Why yes, the road is there.
   And now it seems the road will always be;
Not white, not soft, not fair,
   But hard and straight as strange eternity.

Exactly What Happened

Seated on the bed in his sleazy hotel room, Neil Keller allowed himself another short drink from the whiskey bottle and again picked up the hammer. It was a tiny instrument, with a head little larger than the head of a match. Keller raised it to his mouth, pushed back his upper lip with a finger, and gave one of his front teeth a firm tap.

The tooth moved under the blow. Wincing, Keller gave it a few more taps, then shifted to another tooth. It moved also—they were both loosening up nicely. Keller worked on them slowly but steadily, stopping only for an occasional painkilling drink.

Relatively speaking, there was not a great deal of pain —nothing at all compared with what it had been a month ago. It had been real hell then, back when he had begun the job of loosening two perfectly sound teeth—getting them to the point where they could be finally removed with only one more hour's steady effort.

Now, however, the agony was over, and he had nothing more unpleasant to look forward to than killing Jake Goss. One-Eyed Jake with the missing teeth, the mushy voice, the mole on his right cheek—a guy with a face you could never forget.

Jake had been pretty nice to Keller. Jake had kind of taken a fancy to him when Keller first holed up in this fleabag, and it was through Jake's recommendation that he'd got his job as night janitor in the Wexler Building—Jake was the night watchman.

He was stupid and boastful, this Jake Goss—a guy that had to spread around everything he knew. Still, he'd been pretty nice, so Keller sort of hated to kill him. And yet he couldn't help grinning a little when he thought about it.

It was so damned funny, you see. Really a riot. Keller was going to kill Jake, but it was Jake who would be tagged for murder! The murder of Neil Keller. He, Keller, would kill Jake and knock over Old Man Wexler for a hundred grand or better. But the cops—ha, ha—the cops would be looking for Jake.

Chuckling, Keller turned sideways on the bed and glanced down at the morning newspaper. It was open at the realty columns, where a story in small type announced the transfer by Otto J. Wexler of a certain piece of real estate —"assessed valuation $50,000."

Being assessed at $50,000, it would have sold for at least twice that much. Jake Goss had loftily explained this obvious fact to him one morning, while pointing out a similar item in the newspaper.

"See that the old man sold a house yesterday for ten thousand," he had said. "That means he's got maybe twenty grand in his safe tonight."

"Here you mean?" Keller had said, incredulously. "You mean he keeps that kind of dough up in his office—his apartment?"

"Yep. Getting his money out of real estate as fast as he can, and the kind of deals he's putting it into—not really illegal, y'know, but just a little shady—stuff that the banks won't touch, and with the kind of interest they can't charge."

Wexler was in the loan shark business in a big way, Jake explained, and he was expanding rapidly. "I know, see?" he went on, his one eye gleaming pridefully. "Me and

Wexler are like that. Why, there ain't a morning passes that I don't drop in on him for a cuppa coffee. The old guy don't trust most people, so I guess he gets pretty lonesome. But—"

"Yeah, yeah, sure," Keller had cut in impatiently. "You have coffee with him, and he trusts you. But he wouldn't be sucker enough to keep any big dough *here*. He's kidding you about that."

"The hell he is! You mean, he'd be afraid of getting robbed? How's anyone going to rob him?"

Keller had hesitated. How? Well, now that he stopped to think about it, a robbery didn't look so simple. The old man's office-apartment was thoroughly burglar-alarmed. The building's doors were locked at night, and no one could get in or out unless Jake let them. Of course, one of the tenants could stick a gun in Jake's ribs, or—

Keller mentioned this possibility to the one-eyed man. Jake shook his head.

"So suppose some holdup artist did get in here. Suppose he got past them burglar alarms, and made the old man come across. What good would it do him? This building is right down in the middle of town. There's cops going by all night long. A guy wouldn't get ten feet from the door before they put the cuffs on him."

"Yeah," Keller nodded thoughtfully. "I guess that's right, isn't it?"

"Now, you or me," Jake said. "Suppose you or me tried to rob Wexler. He'd open the door for us, sure, so that would take care of one hurdle. And we wouldn't have any trouble getting out of the building or any trouble with the cops. But how far would we get? The robbery would be discovered in a few hours. They'd know that we did it, just because we've gone, and they'd have our descriptions down pat. Which is just the same as saying they'd have us cold. Oh, maybe we could take it on the lam for a little while, but sooner or later—"

"I guess you're right," Keller had nodded. "It just couldn't be done, Jake."

And he had laughed silently, contemptuously, as he spoke . . .

The two front teeth were out now. Keller stood in front of the lavatory mirror, snapping a black patch over one eye, applying an artgum mole to one cheek, stippling freckles across his nose, and thickening his brows with color pencils.

He put on his brown uniform cap. He slumped his shoulders, the way Jake slumped his. Then—well, nothing then. That was all there was to it. Except for the extraction of the teeth, the entire transformation had taken only a few minutes, yet it had made him into another man.

Naturally, he couldn't keep up the masquerade indefinitely. Given enough time, someone was bound to see through it. But no one would be given that much time. Not Wexler, after he'd been slugged and tied up. Not the cops, as Keller left the building.

Thus, they would swear that he was Jake, that it was Jake who had pulled the robbery and brazenly walked away with the loot.

They would have no suspicions—nor the opportunity to prove them—that he might not be Jake.

Keller studied his reflection in the mirror, mouthing silent words, grimacing experimentally. Those teeth—he would get the gaps filled later on. Meanwhile, as long as he was careful about smiling and talking, no one would even know that two teeth were missing.

He removed the eyepatch and mole, then scrubbed his face thoroughly. Wrapping the patch and color pencils in a handkerchief, he stuffed them into his pocket and left the hotel.

At the railroad station he retrieved a large briefcase from a rental locker. Proceeding to the men's room, he gave the attendant fifty cents and was admitted to a dressing cubicle. Some twenty minutes later he emerged, smartly attired, his work clothes stuffed into the briefcase, and taxied to a nearby hotel.

He had registered there several times before to establish his identity—or, rather, his false identity. So the doorman and bellboy greeted him as Mr. Jennings, and the clerk assured him that they were delighted to have Mr. Jennings back as a guest again.

"Going to have you with us for a while, sir?" he inquired, as he assigned a room to Keller. "Or is this another one of your flying trips?"

"Looks like a real quickie this time," Keller said briskly. "I have to close a deal tonight and head back to Chicago in the morning. Just hope I can squeeze in a few hours' sleep."

"Well, I hope so, too." The clerk frowned with professional warmth. "You drive yourself too hard, Mr. Jennings."

Arriving at his room, Keller dismissed the bellboy with a generous tip and received generous thanks in return. Then, as the youth departed beaming, Keller's own smile faded and he was filled with an uneasy sense of depression. It was a familiar feeling—one he experienced every time he came to this hotel.

Probably, he supposed, it derived from the way he was made welcome here, from the establishment's friendliness toward him. Its bought-and-paid-for, good-business kind of friendliness. For at such times it was borne home to him that he had never exactly been laved in the warmth of real friendship. Axiomatically, it was impossible.

Genuine friendship was a sharing arrangement. You knew a man's problems, his secret hopes and aspirations, and he knew yours. And you sympathized with and wished the best for one another.

That was real friendship—always a matter of give-and-take. So if you were strictly a taker, as Keller was, it obviously wasn't for him. He couldn't let a man know too much about him. Not only that, but he couldn't let himself know very much about the other man. If he did, you see, he might weaken. He might get to feel sorry for the man to the extent of letting him slip away.

Take Jake Goss, now—one-eyed, gap-toothed Jake. What was his background? Did he have a wife somewhere, or a sweetheart? How had he lost his eye and those teeth? Was his dullness, his absorption with gossip, only a protective reaction to lifelong failure? Was it his way of shedding the blame for his lack of achievement?

Jake was still a young man—little older, at least, than Keller. Yet he seemed quite content to go on forever in a cheap, monotonous, dead-end job.

Why? How could he have so little ambition? What had imprinted him so indelibly with the stamp of stupidity? What made the guy tick?

Sprawled on the bed, Keller let his eyes drift shut, dismissing the many questions.

He didn't know any of the answers—he didn't want to know them. For the sake of his future comfort and his present plans, it was better to leave Jake as he was—a human question-mark. A human zero who was soon to be erased.

Keller slept a few hours. Then, carrying his briefcase, he hurried out of the hotel and returned to the railroad station.

In the men's room he changed back into his work uniform. His business suit went into the briefcase, which he again placed in the locker. The suit would be rumpled, of course, but that was all right. When he went back to the hotel in the morning, he would look about as he should— as a man would look who had been up all night at an important conference.

Keller ate supper, then went to the Wexler Building. Mindful of his missing teeth, he greeted Jake cautiously, just a little nervously. But the one-eyed man obviously didn't notice. He was grumpy, in a bad mood about something or other. He didn't want to talk or be talked to, and he made it apparent.

That suited Keller perfectly, of course. Loading his pails and mops onto one of the elevators, he ascended to the top floor of the building and began his nightly work.

The hours passed slowly. At three in the morning he

took over Jake's duties while Jake went out to eat. And at 3:30, on Jake's return, he himself went out for half an hour.

When he came back to the building Jake admitted him surlily, still grumpily silent. And Keller lowered his elevator to the basement.

The trip was routine at this hour of the morning. The incinerator, burdened with the night's accumulation of waste, was frequently in need of adjusting. So Keller adjusted it, opening its dampers to their widest. He listened to the responding roar of the flames and nodded with grim satisfaction:

That would take care of Jake—that and a few heavy blows from a steel poker. Between the two things, the poker and the fire, Jake would lose his one-eyed, missing-toothed identity. In effect, Jake would become Neil Keller.

Keller took out his wallet and stripped it of money. Then, with its identification cards intact, he tossed it into a dark corner and returned to the elevator.

Old man Wexler was an early riser. He was always up by six or before. At 6:30—never earlier—Jake Goss stopped by to share a cup of coffee with him. So at five minutes before six . . .

Keller parked the elevator on the second floor and took the make-up and eyepatch from his pocket. Working with practiced skill, he assumed the appearance of Jake Goss. He used extra care this morning, and the transformation was not merely good but was near-perfect—indeed, so perfect that even he was startled.

He stared at himself in the elevator mirror, fascinated by Jake's face, even a little frightened by it, actually believing—as the cops and Wexler were certain to—that he *was* Jake Goss.

It was 6:15 when he left the elevator and took to the stairs. At 6:20, having ascended two flights, he stood before the door of Wexler's apartment-office, sniffing the aroma of freshly brewed coffee, making one last swift check-through of his plans.

> *Let's see,* he thought; *I give the old man a couple of medium-good pokes, just enough to make him behave without knocking him out. Then, as soon as he opens the safe, I bind and gag him, put him in the bedroom, and come back by the door to wait for Jake. And when Jake shows up at 6:30—*

But there was no use in going through that again. Besides, there wasn't time. Killer raised his hand and knocked.

The door opened abruptly.

Keller said, "Okay, Wexler! This is a—"

And that was all he said.

For suddenly his vocal cords, his face, his entire body seemed paralyzed. And he could only stand there helplessly and stare.

Not at Wexler, but at Keller. Yes, at Keller!

He, Neil Keller, was staring at Neil Keller.

Then something crashed down on his skull, and when he recovered consciousness he was in the basement. And the other Keller was standing over him, a heavy steel poker in his hands.

He didn't live very long after that—not long enough to solve the simple riddle of the other Keller. And, certainly, it was a simple enough riddle.

After all, if facial blemishes can be put *on* with makeup, they can be *concealed* with make-up—right? And if teeth can be *removed* they can also be put *in*—correct? And a glass eye is rather easily purchased—right?

Or, getting down to cases, if you can easily assume the appearance of another man, why can't he just as easily assume yours?

Well, you see how it was. But Neil Keller didn't. He didn't have the time.

In his last brief moments all he saw was himself. The one man he had not guarded against. The one man every man faces sooner or later. All he saw was that he was about to be murdered by himself—which, in a sense, was exactly what happened.

The Threesome
in Four-C

There they go again," I said. "Two o'clock in the morning, and they're up there running a footrace."

"Please, darling..." Ellen's voice shook as she tried to pull me back down in the bed. "Don't start anything. I—I just can't take any more!"

"Me start something?" I said. "All I'm trying to do is get some sleep. Just listen to that, will you? They'll be coming through the ceiling in a minute!"

"I'm listening," Ellen said dully. "I've listened."

"Do you know what I think? I think it's the same outfit that was in the last place. They had the apartment next to us there, and now they're up above."

"Yeah," said Ellen. "Oh sure. That's all they have to do, just follow us around."

"Well, it sounds like them. The same woman and her two little kids. They had the—"

"All right! And the next place we go to they'll move right in with us!" She laughed hysterically. "Now, lie down, will you? Oh, God, darling, please lie down and go to sleep!"

"How can I?" I said. "I'm going to call the manager."

"No! You mustn't! You know what—you know there's

nothing he can do about it. He's told you and I've told you that—"

"He'd better do something about it," I said. "He'll do something after I get through talking to him."

"Don't!" She snatched the phone out of my hands. "I'll call, darling. You go take a couple of sleeping pills."

"Well, all right," I said. "But be sure you make it strong."

"I will. Now, please go take the pills," she said, and her voice followed me as I started for the kitchen:

"Mr. Dorrance? This is Mrs. Clinton in Apartment Three-C...That's right, Three-C...I'm sorry to disturb you, but you simply must make the people above us quiet down...Yes, they are. They most certainly are...I see. You'll have to dress, and it'll take you a little while. But just as soon as you can...Thank you very much, Mr. Dorrance."

"Well?" I said, as she entered the kitchen. "What did he say?"

"He'll take care of it, just as soon as he can. Did you take the pills, darling?"

"I took them," I shrugged. "Not that they'll do any good. Nothing does any good when that racket starts."

"They will if you give them a chance. Now, come on back to bed, and by the time Mr. Dorrance—"

"What's the matter with that woman, anyway?" I said. "If she wants to romp with her children why doesn't she do it in the daytime?"

"Please, darling..."

"She isn't being kind to them," I said. "I like children, myself. You know how fond I am of them, Ellen. Why, if anything ever happened to a child of mine, I'd—I'd... You didn't call Dorrance, did you, Ellen? You just pretended to."

"All right," she said harshly. "I didn't. And you're not going to either! If you don't care anything about yourself, you can think of me."

"I'm going to stop that noise," I said. "I'm going to get some sleep. Everyone's entitled to a little sleep."

"You'll get some, all right! How long do you think you can get away with this stuff? Don't you realize that we were lucky to get out of the last place without—*No! You can't!*"

"Why not?" I hefted the broom. "I'm just standing up for my rights, Ellen. That's all."

"Sure, and you're a citizen, aren't you? A darned well-known citizen! So well-known that you have to disguise yourself with a mustache and dyed hair, and—*No!*"

"Quiet!" I yelled, and I pounded the ceiling with the broom. "Stop it, stop it, stop it!" And I ran from room to room, pounding. "Quiet! Stop it! I c-can't take any more! I—I—Ellen—" I paused in the living room, breathing hard, listening. "I believe that did it, Ellen."

"Yes," she said. "That did it."

"What happened?" I said. "When did you get dressed? How long was I . . . ?"

"Goodbye," she said, opening the door. "Goodbye, period."

"Paragraph," said one of the two men who walked in. "What's going on up here?"

"I'd like to know myself," I said, looking past them to address Dorrance. "What's the meaning of this? Who are these men?"

"I've warned you," Dorrance said. "I've told you and told you that—"

"Save it." The two men studied me, narrow-eyed. "What's your name, mister?"

"Clinton. Now—"

"Huh-uh. Where's your wife?"

"My wife? Why, this is my wife right here."

"Maybe. Must think a lot of her, all right. But we're talking about the other one."

"Other one?" I said. "I have no other wife."

"Uh-huh. And you don't have two kids either, do you? Not any more, you don't."

"I—I just don't understand," I said. "I'm really very fond of children. I hated to complain, but the noise has been going on night after night—right above us, you know, in Apartment Four-C; a woman and two youngsters —and I couldn't get any rest and . . . You see how it was, don't you? I didn't mean to cause any disturbance, but it's gone on and on—always, wherever we move to, there's the same woman and her children. And . . ."

"They won't bother you much longer. Come on. You too, sister."

"Come on?" I said. "Where? Why?"

"You're under arrest. Murder. Triple murder."

"N-no!" I said. "You're making a mistake. I'm just a little nervous and excited, and—Tell them, Dorrance! Tell them what I've been through. If it wasn't for that family up in Four-C—"

"I told them," Dorrance said wearily. "I told you. Apartment Four-C is vacant."

Thompson readers will recognize the setting and a key plot device from this 1946 true crime story, since Jim borrowed them for his first crime novel, 1948's *Nothing More Than Murder*.

The Dark Stair

by County Evidence Officer Chester L. Stacey, La Tumara, Texas

Technical Sergeant Raymond P. Clinton rose reluctantly from his seat in the Palace Theatre. The last show of the evening was over. It was the night of September 18, 1944; and in another hour, at midnight, his twenty-four-hour pass would expire.

Yawning, he went up the aisle, almost the last of the few patrons of the late show. He reached the lobby, but with his hand on the exit door he hesitated. It was a two-mile walk from the city of La Tumara, seat of the county of the same name, to the airbase. After a moment's reflection, he turned away from the door and went down the steps that led to the basement lounges.

A few feet down, a dimly burning red light cast a weak glow over a landing from which accessory stairways branched off at right angles. Sergeant Clinton took the stairway to the left to the men's lounge. Halfway down, the steps again angled sharply. The soldier found himself in almost absolute darkness. Fumbling in his pocket, he drew out a match and struck the head with his thumbnail.

"These movie people certainly must be hard up," he

grumbled to himself. "Can't even afford to have a light on. It's a wonder someone doesn't fall down and break——"

His mutterings died in a gasp of horror. The match flared and grew dim. The flame touched his fingers, and he did not know it. The light flickered and disappeared. He was in the dark again.

He snapped out of his momentary paralysis, started backing up the stairs, then turned and hurled himself up them three at a time.

From her parked car in front of the Palace, Mrs. L. C. Farrell, wife of the owner of the theatre, saw Clinton dash out and look anxiously up and down the street. Rolling down the window, she called to him:

"Something wrong, Sergeant?"

Gratefully, he hastened out to the curb. "There's a dead man in there!" he exclaimed. "He's down at the foot of the stairs to the restroom! I've been looking for someone to——"

"A dead man?" interrupted Mrs. Farrell. "Are you sure?"

"Well, I——He looks like——"

"Probably some drunk who decided to take a nap," said Mrs. Farrell. "They will do that, now and then."

Smiling deprecatingly, she opened the door of the car. Not for nothing had she been the wife of a showman for almost ten years. She rebelled, instinctively, against anything that might alarm a squeamish and fanciful public.

"My husband owns this theatre," she explained. "I'll run in and tell him about it."

"He's not in there. There's no one in there," said Clinton flatly. "And I'm pretty sure that man is——"

"Oh, well, he's probably up in the projection booth, then."

Crossing the walk to the now unoccupied cashier's cage, she opened the door and turned on the light. There was a short ladder affixed to the back wall. She climbed up it a couple of rungs, and tapped on a trap door in the ceiling.

The door opened and Lem Skidmore, the projectionist, looked down at her.

"Is my husband up there, Lem?"

Skidmore shook his head. "He looked in at ten-fifty, just before I put the last reel on. Haven't seen him since then."

"Well, I wonder where he could be?"

Skidmore muttered something under his breath. He slammed the door shut.

Mrs. Farrell stepped down from the ladder, coloring. The projectionist was something of an institution around La Tumara. Back in the days of silent pictures, long before the Palace had been built, he had owned and operated a theatre called the Rex. After the Palace had opened, and the Rex had failed, he had gone to work for Farrell.

Since the loss of his business, he had drawn more and more into himself, deliberately discouraging friendships. Tales of his sourness and bad temper were numerous about the town. But this was the first time he had ever been openly rude to Mrs. Farrell.

She closed the door of the cashier's booth, then turned again to Sergeant Clinton.

"Mr. Farrell must still be inside," she said. "Will you go in with me? I won't keep you but a moment or two longer."

"He's not inside, lady," Clinton replied emphatically.

"But he must be. You must have seen him. He was wearing a black and white checked sports jacket and gray trousers, and—What's the matter?"

Sergeant Clinton gulped.

"L-lady," he stammered. "You'd better sit down some place."

"Sit down? What for?"

"Because that dead—that man I saw—that's the way he's dressed."

Deputy Sheriff Joe Todd, who was in the Elite Cafe across the street from the theatre, was the first officer to reach the scene of the tragedy. He immediately summoned our county physician, Dr. E. E. Hutchinson, then called Sheriff Isaac R. Carter and me from the lodge meeting we were attending.

Carter and I arrived to find that the body had been moved up into the lobby. Hutchinson had already pronounced Farrell dead—by strangulation.

Deputy Todd looked at the big, gray-haired Sheriff apologetically. "I didn't want to move the body," he explained, "but Doc thought—"

"I thought there might be chance for artificial respiration," interrupted Hutchinson. "Unfortunately, I wasn't quite soon enough. A few minutes earlier I might have swung it."

"How did it happen, Joe?"

"Well, it was a blamed queer thing." Todd scratched his head. "I reckon I'd better show you."

The lights had been turned on over the basement stairs again. The deputy led the way down them to the door of the men's lounge, and then knelt on the landing.

"You see, there's a space here of about four feet between the foot of the stairs and the door," he pointed out. "And the door opens outward. Farrell was lying with his head and neck across the threshold, and the weight of his body was holding the door shut, strangling him."

"The stairs were dark, you say?" Carter inquired.

"Yes. Lem Skidmore tells me that Farrell had him cut the lights off every night at ten-thirty. He wanted to discourage people from coming down here late. It took him just that much longer to close up, and some of these night owls were pretty hard on fixtures and equipment.

"Farrell himself, of course, could make his rounds about as well in the dark as he could in the light. And there's a wall switch inside the lounge in case someone did want to use it."

There was a heavy silence as Todd stood up, brushing at his knees. Then Hutchinson laughed shortly.

"I imagine we're all thinking the same thing, Sheriff Ike. This merely looks like an accident. The appearances don't stand up under analysis. There's nothing on these stairs for a man to trip or slip on. The door has an automatic closing device on it; it wouldn't have been standing open for Farrell to thrust his neck through so conveniently. Finally, he wouldn't have remained there to strangle unless he was unconscious."

Carter nodded agreement to these conclusions. "Go on, Doc."

"Well, he was stunned, all right. He's got a lump over his left temple, and it didn't come from falling. Looks as if he had been blackjacked."

The sheriff turned to Deputy Todd. "Are all the employees gone, Joe?"

"Yes. Little Tommy Marble, the youngster who takes tickets, leaves at ten-thirty. Mrs. Converse, the cashier, leaves a few minutes later. She was over in the Elite Cafe having some coffee when we heard about this. I had her drive Mrs. Farrell home."

"What about Lem Skidmore?"

"I sent him home, too. He was all broken up when he heard about Farrell."

"Lem broken up about Farrell?" Carter could not conceal his surprise.

"He certainly seemed to be," the deputy said.

Sergeant Clinton, who had remained on the scene at Todd's request, was becoming an increasingly anxious witness to the proceedings.

"Can I go now, Sheriff?" he asked nervously. "I've told Mr. Todd all I know, and I'm going to be over leave in about ten minutes."

Carter gave him a reassuring smile. "In about five minutes you'll be back at your post, Sergeant. Mr. Stacey and I will drive you out. Come along, Chet."

Leaving Joe and Doc to supervise the removal of the body, Sheriff Ike and I drove Clinton to his post. The soldier seemed greatly upset by the showman's death.

He was inclined to blame himself for not having rescued Farrell.

"I knew he wasn't just some drunk," he insisted. "I

shouldn't have ever allowed her—Mrs. Farrell—to delay me. I'd have moved him myself, but the Army teaches us to be careful about that sort of thing."

"You did all you could," said Carter soothingly.

"No, I didn't. I knew the man was dead or nearly so; and yet I wasted five minutes arguing with her and waiting while she talked to the projectionist."

The sheriff started to reply, but for some reason changed his mind. We said goodnight to the sergeant and drove back to town.

Lights were still burning in the Farrell home at 1153 East Elm Street, so Carter turned into the driveway. Mrs. Elizabeth Converse, attractive young cashier of the Palace Theatre, answered the door. Stunned by the news that the "accident" had been murder, she controlled herself with an effort. She declared positively that robbery could not have been the motive, since the day's receipts were locked in the safe in the cashier's booth—a statement which we subsequently found to be correct.

"When did you last see Farrell?" Carter asked.

"It must have been around ten-forty-five," replied Mrs. Converse. "We stop selling tickets at ten-thirty, and it usually takes about fifteen minutes to check up. When I left, Mr. Farrell was starting up the ladder to the projection booth."

"Did he go up to the booth every night at about that time?"

"Yes, it was part of his regular schedule. First he checked with me then he looked in on Lem to see that everything was all right with him. Finally, he took a turn around the theatre looking for fires and sleepers and so on."

"Do you know of anyone—did you see anyone go into the show tonight who might have had a motive for killing him?"

The young woman shook her head. "No. But, of course, someone could have gone in after I left."

Sheriff Ike looked through the open door into the dimly lighted living room.

"I wonder if Mrs. Farrell could see us a few minutes?"

"Why, I don't know whether she's able—" Mrs. Converse began. Before she could say more Mrs. Farrell called out, inviting us in.

A trim, dark-eyed brunette in her early thirties, she was lying on the brocade lounge in a quilted robe. Considering the circumstances, she seemed remarkably self-controlled. She held up a hand as Carter started to explain the reason for our visit.

"I heard what you told Elizabeth. What do you want to ask me?"

"Do you know of any one who might have killed your husband?"

"I certainly do!" Mrs. Farrell's eyes flashed. "Lem Skidmore hated Larry for breaking him in business. I told Larry it wasn't safe to have him working there, but he just laughed at me. He never would listen to anything I said."

Ike ignored the edge of bitterness in her voice. "How long had you been waiting for your husband tonight?"

"About an hour. Since ten o'clock."

"Then, wouldn't you have seen Skidmore if he'd left his booth and gone down into the show?"

"But it was eleven o'clock before I parked in front of the theatre. Up until then, I was around in the alley, in the rear."

"Oh?" drawled Carter.

"Sometimes Larry liked to slip out before closing time to get a bite to eat. He didn't want me to park in front because it would take up space that some customer might need, so I always waited in back until eleven."

"You didn't wait inside because you'd already seen the picture?" the sheriff suggested.

"Yes, I had. I saw it twice the first day it was here."

Ike fumbled thoughtfully with a packet of brown cigarette papers, then returned them to his pocket. Of the old school of Westerners, he still refrained from smoking in the presence of women.

"How could Skidmore have left his booth without interrupting the show?" he inquired.

"Oh, the projectors will run themselves until they reach the end of a reel. Unless something goes wrong, of course."

"I didn't know that," Carter confessed. "We'll check on Lem. Now, can you think of anyone else?"

Mrs. Farrell hesitated, then said slowly, "Well there's Mr. Prentice. I saw him come out of the show tonight."

"He must have gone in after I left," interposed Mrs. Converse. "I didn't sell him a ticket."

"Did you notice anything unusual about him?" asked Carter.

Mrs. Farrell hesitated again before replying. "I thought he seemed rather nervous and agitated," she admitted reluctantly. "But it could have been my imagination."

Joseph A. Prentice owned the Rex Theatre building. He had leased it to Lem Skidmore under the not uncommon arrangement of a flat monthly rental or a percentage of the receipts, whichever should be greater. Normally, the percentage rental exceeded the base rate by several times, and was the only one that provided Prentice a profit.

When Farrell built the Palace Theatre and the Rex failed, the percentage rental, of course, disappeared. Farrell took over Skidmore's assets, the lease among them, and boarded the Rex up. Prentice was thus tied to a rental, for many years to come, which barely paid his taxes—if it did that.

Fearing competition, Farrell would not give up the lease. Neither would he operate the show himself, since to do so would double his overhead without any proportionate increase in income. He offered to cancel the lease providing Prentice would remodel the building for use by some business other than a theatre. But Prentice was unwilling to do this unless Farrell would defray the cost; for the reconversion of a theatre building is a very expensive process.

So matters had stood down through the years. Neither man was the type to indulge in street brawls, but they were not above exchanging sharp words and snubs whenever the opportunity offered.

"It was very embarrassing," Mrs. Farrell related. "You can't avoid people in a town as small as this, and—well, I've always felt rather guilty. I've told Larry I thought he was in the wrong; but he would never listen to me."

It was two o'clock in the morning when we left the Farrell residence. In our section of the country, an officer does not disturb a man at that hour unless to make an arrest; and we were certainly not prepared to arrest Prentice. At any rate, we were confident that he would come to us, as soon as news of the murder spread. Our belief proved correct.

Not more than thirty minutes after we had opened our offices the following morning, Joseph Prentice came in.

He was in a highly nervous state. His hand trembled as he reached for a chair and sat down.

"I've just heard that Larry Farrell was murdered last night. I—I must have been there when it happened. I thought I'd better come in right away."

"We're glad you did," said Ike soberly. "But what makes you think you were there when it happened?" he asked.

"I—because I saw him at ten minutes of eleven, and he wasn't seen alive after that. I went in at ten-fifty and I left when the show closed, and—"

"Let's start at the beginning," Carter suggested. "You weren't on good terms with Farrell. How did you happen to be at the show? And how do you place the time?"

"Well, it was like this," Prentice began, wiping his forehead with his handkerchief. "Farrell called me late yesterday afternoon, and asked me to drop in on him around closing time. I couldn't see that I had anything to lose, so I went. He was just coming down the ladder from the projection booth, and I went on inside. I stood in back, waiting for him, and I saw that Lem Skidmore had missed his changeover. That's how I know about the time. I suppose he got to talking to Farrell, and—"

"Hold on a minute," Carter interrupted. "What is this changeover business?"

"A changeover," said Prentice, "is when the operator switches from one projector to another. If he forgets to switch, there are a lot of white flashes and numbers on the screen, indicating the end of a reel. You've probably seen it happen yourself."

Sheriff Ike nodded. "And the time?"

"A reel of film takes just about ten minutes to run. Lem missed his changeover on the last reel. So I must have gone in at ten-fifty."

"Then what happened?"

"Farrell passed by me and shoved some papers in my hand. I couldn't see what they were in the dark, of course, and I supposed he'd want to talk to me when the show was over. So I just stayed there in the back, watching the picture. When it ended, the house lights flashed on and I looked at the papers. I never got such a surprise in my life. I was so excited I forgot to wait for Farrell to thank him."

"Thank him for what?"

"For these."

Prentice dug into the pocket of his coat and produced two folds of paper, tossing them onto the sheriff's desk. I read them over Carter's shoulder. One was a cancellation of the lease on the Rex. The other was an agreement to pay Prentice quarterly installments of $1,000 each until the cost of remodeling the building was covered. The papers were dated as of the previous day. Both were signed by Farrell, and notarized.

While the sheriff pretended to study them, I stepped into an adjoining office and called the notary. She was Miss Nina Birch, of 455 Front Street. She said that Farrell had signed the papers in her presence at about three o'clock in the afternoon of the preceding day. Because of their brevity, she remembered the contents well, and could recite them from memory.

I gave Carter a slight nod as I went back through the

door, and he handed the documents across the desk to Prentice.

"Did you have any previous indication that Farrell meant to straighten things up with you?" he asked.

"Well, yes and no," replied Prentice. "I'd heard that Mrs. Farrell felt I'd been mistreated and was trying to get her husband to do the right thing. Then, about a month ago, Lem Skidmore told me that Farrell would probably be willing to cancel the lease without my agreeing not to re-open the building as a show. You know, a lot of showmen have been getting into trouble lately for acting in restraint-of-trade. Skidmore wanted me to take the show back, and let him run it for me."

"And you refused?"

"Yes, I'd lost so much money on that building that just getting the lease cancelled wasn't a satisfactory adjustment any more. On top of that, I was pretty sure that Farrell had all the good pictures under contract to the Palace. It seemed best to take the little rent I was getting, and hope that Farrell would make things right with me, eventually."

Carter thanked him for coming in, then escorted him to the door. Turning back, he looked at me quizzically.

"What's the matter, Chet? You don't still suspect Prentice, do you?"

"Why not?" I asked. "He admits he didn't know what the papers were until after the show was over. And until he knew, he had a motive."

Ike shook his head in smiling reproof. "Murder is the last resort of even a hardened criminal, Chet. Prentice certainly isn't that. He'd been expecting Farrell to make amends; that's why he called on him. After Farrell handed him those papers he surely would have examined them before taking any violent action. Even without the papers, he'd probably have waited to see what Farrell had to offer before he did anything."

"You're right," I admitted. "What do we do now?"

Carter did not answer immediately. He seemed to be

thinking over something he had just said. Abruptly, he came out of his reverie. "Let's go see Lem Skidmore."

We found the elderly projectionist inside the theatre, making some adjustments in the sound speakers on the rear of the stage. Questioned, he admitted making the proposition to Prentice that the latter had claimed he had made. But, he declared, he had done it at Farrell's suggestion. The latter had been worried about the restraint-of-trade suits. He was sure that Prentice would not be able to obtain enough good pictures to provide any very harmful competition.

"So you never intended managing the show for Prentice?" asked the sheriff.

"Of course not!" Skidmore exclaimed. "What chance would I have had, competing with a man like Farrell? I was just trying to help him out of a hole."

"Wasn't that just a little out of your regular line of duty?"

"I'd have gone a lot further," replied Skidmore vigorously. "He was the best friend I ever had. The equipment in that old show of mine was all run down, and Prentice was grabbing all the profits with that percentage lease, and I'd made some bum picture contracts. I was running behind every day, but I didn't know how to let go. Then Farrell came along and took the whole thing off my hands and gave me a good job to boot. Yes, sir; I thought the world of Mr. Farrell."

Carter grinned dryly. "You kept your feelings pretty well to yourself, Lem. I always figured you were sore at him."

"Everyone did," Skidmore replied. "I never could see that it was any of their affair, though, and neither could Farrell."

He expressed a strong desire to lay hands on the murderer, but he could offer no clue as to the killer's identity.

"I suppose Mrs. Farrell will be running the show now," Carter suggested. "Will you keep on working here?"

"Don't know whether I will or not," said Lem shortly. "If she gets to botherin' me, I may try to talk Prentice into opening the Rex. We could put her out of business as easy as Mr. Farrell put me out."

"I see." The sheriff deliberately overlooked the significance of the statement. "Mrs. Farrell bothers you quite a bit, does she?"

"She's always butting into things." Lem scowled. "Lately, she's been wanting to hold a matinee every time we have a screening. When Farrell told me about it last night, it made me so mad I missed a changeover."

"A screening? What's that?"

"Well, every time we get a new picture in, I run it once before we show it to the public. Check to see that it's in good condition. Of course, the film exchanges are supposed to do that, but sometimes they slip up."

Carter nodded. "How was the picture you played last night? Pretty good?"

"All but the ending. It was kind of disappointing. If you want to see it, it'll be playing over in Wheat City in three days."

"It doesn't show anywhere else around here before then?"

"No. I'll tell you what, though: If you want to get an idea of what it's about, I can give you the press-book on it."

He lumbered up the aisle and out of the door to the box office, returning after a minute or two with the "book." In size and appearance it looked very much like a tabloid newspaper.

"The picture exchanges send us these with every picture we play," Skidmore explained. "They're full of promotional and advertising schemes. Of course they exaggerate how good a picture is; but this'll give you the plot, at least."

Carter thanked him and tucked the paper under his arm. Carelessly, he jerked his head at the rear exits, indicating the brass rods that stood out horizontally from each door. "I see those contraptions in lots of places," he remarked. "What do you call them?"

"Those are panic-bars," Lem explained. "Every fire exit has to have them. If you just fall or stumble against one the door will open."

"How do you open the door from the other side—the alley?"

"You don't. If the door could be opened from the outside, people would slip in through the exits instead of buying tickets."

"Couldn't you lock them?"

"It's against the law to lock a fire exit."

Carter and I went back to the car. He sat down heavily behind the wheel.

"Well, Chet," he said, "it looks like we've hit another blank wall. No one but Prentice has a very good alibi; but they're good enough. If there was some way, now, that Mrs. Farrell could have opened those alley doors . . ."

"Couldn't she have left her car there and walked around to the front?"

"She could have. But it would be a risky thing to do; as risky as it would have been for Lem to leave his projectors and go down into the theatre. Either one of those things could and may have happened. But unless you could prove—" He left the sentence unfinished. "Maybe we're narrowing our field a little too much, Chet. Maybe we're overlooking some bets."

"I don't get you," I said. "You're not thinking that Mrs. Converse or Sergeant Clinton might be mixed up in this? What motive could they have had?"

He shook his head. "Murderers don't always have motives that seem logical to other people. I've known some that didn't appear to have any at all."

"But Mrs. Converse was—"

"Don't jump the gun on me, Chet. I haven't said that either she or Clinton is involved. I'm just saying that we can't afford to eliminate anyone."

Opening the press-book, he began looking through the pages until he came to a résumé of the picture. He read it, frowning, and then handed it to me to read.

"Well?" I asked, when I had handed it back.

"Couldn't see anything disappointing about that, could you? Sounded like a bang-up ending to me."

"Maybe the publicity writer was exaggerating a little."

"He must have been exaggerating a whale of a lot. Lem knows a picture with a poor ending when he sees it. I don't see how—" He jerked his head suddenly, spraying cigarette ash over the steering wheel. A grim smile came to his lips.

"I think you and I ought to see that picture, Chet; Lem says it'll play in Wheat City in three days. Do you suppose your wife could spare you away from home for a while?"

"Why, of course," I replied. "But it's only forty miles to Wheat City."

"We're not going to Wheat City. We're going to San Deraldo."

We drove all night, taking turns at the wheel, and arrived in San Deraldo early the following afternoon. After registering at a hotel and cleaning up a little, we presented ourselves at the exchange—the booking offices—of the film company that owned the picture the Palace had shown on the night of the murder.

Dennis Baumgartner, the exchange manager, greeted us cordially. But his warmth underwent a natural waning as Sheriff Ike explained the purpose of our visit.

"I've never seen the picture," he admitted, "but from all reports I've had I believe it's a first-class film. Of course, we can't hope to please everyone."

"Do you have the picture on hand now?"

"Yes. We just got it back from the Palace. Would you like to take a look at it?"

We said we would, and Baumgartner spoke a few words into his telephone. "Just come along with me," he said, arising. "I think I'd like to see it, too."

We followed him to the screening room, actually a small theatre, and sat down. Almost immediately the room went dark and the projectors in the rear began to hum. Then the picture flashed on the screen.

When it was over, the lights came on again. Baumgartner's face was a picture of dismay.

"Say," he exclaimed, "this is lousy!"

"It's not real good," Carter agreed. "It kind of leaves things hanging up in the air. I was wondering: Do you have more than one copy of the same picture?"

"Oh, yes. We couldn't keep up with our bookings with only one print."

"What does an exhibitor do after he gets through showing a film? Does he sent it on to the next exhibitor or back here?"

"He sends it back here, and we check it over before it goes out again."

"How do you examine a print for damage?"

Baumgartner smiled thinly. "I see what you're getting at, sheriff. But you're barking up the wrong tree. Come along; I'll show you."

He took us into an adjoining room where several girls clad in smocks sat in front of a long bench. Under a brilliant light, a reel of film slowly unwound before each of them. It was virtually impossible, Baumgartner declared, for them to overlook a flaw.

Carter nodded his satisfaction. "I'll admit that Farrell's picture wasn't damaged," he said. "Now, can you tell me what other shows played the picture before he got it?"

"No other theatre in Texas had it."

"But some others in this film district did?"

Baumgartner's eyes widened in surprise. "I didn't think you knew anything about show business, Sheriff."

"I don't. You're right on the border here; it's just common sense to assume that you'd do some out-of-state business."

"You're right, of course. Normally, the closest exchange gets the business, regardless of state. For instance, our Denver, Colorado, exchange serves part of Nebraska. Our

Omaha, Nebraska, exchange serves part of Iowa. Our—" Baumgartner broke off abruptly, an amazed grin spreading over his face. "By George! Now I see what you're getting at."

"I'm glad you do," drawled Carter. "By the way, I notice that the exits in your screening rooms are equipped with panic bars. Is there any way those doors can be opened from the outside?"

"No, there isn't. Why—"

"Would you mind if Mr. Stacey experimented with them a little?"

Baumgartner gave his consent, and I went back through the screening room and out the exit. The outer surface of the door was perfectly smooth. There wasn't a knob or protuberance of any kind to get a grip on. I tried to grasp the door between its edge and the casing, and got a broken fingernail for my trouble. I tried to pick the catch with my penknife and succeeded only in breaking the blade.

By this time, of course, I was not in the best of humor. Peevishly, I drew my foot back and kicked the door at the base.

Inside, the panic bar swung up and banged downward— and the door opened.

The sheriff was just entering the room from the other side. He nodded approvingly as we went out into the street.

"I knew you'd find a way to do it," he said. "Now, let's go get a bite to eat, and I'll tell you what I found out."

We started home the following morning. As we drove leisurely and stopped overnight, it was evening of the next day before we reached La Tumara.

Acting upon Carter's instructions, I called upon all the principals in the case—Mrs. Farrell, Mrs. Converse, Lem Skidmore, Joseph Prentice and Sergeant Clinton. I told each of them to be at the sheriff's office the next morning at ten o'clock, advising them that their presence was necessary to clear up the murder. Further than that, on Carter's advice, I did not elaborate. To secure Sergeant Clinton's presence, it was necessary for me to confer with his commanding officer, Captain Orson X. Cardwell. Captain Cardwell, who had been an attorney in private life, gladly cooperated as soon as the matter was explained to him.

The following morning at ten o'clock we were all assembled in Sheriff Ike's office. Also in attendance were Deputy Todd, County Attorney Max Radford and the latter's secretary, Miss Jeanne Norton. Carter motioned for Todd to close the door, then looked around the circle of tense and puzzled faces with an air of embarrassment.

"I'm sorry to bring you folks together in this playacting way," he began. "But it looked to me like the only way to get this thing cleared up. To put it plain, you all had the chance to kill Mr. Farrell. You all could have had a reason for killing him. I'll admit I don't know what it would be, in every case. But I can make a few guesses. Just guesses. I'm not accusing anyone of anything."

Sheriff Carter, as he would be the first to admit, is not an accomplished speaker; in the present situation he was easily the most discomfited person in the room. For once, however, his difficulty proved to be an advantage. Everyone began to smile and relax. Mrs. Farrell nodded sympathetically.

"We know this isn't easy for you, Sheriff," she said. "Go right ahead. You can start in with me, if you want to."

He explained haltingly that she might have wanted to run the Palace herself. He also explained, to the apparent surprise of those familiar with the theatre operation, that the exit doors could be opened from the outside.

"What about me?" asked Mrs. Converse.

"Well, you could have been short in your accounts, and Mr. Farrell found out about it."

"But I was in the Elite Cafe at ten-forty-five. Your own deputy will tell you so."

"If I know Joe Todd," drawled Carter, "he doesn't look at his watch when he's eating."

There was a ripple of laughter at the witticism. The sheriff continued:

"Sergeant Clinton had a bit of hard luck in discovering the body. Soldiers don't have a whole lot of money. I know I never did back in '17. If I'd been in his shoes back in those days, people might have got some wrong ideas. They might have figured I tried to hold Farrell up, got scared and killed him, then reported the 'accident' to make myself look good.

"Well, I reckon that's enough guessing. Guessing from a man in my job is liable to cause hard feelings. You can all see that—"

"Now wait a minute," Lem Skidmore interrupted. "Conceding that I had a reason to kill Mr. Farrell, which I didn't, how could I go climbing down the ladder, right out there in the open, without someone seeing me?"

"Why couldn't you?" asked Carter. "The ticket-seller's booth was dark. All the front lights were turned off. And the record shows that people climbed up and down that ladder pretty freely. But let's cut out the guessing.

"Mrs. Converse, did you see the picture that was being played the night Mr. Farrell was killed?"

"Yes," the cashier replied. "I saw it when Lem screened it."

"So you had no reason, after you'd finished work, to go in the show and look at it some more?"

Mrs. Converse hesitated. "Well—you could put it that way."

The sheriff leaned forward, looking searchingly around the room.

"All right," he said. "Here's the situation as I see it. Whoever killed Mr. Farrell prepared himself—or herself —with an alibi. They were prepared to state they were so familiar with the show that they had no reason to see it again, or that they were watching it at the time of the murder. Sergeant Clinton and Mr. Prentice, and perhaps Lem Skidmore, fall into the latter class. The others of you are in the former class."

"Couldn't Clinton and Prentice have seen the picture before the last show?" Skidmore asked.

"They could, but they didn't. Clinton was on a twenty-four-hour pass, and he's able to account for all of his time. Prentice never patronized the Palace for obvious reasons.

"Chet, will you pass around these tablets and pencils?"

I distributed the five pads of paper and the five pencils to the puzzled group. Carter concluded his dissertation:

"Mr. Farrell was killed during the last reel of the picture. For the benefit of Mr. Prentice and Sergeant Clinton, I'll point out that there was an interruption in the picture between the last reel and the others when Lem missed the changeover. The rest of you are sufficiently familiar with show business to gauge what the last reel included.

"Now I want each of you to write down what was in the last reel."

There was a worried, low murmur of protest.

"That picture's been playing at Wheat City," Skidmore pointed out. "How do you know the murderer didn't slip over there and see it to give himself an alibi?"

The sheriff looked flustered. "That's a good question. Did any of you see the picture at Wheat City?"

There was a general shaking of heads; Lem let out an indignant snort.

"You don't think they'd admit it if they did, do you? It'd be the same as saying they were guilty."

Carter reddened, but said nothing. There was nothing to say. Mrs. Converse spoke up.

"I don't see what this is going to prove, anyway, Sheriff," she said. "After all—"

"Do you know what was in the last reel?" asked Carter sharply.

"Of course I do. I'm sure I do."

"Write it down, then."

Sergeant Clinton wet his lips. "Sheriff, I—well, I wasn't trying to remember what I saw. I don't—"

"Don't bother about little details, Sergeant. All I want is the action—what the actors actually did. You can remember that if you think hard."

"But—"

"Try," said Carter firmly.

The ensuing twenty minutes, I think, were the longest in my career. Lem Skidmore was the first to hand in his tablet. Following him was Mrs. Converse, then Prentice and Mrs. Farrell. Sergeant Clinton was the last to finish.

The sheriff shook his head as he looked at his tablet. "You're right, Sergeant. You didn't remember much."

"I told you I couldn't," Clinton protested.

"Mmm. So you did! Lem, you did a pretty good job. About the same as Mrs. Farrell. Your description is very complete, Mr. Prentice. Mrs. Converse, you didn't do badly either."

Carter dropped the tablets on the desk; he was suddenly no longer ill at ease.

"As Mrs. Converse tried to point out," he began, "whether or not you could or couldn't remember this picture doesn't prove a thing. No jury in the world would have accepted your failure as proof of guilt. If any or all of you had simply sat back and refused to write, I'd have had to excuse you and forget it. However, I was pretty sure you wouldn't do that. I was particularly sure the murderer wouldn't. No murderer ever feels safe. He keeps on trying to establish his innocence until he's caught or dies.

"The picture—or I should say, the print of it—which was shown at the Palace, had two or three minutes of action omitted from the last reel. It had been cut by the censors of another state where the print was shown.

"Their censorship rulings differ from ours, and the print went to the Palace through error. It was an easy error to make; the film wasn't damaged. The objectionable part had been removed, and the film neatly spliced again.

"That was the print that four of you saw. Another one— one intended for Texas distribution and without the cuts— played at Wheat City. That's the one you saw, Mr. Prentice."

Everyone sat looking at Carter expectantly, waiting for him to go on. Realization that he had finished came slowly.

It was a full minute before even Prentice realized that he had been accused of murder.

The statement caught him completely by surprise, just when he was feeling safest, as the sheriff intended it should.

"What d-do y-you mean?" he stammered. "Farrell and I had settled all our difficulties."

"No, you hadn't. And you'd given up all hope of getting a settlement out of him. You knew how Mrs. Farrell felt about the matter.

"You were sure, if her husband was out of the way, you'd get what you wanted. So you killed him. You made it look like an accident. You didn't count on being seen, and—"

"I tell you—!" Prentice's face was contorted with fear.

"I'll tell you," Carter continued relentlessly. "The more I thought about your story the more loopholes I saw in it. Farrell didn't like you any better then you liked him. He didn't want anything to do with you. If he made an adjustment with you, it would be because he had to. He wouldn't have seen you personally. He mailed those papers to you, and you received them—the morning after you'd killed him.

"I couldn't prove that. But you could—and you did. This description of the last reel of the picture, which you did not see at the Palace, gives you away. You killed Farrell, and"—Carter paused, letting the words sink in—"you did it for nothing. If you'd waited just one more day— think of it, Prentice—just one more day—"

Prentice was as pale as death. He looked around at the wall of cold, accusing faces, and quickly averted his eyes. Sweat burst from his forehead. He opened his mouth to speak, then slowly closed it again. Suddenly he buried his face in his hands and wept.

That evening, in his cell in the county jail, he made a confession to the crime.

He had, he said, gone to the Palace only with the intention of talking to Farrell. Standing in the rear of the seats, he had nervously drawn out his pocketknife and was paring his nails when the showman came in. Farrell had brushed past him without a word and gone down to the lounge. Prentice, angered by the snub, had followed him. He ran into him at the turn of the steps, as he was coming up. He still had the knife in his hand. Farrell, accustomed to the darkness and seeing the knife, misconstrued the situation. He flung his arms around Prentice, and the latter, surprised and panic-stricken by the attack, lashed out blindly.

He struck Farrell with the knife, knocking him unconscious.

The reasoning behind Prentice's actions from then on were not even clear to himself, he claimed. Perhaps he intended dragging Farrell into the lounge and trying to revive him. Perhaps he was merely following the age-old instinct to conceal, however foolishly, the evidence of a crime. At any rate, he had started into the lounge with Farrell when his overwrought nerves had forced him to drop the showman and flee the place.

He was horrified, he declared, when he learned that he had inadvertently strangled him.

But the same fate that had made him a murderer seemingly provided him with an escape in the form of the papers Farrell had mailed him. So he had lied about the interview and to reinforce the lie had gone to Wheat City to see the picture.

Prentice went on trial on November 7, 1944, in the District Court of Judge Robert Lee Arrowman. Under the vigorous attack of County Attorney Radford, his story of Farrell's death lost much of its credibility. It was shown that the knife with which he had slugged Farrell had been purchased on the day of the crime. It was further shown that although he was practically without ready cash, he had promised several creditors substantial payments in the immediate future only a few days before the showman was killed.

In other words, there was strong evidence of premeditation.

Moreover, a person who attempts to conceal his guilt of a felonious act, even though the act may have been unintentional, is always at a disadvantage in a court of law. There is always a suspicion that he used the interim before his apprehension to concoct a plausible story. There is a sinister implication that he would have been willing to see an innocent person pay the penalty for his act.

On November 23, the jury returned a verdict of guilty, with a recommendation for leniency.

Prentice was sentenced to forty years in the state penitentiary.

In conclusion, I would like to say that the Palace is thriving under Mrs. Farrell's management, and she and Lem Skidmore have long since settled their trifling and largely imaginary differences. With Mrs. Converse in the cashier's booth, the show goes on pretty much as it always did—except that the basement lights are never turned off until closing time.

Forever After

It was a few minutes before five o'clock when Ardis Clinton unlocked the rear door of her apartment and admitted her lover. He was a cow-eyed young man with a wild mass of curly black hair. He worked as a dishwasher at Joe's Diner, which was directly across the alley.

They embraced passionately. Her body pressed against the meat cleaver concealed inside his shirt, and Ardis shivered with delicious anticipation. Very soon now, it would be all over. That stupid ox, her husband, would be dead. He and his stupid cracks—all the dullness and boredom would be gone forever. And with the twenty thousand insurance money, ten thousand dollars' double indemnity...

"We're going to be so happy, Tony," she whispered. "You'll have your own place, a real swank little restaurant with what they call one of those intimate bars. And you'll just manage it, just kind of saunter around in a dress suit, and—"

"And we'll live happily ever after," Tony said. "Just me and you, baby, walking down life's highway together."

Ardis let out a gasp. She shoved him away from her, glaring up into his handsome empty face. "Don't!" she

48

snapped. "Don't say things like that! I've told you and told you not to do it, and if I have to tell you again, I'll—"

"But what'd I say?" he protested. "I didn't say nothin.'"

"Well . . ." She got control of herself, forcing a smile. "Never mind, darling. You haven't had any opportunities and we've never really had a chance to know each other, so—so never mind. Things will be different after we're married." She patted his cheek, kissed him again. "You got away from the diner, all right? No one saw you leave?"

"Huh-uh. I already took the stuff up to the steam table for Joe, and the waitress was up front too, y'know, filling the sugar bowls and the salt and pepper shakers like she always does just before dinner. And—"

"Good. Now, suppose someone comes back to the kitchen and finds out you're not there. What's your story going to be?"

"Well . . . I was out in the alley dumping some garbage. I mean"—he corrected himself hastily, "maybe I was. Or maybe I was down in the basement, getting some supplies. Or maybe I was in the john—the lavatory, I mean—or—"

"Fine," Ardis said approvingly. "You don't say where you were, so they can't prove you weren't there. You just don't remember where you were, understand, darling. You might have been any number of places."

Tony nodded. Looking over her shoulder into the bedroom, he frowned worriedly. "Why'd you do that now, honey? I know this has got to look like a robbery. But tearin' up the room now, before he gets here—"

"There won't be time afterwards. Don't worry, Tony. I'll keep the door closed."

"But he might open it and look in. And if he sees all them dresser drawers dumped around, and—"

"He won't. He won't look into the bedroom. I know exactly what he'll do, exactly what he'll say, the same things that he's always done and said ever since we've been married. All the stupid, maddening, dull, tiresome—!" She broke off abruptly, conscious that her voice was rising. "Well, forget it," she said, forcing another smile. "He won't give us any trouble."

"Whatever you say," Tony nodded docilely. "If you say so, that's the way it is, Ardis."

"But there'll be trouble—from the cops. I know I've already warned you about it, darling. But it'll be pretty bad, worse than anything you've ever gone through. They won't have any proof, but they're bound to be suspicious, and if you ever start talking, admitting anything—"

"I won't. They won't get anything out of me."

"You're sure? They'll try to trick you. They'll probably tell you that I've confessed. They may even slap you around. So if you're not absolutely sure . . ."

"They won't get anything out of me," he repeated stolidly. "I won't talk."

And studying him, Ardis knew that he wouldn't.

She led the way down the hall to the bathroom. He parted the shower curtains, and stepped into the tub. Drawing a pair of gloves from his pocket, he pulled them onto his hands. Awkwardly, he fumbled the meat cleaver from beneath the shirt.

"Ardis. Uh—look, honey."

"Yes?"

"Do I have to hit you? Couldn't I just maybe give you a little shove, or—"

"No, darling," she said gently. "You have to hit me. This is supposed to be a robbery. If you killed my husband without doing anything to me, well, you know how it would look."

"But I never hit no woman—any woman—before. I might hit you too hard, and—"

"Tony!"

"Well, all right," he said sullenly. "I don't like it, but all right."

Ardis murmured soothing endearments. Then, brushing his lips quickly with her own, she returned to the living room. It was a quarter after five, exactly five minutes— but *exactly*—until her husband, Bill, would come home.

Closing the bedroom door, she lay down on the lounge. Her negligee fell open, and she left it that way, grinning meanly as she studied the curving length of her thighs.

Give the dope a treat for a change, she thought. *Let him get one last good look before he gets his.*

Her expression changed. Wearily, resentfully, she pulled the material of the negligee over her legs. Because, of course, Bill would never notice. She could wear a ring in her nose, paint a bull's-eye around her navel, and he'd never notice.

If he had ever noticed, just once paid her a compliment . . .

If he had ever done anything different, ever said or done anything different at all—even the teensiest little bit . . .

But he hadn't. Maybe he couldn't. So what else could she do but what she was doing? She could get a divorce, sure, but that was all she'd get. No money; nothing with which to build a new life. Nothing to make up for those fifteen years of slowly being driven mad.

It's his own fault, she thought bitterly. *I can't take any more. If I had to put up with him for just one more night, even one more hour . . . !*

She heard heavy footsteps in the hallway. Then, a key turned in the doorlatch, and Bill came in. He was a master machinist, a solidly built man of about forty-five. The old-fashioned gold-rimmed glasses on his pudgy nose gave him a look of owlish solemnity.

"Well," he said, setting down his lunch bucket. "Another day, another dollar."

Ardis grimaced. He plodded across to the lounge, stooped, and gave her a half-hearted peck on the cheek.

"Long time no see," he said. "What we havin' for supper?"

Ardis gritted her teeth. It shouldn't matter, now; in a few minutes it would all be over. Yet somehow it *did* matter. He was as maddening to her as he'd ever been.

"Bill . . ." She managed a seductive smile, slowly drawing the negligee apart. "How do I look, Bill?"

"Okay," he yawned. "Got a little hole in your drawers, though. What'd you say we was havin' for supper?"

"Slop," she said. "Garbage. Trash salad with dirt dressing."

"Sounds good. We got any hot water?"

Ardis sucked in her breath. She let it out again in a kind of infuriated moan. "Of course, we've got hot water! Don't we always have? Well, don't we? Why do you have to ask every night?"

"So what's to get excited about?" he shrugged. "Well, guess I'll go splash the chassis."

He plopped off down the hall. Ardis heard the bathroom door open and close. She got up, stood waiting by the telephone. The door banged open again, and Tony came racing up the hall.

He had washed off the cleaver. While he hastily tucked it back inside his shirt, Ardis dialed the operator. "Help," she cried weakly. "Help . . . police . . . murder!"

She let the receiver drop to the floor, spoke to Tony in a whisper. "He's dead? You're sure of it?"

"Yeah, yeah, sure I'm sure. What do you think?"

"All right. Now, there's just one more thing . . ."

"I can't, Ardis. I don't want to. I—"

"Hit me," she commanded, and thrust out her chin. "Tony, I said to hit me!"

He hit her. A thousand stars blazed through her brain and disappeared. And she crumpled silently to the floor.

When she regained consciousness, she was lying on the lounge. A heavy-set man, a detective obviously, was seated at her side, and a white-jacketed young man with a stethoscope draped around his neck hovered nearby.

She had never felt better in her life. Even the lower part of her face, where Tony had smashed her, was surprisingly free of pain. Still, because it was what she should do, she moaned softly; spoke in a weak, hazy voice.

"Where am I?" she said. "What happened?"

"Lieutenant Powers," the detective said. "Suppose you tell me what happened, Mrs. Clinton."

"I . . . I don't remember. I mean, well, my husband had just come home, and gone back to the bathroom. And there was a knock on the door, and I supposed it was the paperboy or someone like that. So—"

"You opened the door and he rushed in and slugged you, right? Then what happened?"

"Well, then he rushed into the bedroom and started searching it. Yanking out the dresser drawers, and—"

"What was he searching for, Mrs. Clinton? You don't have any considerable amount of money around do you? Or any jewelry aside from what you're wearing? And it wasn't your husband's pay-day, was it?"

"Well, no. But—"

"Yes?"

"I don't know. Maybe he was crazy. All I know is what he did."

"I see. He must have made quite a racket, seems to me. How come your husband didn't hear it?"

"He couldn't have. He had the shower running, and—"

She caught herself, fear constricting her throat. Lieutenant Powers grinned grimly.

"Missed a bet, huh, Mrs. Clinton?"

"I—I don't know what you're—"

"Come off of it. The bathtub's dry as an oven. The shower was never turned on, and you know why it wasn't. Because there was a guy standing inside of it."

"B-but—but I don't know anything. I was unconscious, and—"

"Then, how do you know what happened? How do you know the guy went into the bedroom and started tearing it apart? And how did you make that telephone call?"

"Well, I . . . I wasn't completely unconscious. I sort of knew what was going on without really—"

"Now, you listen to me," he said harshly. "You made that fake call of yours—yes, I said *fake*—to the operator at twenty-three minutes after five. There happened to be a prowl car right here in the neighborhood, so two minutes later, at five-twenty-five, there were cops here in your apartment. You were unconscious then, more than an hour ago. You've been unconscious until just now."

Ardis' brain whirled. Then, it cleared suddenly, and a great calm came over her.

"I don't see quite what you're hinting at, lieutenant. If you're saying that I was confused, mixed up—that I must have dreamed or imagined some of the things I told you—I'll admit it."

"You know what I'm saying! I'm saying that no guy could have gotten in and out of this place and done what this one did in any two minutes!"

"Then the telephone operator must have been mistaken about the time," Ardis said brightly. "I don't know how else to explain it."

Powers grunted. He said he could give her a better explanation—and he gave it to her. The right one. Ardis listened to it placidly, murmuring polite objections.

"That's ridiculous, lieutenant. Regardless of any gossip you may have heard, I don't know this, uh, Tony person. And I most certainly did not plot with him to kill my husband. Why—"

"He says you did. We got a signed confession from him."

"Have you?" But of course they didn't have. They might have found out about Tony, but he would never have talked. "That hardly proves anything, does it?"

"Now, you listen to me, Mrs. Clinton! Maybe you think that—"

"How is my husband, anyway? I do hope he wasn't seriously hurt."

"How is he?" the lieutenant snarled. "How would you be after gettin' worked over with—" He broke off, his eyes flickering. "As a matter of fact," he said heavily, "he's going to be all right. He was pretty badly injured, but he was able to give us a statement and—"

"I'm so glad. But why are you questioning me, then?" It was another trick. Bill had to be dead. "If he gave you a statement, then you must know that everything happened just like I said."

She waited, looked at him quizzically. Powers scowled, his stern face wrinkling with exasperation.

"All right," he said, at last. "All right, Mrs. Clinton. Your husband is dead. We don't have any statement from him, and we don't have any confession from Tony."

"Yes?"

"But we know that you're guilty, and you know that you are. And you'd better get it off your conscience while you still can."

"While I still can?"

"Doc—" Powers jerked his head at the doctor. At the man, that is, who appeared to be a doctor. "Lay it on the line, Doc. Tell her that her boyfriend hit her a little too hard."

The man came forward hesitantly. He said, "I'm sorry, Mrs. Clinton. You have a—uh—you've sustained a very serious injury."

"Have I?" Ardis smiled. "I feel fine."

"I don't think," the doctor said judiciously, "that that's quite true. What you mean is that you don't feel anything at all. You couldn't. You see, with an injury such as yours—"

"Get out," Ardis said. "Both of you get out."

"Please, Mrs. Clinton. Believe me, this isn't a trick. I haven't wanted to alarm you, but—"

"And you haven't," she said. "You haven't scared me even a little bit, mister. Now, clear out!"

She closed her eyes, kept them closed firmly. When, at last, she reopened them, Powers and the doctor—if he really had been a doctor—were gone. And the room was in darkness.

She lay smiling to herself, congratulating herself. In the corridor, outside, she heard heavy footsteps ·approaching;

and she tensed for a moment. Then, remembering, she re-laxed again.

Not Bill, of course. She was through with that jerk for-ever. He'd driven her half out of her mind, got her to the point where she couldn't have taken another minute of him if her life depended on it. But now. . .

The footsteps stopped in front of her door. A key turned in the lock, the door opened and closed.

There was a clatter of a lunch pail being set down; then a familiar voice—maddeningly familiar words:

"Well. Another day, another dollar."

Ardis' mouth tightened; it twisted slowly, in a malicious grin. So they hadn't given up yet! They were pulling this one last trick. Well, let them; she'd play along with the gag.

The man plodded across the room, stooped, and gave her a half-hearted peck on the cheek. "Long time no see," he said. "What we havin' for supper?"

"Bill . . ." Ardis said. "How do I look, Bill?"

"Okay. Got your lipstick smeared, though. What'd you say we was having for supper?"

"Stewed owls! Now, look, mister. I don't know who you—"

"Sounds good. We got any hot water?"

"Of course, we've got hot water! Don't we always have? Why do you always have to ask if—if—"

She couldn't go through with it. Even as a gag—even someone who merely sounded and acted like he did—it was too much to bear.

"Y-you get out of here!" she quavered. "I don't have to stand for this! I *c-can't* stand it! I did it for fifteen years, and—"

"So what's to get excited about?" he said. "Well, guess I'll go splash the chassis."

"Stop it! STOP IT!" Her screams filled the room . . . silent screams ripping through silence. "He's—you're dead! I know you are! You're dead, and I don't have to put up with you for another minute. And—and—!"

"Wouldn't take no bets on that if I was you," he said mildly. "Not with a broken neck like yours."

He trudged off toward the bathroom, wherever the bathroom is in Eternity.

The Cellini Chalice

1

It was late afternoon when Mitch Allison reached the last shabby house in a shabby block of houses, and he was cursing himself for eighteen kinds of a sap. He hadn't made a nickel all day. He hadn't made bean money all week. Well, if this was the best Doc Krug could do for a hustling man, he, Doc Krug, could shove it. Doc was supposed to be a sharpie. Supposedly, he could always put a fast boy next to a good thing. But all he'd put Mitch next to was being broke.

Mitch knocked on the door of the house. He waited a second, then pounded, adding an angry kick for good measure. The door opened suddenly, and a redhead glared out at him. She was young, built like a brick henhouse in a windy country. Judging by the nightgown beneath her half-opened robe, she had been asleep.

"Beat it!" she snapped. "Whatever you're selling, I don't want any."

Mitch smiled apologetically, flashing one of Doc Krug's business cards. The card identified him as an associate of Krug's and Company, San Diego's largest buyer of precious metals and old jewelry.

"I'm not selling a thing, lady. I'm here to—"

"Yeah, yeah, I know." The girl cut him off impatiently. "I've heard the spiel before. What would I have that was worth any dough?"

Mitch's smile vanished. He was about to say that she had plenty that was worth dough, and that she was doubtless selling it regularly. But then he saw the thing—the cup or the bowl or whatever the hell it was. And the insulting words died in his throat.

"I'm terribly sorry to have disturbed you, madam," he said earnestly. "I did hope you might have some old trinkets I could purchase, but since you haven't . . ." He gave her a courtly bow. The girl's face and her voice softened.

"I really don't have a thing, mister. And I'm sorry if I was rude. You see, I work all night in a restaurant and—" She broke off with a gasp. "What's the matter? For God's sake, what's the matter?"

Mitch didn't answer. He simply moaned, clutching his heart, his handsome face contorted with pain. The girl's reaction was exactly what he hoped it to be. She was one of those tough babies. All the toughies had a soft streak; they were easier to handle, really, than the so-called softies.

So, less than a minute after he had gone into his act, he was seated in the living room, sipping at the glass of water which she held to his mouth.

Bent over him as she was, she gave him plenty to look at. Unfortunately, he couldn't be bothered, at the moment. His seemingly closed eyes were fixed on a shelf near the window, attempting to appraise the cup-shaped object which stood there betwixt a withering potted plant and a battered alarm clock.

Doc Krug had tired to drum some knowledge of antiques into him. It was necessary, Doc pointed out, if Mitch was to work with him in fencing hot items. Moreover, Mitch had the hustler's instinct for something good—for a tangible or intangible that could be turned for a big dollar. Still, he had no real idea of what the thing on the shelf was worth.

All he knew was that (1) it must be worth a wad, and (2) he'd get it away from the babe if he had to slug her.

"Better now?" Her anxious voice interrupted his thoughts. "Answer me, please!"

Mitch allowed his eyes to flutter open. He gave her a brave, weak smile.

"I'm all right, now, thanks to you. You saved my life, Miss—Miss—"

"Turner. Peggy Turner. What was it, your heart?"

Mitch nodded. "It's my own fault, I suppose, for leaving the hospital this morning. But I'd been there for so long. Two years of lying on my back, accepting charity..."

"Charity?" She frowned at him suspiciously.

Mitch continued, lying with the smoothness of long practice, "My good friend Doctor Krug lent me some clothes. He gave me this job, and a little money to work with. I wish I could justify his faith in me. But"—he sighed heavily—"I haven't made a purchase all day, and it doesn't look like I will. So the only honorable thing for me to do is to quit."

"But—what will happen too you? How will you live?"

"It doesn't matter," Mitch said gently. "I don't have long to live, anyway."

It went against his hustler's pride to deal out such terrible corn. But Peggy Turner was lapping it up. Timidly, she suggested lending him a few dollars. He refused it with a firm smile of thanks.

"I do wish you something I might buy from you, Miss Turner, but since you haven't, I'll—"

"I really don't, Mr. Allison. Honest, I don't." Her tear-dimmed eyes strayed to the shelf. "Except maybe that old goblet. But I doubt that'd be any good to you."

"I'm afraid not," Mitch said doubtfully. "Of course, it wouldn't hurt to look at it."

She handed it to him. Mitch examined it, his lips pursed deprecatingly to conceal his excitement. Its finish was dull, greenish with age. Each of the four grime-obscured handles was formed in the shape of a different figure, a mermaid, a knight and so on. The under-rim was a metallic circle of lace—filigree—as exquisite as it was intricate.

"Kind of cute, isn't it?" the girl said. "I was trying to remember where I got the thing."

"Yes," Mitch murmured. "It is kind of cute."

He hefted it casually, deciding that it was undoubtedly gold. Of course, lead or some other base metal would weigh heavily, too. But it seemed unlikely that any metal but gold would have received so much careful workmanship.

It just wasn't done, Krug had explained to him. Diamonds were not mounted in tin. Expert craftsmen did not spend their valuable time on the intrinsically cheap.

He looked up suddenly. There was a peculiar expression on the girl's face, something that seemed strangely close to amusement. It disappeared immediately, so swiftly that he was not sure he had seen it. He decided that he hadn't, that it was only his guilty imagination, and the tension drained out of his body.

"Well," she said. "Is it worth anything, Mr. Allison?"

"Well," Mitch said. "It's not completely worthless."

"I see."

"There's a little silver in it. Just plate, you know, but it is worth *something*."

"Yes?"

"Well," Mitch squirmed inwardly. Was she wise? Was she just leading him on, building up to a horse-laugh? "Well, I have to make a little profit. Not much, only fifty cents or so, or maybe a dollar."

"Yes?"

"I can offer you two dollars for it," Mitch said.

The girl choked, and burst into laughter.

Mitch's eyes flashed venomously. He got a firm grip on the cup, and pushed himself up from the chair. One of his hands balled into a fist.

"Please," Peggy Turner gasped. "Please forgive me, but—"

"Sure," said Mitch grimly. "Sure, I'll forgive you."

"You poor innocent, you! You poor helpless thing! Of course I won't sell you that cup!"

"Of course you won't," Mitch said, and drew a bead on her chin.

He'd slugged plenty of dames for less reason. Socking this one would be both pleasurable and profitable. By the time she stopped listening to the birdies he'd have the cup to Krug and be miles away.

"I wouldn't think of taking your money," she said. "I'll give you the cup."

She wrapped it in a paper bag to carry.

As he started down the street toward town, he thought he heard another burst of half-hysterical laughter. But a train was passing so he wasn't sure. It wasn't something to be bothered about, anyway. She was just a nut—one of those babes who laughed instead of crying. Now that he had the cup, she could laugh her pretty red head off for all he cared.

2

Coming out of the public library, Mitch knew a moment of regret for his lack of a formal education. He hadn't known where to look for the information he wanted. He didn't know the names of any of the old geezers, silversmiths and gold workers, whose craftsmanship the cup might be. He could have asked the librarian for guidance but he guessed that wouldn't have helped him much. If this thing was as rare as he hoped, there would be no picture of it. If there was a picture, it would certainly not be labeled with a price tag. And without price tags, Mitch Allison was lost.

He knew when something was valuable: a hustler was born knowing. He could not, however, say how valuable it was nor why it was valuable at all.

Under the circumstances, Doc Krug would probably give him a rooking. Or try to. But there was little to be done about it. About all he could do was hold the rooking down to a minimum, to drive the best bargain which his ignorance of values would permit.

Doc's shop was on a side street in the outer edge of the business district. The sign on the door read: KRUG—ANTIQUES, *Dealer in Precious Metals*. A display of old coins and ancient silverware gleamed dully behind the dusty windows. Inside were two long rows of showcases, divided by a narrow aisle, extending to the grilled workroom-office at the rear.

Doc was a short, fat little man. His bald hard-looking head looked like it had been put on with an ice cream dipper. As Mitch came in, he dropped the loupe from his eye and dimmed the brilliant light of his work lamp.

Ignoring Mitch's greeting, he opened the wicket and held out his hand.

"There was a wrist-watch on my workbench this morning," he said. "After you left, it was no longer there. You will return it, please."

"Why not?" Mitch handed it back to him with a shrug. "It's not worth a five-spot."

"So." Doc nodded. "Otherwise, you would not have stolen it. Only the cheap, the shoddy, do you have an eye for. Apparently, you are traveling under false colors. Apparently, there is another Mitch Allison—a truly fast boy, not a clown who could not hustle a dime at a world's fair— and you have taken his name."

He shook his head contemptuously.

Mitch reddened. "Look who's talking," he sneered. "If you're sharp, then I'll shave with a wet noodle! How the hell the word ever got around Los Angeles that you were the guy for a hustler to come to—"

"A real hustler. A boy who recognizes his opportunities, such as I have wasted on you. You yourself know many such men: None of them, I believe, has ever accused me of a lack of sharpness."

Mitch had to admit it, but he did so silently. How Doc had got his reputation he didn't know, but all the fast boys spoke highly of him.

"I send you to a good neighborhood," Doc continued, "and you do nothing. I send you to a poor neighborhood, a place where all of my former associates have done well, and still you do nothing. You lack nerve, presence, intelligence. You expect to swindle a pro, yet you cannot cheat a housewife."

"I can't, huh?" Mitch's face was scarlet. "What do you think I've got in this sack?"

"Bananas?" Doc guessed. "Have you raided a fruit stand, you oh-so-daring young man?"

Mitch ripped the sack from the cup. He set it in the window of the wicket, forcing himself to calm down, realizing that Doc was angering him deliberately.

Had he glimpsed the cup over the top of the sack? Had its outline against the paper hinted of its value? Mitch thought, yes—hence Doc's attempt to upset him. But there was nothing to bolster the hunch in the fat man's expression.

"I apologize," Doc said. "It was a trash pile you raided, not a fruit store."

Mitch shrugged carelessly and reached for the cup. "I'll just take it along with me," he said. "Save you the trouble of throwing it away."

"Wait."

Mitch grinned.

"I-I did not say it was worthless. Taking a second look at it, I can see that it contains silver. Almost—well, two or three dollars' worth."

"How much?" Mitch cupped a hand to his ear. "I don't hear so well, Doc?"

"Five dollars. Well, ten then. Little silver it has, but the design is nice, indeed quite interesting."

"Little silver it has," Mitch nodded mockingly. "But gold, Doc, of gold it has much. A good half-pound I'd say of about eighteen carat."

"Nonsense! It is no better than a thick silver-plate. Perhaps only a fill."

"Well, let's see," Mitch said; his hand reached for a rubber-corked bottle. "Let's just—"

"Imbecile!" Doc jerked the bottle out of reach, his face turning white. "Fool! Better you should have acid on your head than on this—this—"

His voice died foolishly. His eyes wavered under Mitch's knowing gaze, and he heaved a sigh of surrender. "All right," he said. "Beneath this shamefully tarnish exterior is a very good grade of gold."

"Go on."

"It is antique, very old. Truly a work of art. In all my years in the business, I have seen nothing quite so fine."

"It kind of got me, too," Mitch confessed, a little wonderingly. "But go on, Doc. The business."

Doc Krug spread his fat hands. "I will tell you the truth, Mitch. An object such as this is above price. It is as valuable as one's sense of beauty is great. I might say it was worth fifteen hundred dollars. Or two thousand. Or even twenty-five hundred. And I would be correct in each case. Do you follow me? If one can wait and look long enough, find exactly the right buyer..."

"I can't," said Mitch. "Make me an offer."

"One thousand dollars."

Mitch concealed a start. It was a much better deal than he had hoped for. Gratified as he was, however, he automatically refused. "Come on, Doc. You can do better than that."

"No. I am not absolutely positive that I can resell it for even a thousand. Because it is a work of great beauty, I am willing to gamble. But a thousand is my limit."

"All right," Mitch said. "I guess I'll just keep it then. Try for a deal some place else."

"You are wise to do so," Doc nodded. "Yes, and I would even prefer that you do it. I am not a gambling man. For me to have a thousand dollars tied up indefinitely, perhaps for years—"

"It's a deal for a grand," Mitch said hastily.

Krug gave him a thousand dollars, twenty crisp fifties.

Mitch turned over his buy-slip on the cup, a receipt turned over by Peggy Turner and transferring title to the cup for "one dollar and other valuable considerations."

"And now," Doc said, "I assume that this will be the end of our association. You will be leaving town."

"The first thing in the morning," Mitch agreed. "All I came here for was a stake. Now that I've got it, I'm lighting out of here, fast."

"It is well. As your best friend of the moment may I make a suggestion? Get into some very simple occupation —something akin, say, to stealing from blind men, or robbing very small newsboys. For anything better, you lack the mentality."

Mitch thanked him politely. Then he made a suggestion, a completely impossible one, involving various parts of Doc's anatomy.

"Scum!" Doc hissed. "Hoodlum! Stupid oaf! So easily I cheated you on the cup. Why, in time, I will resell it for—"

"In time," Mitch nodded, "and maybe. It's starting to stick in your craw already, isn't it? Well, goodbye, you fat, bald-headed old . . ." He loosed a hair-curling string of epithets at Krug. Then, he left.

And Doc Krug looked after him, not angrily but pleased, a wolfish smile on his face.

3

Mitch Allison was as lowdown as they come, but his front was strictly high-class. He was capable of courtly manners and language. He ate, drank and wore nothing but the best. So, while he was staying at a second-rate hotel—a place where the guests' backgrounds and misdoings were discreetly ignored—he occupied a parlor suite. He was in the parlor now, on the evening of his sale of the cup.

He had eaten elegantly, as the plates on the linen-covered table testified. In a bucket at the side of his chair there was a large bottle of imported champagne, and in his hand a crystal goblet of the sparkling liquid. He studied it fondly, marveling at the suddenness with which his luck had turned from god-awful to grand.

A week ago he had had nothing, as next to nothing as a hustler can have and keep going. Now he had a thousand bucks, or call it nine hundred after he squared with the hotel. Almost two hundred dollars for each day he'd put in with Doc Krug.

Not bad, he mused comfortably. Not bad for a guy with no education, no family; nothing but a head on his shoulders and the guts to kick back twice as hard as he got kicked!

He could take a stateroom all the way to New York, and still arrive there with a very tidy sum. It wouldn't be as much as he'd like to have, enough to really live it up while he was trying to latch onto something. But—

Mitch Allison frowned thoughtfully. Perhaps he should make another last whirl at Los Angeles. It had seemed wise, a week ago, to get out and stay out of L.A. With three people threatening to kill him—his wife, Bette, among them—it seemed very wise. But his nerves had been a little bad at the time, so maybe he'd considered too hastily.

After all, people had been threatening to kill him for years, without, obviously, carrying the project through. And the sucker you'd trimmed was always the best sucker to trim again. He'd be waiting to get even with you. He'd think that he was wise to all your tricks, and that he would take you this time.

So? Los Angeles or New York? Or, rather, Los Angeles then New York, instead of New York period.

Mitch turned the matter over in his mind . . . There was a soft knock on the bedroom door. He didn't answer it, naturally. He knew no one in San Diego but Doc, and Doc most certainly would not be paying him a call.

Picking up the phone, he spoke softly to the room clerk. The clerk's reply was similarly soft. "None of the employees, Mr. Allison. Someone must have slipped past me. Want the house dick?"

"No, I'll handle it," Mitch frowned, hesitating, and then he grinned. Entering the bathroom, he turned the shower on full blast. He let out a brief, muted bellow, as of a man singing in his bath; then cautiously, noiselessly, he unlocked the bedroom door and returned to the parlor.

If things worked out as he expected them to . . .

They did work out that way, after a few more knocks. The bedroom door opened slowly. It closed again softly. And there in his room, looking frightened but angry and determined, stood the redheaded girl, Peggy Turner.

Mitch scowled. Only Doc knew his address. Had Doc sicced her on him, told her she'd been cheated, just to make trouble for him?

Well, he'd have to do something nice for Doc, too. Yes, he'd do something very nice for him. Meanwhile, first things first.

Mitch took a roll of adhesive from his pocket; a very handy item, he'd found, and nothing that the cops could kick about in case you were searched. He ripped off a piece of it, laid it flat in his palm, and moved back softly into the bedroom.

The girl was at the baggage rack, rummaging through his suitcase. As she straightened, Mitch's hand swooped in front of her face, slapping the tape across her mouth.

She gasped and kicked backward. Mitch bumped her head against the wall, jerked and whirled her and sent her sprawling on the bed. Before she could rise, he was on it with her. Holding her against him, his arms locked around hers.

"Now, listen," he said, his mouth almost against her face. "You want to play rough, I'll do it, but it's my game, baby, and you won't like the way it turns out. So what do you want to do? Play nice—behave yourself—or go out of here without your front teeth?"

Blue eyes blazed at him helplessly. Her throat rippled with the effort to speak.

"You'll behave?" Mitch said. "Just nod for yes."

She hesitated. Then, all the anger went out of her eyes, and tears filled them; she nodded, sobbing.

Mitch took the tape from her mouth. He was all set for a scream or a struggle, but neither came. All the fight had left her, apparently, for she stayed where she was, weeping as helplessly as a baby.

Her body trembled against his as she wept. Trembled in an extremely pleasant way. Mitch gave her a few experimental pats, he stroked her and was met with only token resistance.

"You s-stop that"—but she didn't move away. In fact, she seemed to cuddle a little closer. "First you ch-cheat me, and then y-you—"

"Now, now," Mitch said. "I didn't like it either, baby. It was just business, you know, nothing personal."

"I was sorry for you! I l-lost my job last night and I'm almost broke, but I felt s-sorry for you that—"

Mitch clicked his tongue remorsefully. He murmured that he was most terribly, terribly ashamed of himself, and that he was going to start right now to turn over a new leaf.

"Y-you—you mean,"—she shifted her red head, stared hopefully into his eyes. "You mean you'll—"

"That's just what I mean, honey. We'll split the take right down the middle. Half for you, half for me."

"Ooooh!" she kissed him wildly. "You darling, *darling!* You know what I'm going to do for you?"

"Let me guess," said Mitch, and he increased his patting.

Needless to say, he wasn't going to split Doc's grand with her. The only dough she'd get out of him would be her cab fare, and she wouldn't get that until morning.

"You're so sweet to me, I'm going to be sweet to you. I'll give you half of the eight thousand I get from Doctor Krug."

"Fine. Swell. You'll give . . ." Mitch stared at her.

"Something wrong, darling?"

"N-nothing." Mitch fought to control his voice. "So Doc told you he'd paid me eight grand for the cup?"

"Uh-huh. Well, no, he didn't either, exactly. He came out to the house to see if I had another cup. A chalice he called it, a Cellini chalice, like the one I gave you. And he said if I did have, he'd give me eight thousand dollars for it."

"So?"

"Well, I didn't like him a bit. I mean, I'm an awfully good judge of character—everyone says so. And I knew that was one man I'd certainly have to watch my step with. He was so sneaky looking, so kind of oily and—"

Mitch suppressed a groan of impatience. "You're absolutely right about him, sweetheart. He's a stinker in spades. But what about the eight thousand you're going to get from him?"

"The eight thousand?"

"Yes!"

"For another chalice?"

"God!" Mitch groaned. "Holy God!"

"Now, look," the girl twitched. "You don't need to be so cross about it!"

"Cross? You mean you thought I was cursing?" Mitch laughed hollowly. "Why, I was praying, my pet!"

"Oh, how sweet! Do you always pray at this time?"

"Always," Mitch sighed. "Always and always. Now, please, baby! Take it from the beginning and . . ."

Gradually, he got the story out of her.

Distrustful of Doc Krug, she'd told him that she didn't have another chalice at the house, but that she thought she had one stored away in an old trunk. It was in a warehouse, she'd said, and she couldn't get into it before morning. Actually, it was in a bar—it belonged to the owner—down near the railroad station, where she, or rather a boyfriend she was with at the time, had bought the first one. They'd been just a teensy-bit tipsy that night and the boyfriend had thought it'd make a swell thing to drink beer out of. So he'd bought it from the proprietor for two dollars.

"An awful old grouch," the girl added. "I mean, he didn't act that way the first time, but he was just as mean as he could be tonight. Why, he wasn't using it at all. It was just sitting up there with a lot of old receipts stuffed into it. But when I offered to buy it from him—and I wasn't snippy at all, Mitch; I most certainly wasn't trying to throw my weight around like he said I was . . ."

But anxiety had probably made it seem like she was, Mitch guessed. And apparently the proprietor was one of those stubborn, independent birds. At any rate, he'd told her that if she wanted the cup it would damn well cost her. Either she laid a hundred bucks on the line, or he'd keep it himself.

"And you didn't have the money, so you came to me," Mitch finished. "Where did you say this place was, honey?"

"Just about three blocks from here." She gave him the address. "Could I have my four thousand dollars, honey? I'll go and get the cup, then, and—"

"Certainly, you can have it," Mitch said. "Just as soon as I run out and get some change. It's all in—in big bills. A five-thousand and a three-thousand. I—uh—"

"Three thousand?" the girl frowned. "I didn't know they made three-thousand-dollar bills."

"They just started," Mitch assured her. "I'll be right back, honey. Right back." He literally ran out of the room. He left the hotel on the double, gradually slowing to a thoughtful walk. Take it easy, he cautioned himself. Maybe she misunderstood Doc. Maybe he lied to her deliberately, to get her good and burned with me.

Turning in at a newsstand, he phoned Krug—at his house, since his shop would be closed at this hour. Doc snickered at the sound of his voice. "You have had a nice visitor, yes? When do the doctors think you will recover?"

"She was very nice," Mitch told him. "Nice enough to tell me where I could pick up the duplicate of the Cellini chalice I sold you."

"Please do so. It will confirm my opinions as to your stupidity."

Mitch was silent. Doc laughed with a trace of nervousness.

"I think I have punished you enough, Mitch. Save your much-needed money for traveling expenses. There is no duplicate of the chalice."

"There isn't, huh?" Mitch said. "Well, well."

"Indeed, there isn't, Mitch! If she knows of a similar one, it is certain to be a fake. It would be worthless. It—uh—Of course, if it is a very good fake I might pay a little for it. I would be very happy to examine it, and—"

"You're showing your seams, Doc." Mitch laughed shortly. "Now, lay it on the line and do it fast. That chalice will cost you exactly ten thousand dollars. Do you want it or not?"

"Ten thousand!" Doc squealed like a stuck pig. "But it is a fake, an imitation! It cannot be otherwise. I—"

"Yes or no?"

He heard Doc gulp. "All right, Mitch," Doc said in an agonized whisper. "When . . . ?"

"I'll get in touch," Mitch said, and he banged up the receiver.

He arrived at the block the bar was in, crossed the street and studied it from the other side. It was a wine-and-beer joint, rather than a regular bar. Its four stools and one small booth were empty. The proprietor, a beefy square-faced guy, was lounging behind the counter, reading a newspaper.

Mitch crossed the street, and entered. Taking the front stool, he laid a coin on the counter and ordered a beer. He sipped, and his eyes moved to the top shelf of a tiered whatnot.

It was there, a cup with four figured handles. It wasn't quite so dingy, perhaps, but it was unmistakably the twin of the other chalice. No fake, no imitation. Even from several feet away, Mitch knew that it was genuine. Unerring

instinct told him it was, whispered that here was money—
big money—as it had when he saw the first cup.

He caught the proprietor's eye, nodded.

"That cup," he said. "My wife likes it. I don't like my
wife."

"You got company." The man looked at him stolidly.
"How much you don't like her?"

"A hundred dollars' worth."

"A hundred dollars. And you ain't in no big hurry? You
don't want to give me the rush act?"

"I wouldn't think of it," said Mitch.

"Well, all right. People come here thinking I'm gonna
jump every time they holler frog . . ." The grumbling words
trailed away, as he turned and reached down the cup. He
laid it on the back bar, and began wrapping it in an old
newspaper.

Mitch grimaced wryly. It was no wonder the guy was
running a dump like this. With his temperament, he was
lucky to have any kind of business.

The man turned around again, and set the cup on the
counter. Mitch took the wallet from his hip pocket.

It was empty.

4

The proprietor stared at Mitch, a stubborn frown wrinkling
his forehead. Mitch went on talking, the words issuing
from his mouth in a suave and steady stream. He was very
convincing; the ability to be convincing was his stock in
trade. Slowly, the proprietor softened up.

"All right," he said, at last, "we'll start all over. You
were lying about the dame. You don't like her maybe, but
you're really after the cup. And you want it because it's
worth heavy sugar to you."

"Well. I wouldn't put it that way exactly."

"Put it this way, then. What do I get out of it, and when
do I get it?"

"In twenty-four hours. Just give me twenty-four hours."

"How much in twenty-four hours? And don't give me no stuff about a hundred dollars. The price has gone up."

"Well . . ." Mitch hesitated.

The girl had that grand she'd nicked him for. Since she didn't trust Doc, the grand was all she could offer this guy. So if he was promised eleven hundred or maybe twelve to clinch things . . .

But! Would the girl have picked his pocket if she intended to hang around? It didn't seem likely. She'd have to be a lot dumber than she acted to come near this place. She didn't know anything about antiques; she was scared and distrustful. So she'd taken him for his roll, thinking she was getting four grand instead of one, and now . . .

Still, maybe not. He couldn't be sure, and this was no time to take chances.

"Well?" the proprietor frowned. "What d'ya say, Mac?"

"I'll tell you what I'll do," Mitch said. "Whatever you're offered for the cup I'll give you two hundred more."

"What the hell does that mean? Suppose I ain't offered anything?"

"Then," said Mitch smoothly, "you get two hundred dollars. Fair enough?"

The man frowned uncertainly. He scratched his head, a doubtful look coming into his eyes. "Yeah, I guess so," he admitted. "Two hundred bucks on top of anything, from zero on up. Yeah, that sounds okay."

He gave Mitch a look of surly approval. He said he liked a guy that shot square and didn't rush him and that he'd hold the cup twenty-four hours.

Mitch thanked him warmly, shook hands and left.

He didn't go back to the hotel, naturally. The redhead wouldn't be there; he had no funds to pay his bill. He entered a pawnshop, emerged minus his topcoat and wristwatch and caught a cab to the airport. A little more than an hour later he got out of another cab on Los Angeles' Spring Street and started up the steps to his wife's apartment.

It was above a store building in a rundown neighborhood. Bette made good dough as a burlesque strip, she was always a tight gal with a dollar, and man. Mitch hadn't loosened her up any.

There was a double lock on the door. Two locks, inste. of the customary one, and both of them were new. He wen. to work on them, picked them almost as readily as he had picked all the others and went inside.

It was only a few minutes after ten. Bette wouldn't be home before midnight. Mitch got busy again, searching every nook and cranny of the apartment, searching all the old hiding places and every possible new one. He wound up empty-handed.

There wasn't a dollar in cash in the joint. There wasn't a thing that was hockable for more than a few bucks.

Mitch put back everything as he had found it. He left, not at all dejected, already planning his more subtle return. Meanwhile, there was another prospect on his list, a sucker who, unfriendly as he might be, was also loaded.

The guy's name was Duke English. A pretentious thug with a phony way of talking, he ran a nightclub a few blocks from Bette's apartment.

Mitch strolled into the place. A muscle-bound dancer called The Ape escorted him back to Duke's office. He was very firm about it.

This visit was probably a mistake, Mitch decided. Duke was still as murderously sore at him as he had been a week ago. The Ape knee-booted him into the Duke's office. English greeted him warmly, and Mitch's hunch that he had erred became a conviction.

That was the Duke's way. The sorer he was the more friendly he acted. "Sweetheart!" he said. "Mitch, darling! What a pleasant surprise!"

"Look, Duke," Mitch stammered. "I'm sorry about that little frammis on the booze, and I've come to make it up to you. I've got a—"

"A surprise?" Duke clapped his hands. "I'll be it's money, isn't it? You've come to give me some money!"

"No—yes, that's right," Mitch said hastily. "You put in

leven or twelve hundred with me, well, two grand at the
outside, and—"

"Money!" Duke interrupted him gaily. "Oh, goody!
Ape, lover, our friend is being coy. Will you give him a
little assistance?"

The Ape frisked Mitch. He did a very thorough job of it.
Duke pouted over the result, then leered and fluttered his
eyelids modestly. "Will you put your clothes back on,
dear? I do blush so easily!"

Mitch re-dressed, keeping a wary eye on him. Despite
Duke's talk, his appearance was anything but feminine. He
was small, with the same wiry build and hard, big hands of
a jockey. Without his shoulder-holstered gun, Mitch knew
he was a match for practically any tough customer who
patronized his place. He could joke while kicking a man's
teeth out.

"No money," he said. "Dear, dear. But you spoke about
letting me in on something juicy?"

"That's right! Duke, if you can bank me for two-grand
max, I'll guarantee—"

"It wouldn't involve whiskey, would it? I do hope not!"

"On the level, Duke. I swear it."

"Proceed," the Duke said. "And would you mind, darling? I'll decide whether it's on the level."

Mitch gave him the story, holding out enough details to
prevent Duke's taking over the deal himself. He finished
and Duke frowned thoughtfully and reached for the telephone.

"Long distance," he said. "I'd like to speak to San
Diego, the residence of—"

"Wait!" Mitch broke in. "Doc will lie to you, Duke.
He'll tell you that—"

"Shaddup!" the Ape said.

Mitch shut up. The Ape had tapped him across the
Adam's apple. Duke spoke to Doc, listened and hung up
the receiver. He grinned at Mitch.

"Naughty, naughty! Oh, you naughty boy!"

"Listen!" Mitch begged. "That cup is the McCoy, the real thing! Doc lied to you because—"

"You're excited," the Duke said, solicitously. "You need a drink. Ape, darling, will you get a bottle out of the liquor cabinet?"

"The Scotch?"

"But, of course! Some of that rare old Scotch that our dear friend sold me at a bargain rate."

The Ape took a full quart from the cabinet. He opened it, and thrust it into Mitch's nerveless hands. Mitch stared at it horrified, for naturally it did not contain Scotch or any other kind of whiskey. What it contained was radiator fluid and tobacco juice.

"Drink up!" Duke beamed. "I'll be terribly offended if you don't."

"Listen, Duke. I—"

"You better drink, dear!"

Mitch took a sip of the stuff. He gasped, choked, and his stomach did flip-flops.

"Delicious, isn't it?" the Duke said. "Have another."

"I c-cuh-can't!" Mitch strangled. "I—I—"

"You don't like it? Oh, dear! Ape, why do you suppose the darling doesn't like our Scotch?"

"He's just pretendin'," the Ape said. "He loves it."

"Oh?"

"Uh-huh. Kinda bashful, you know. His mama told him he should never take seconds."

"Why, the shy sweet child! Well, if he won't accept our hospitality, we'll simply have to—"

Mitch made a wild lunge from his chair. The Ape collared him, and slammed him down into it again. He put a hamlike hand over the upper part of Mitch's face. His mouth was forced open, and . . .

It wasn't as bad as he expected. Rather, they didn't give him the full treatment he had expected. After a couple of swallows, the Ape kicked him out into the alley, the kick prompting Mitch's stomach to expel the stuff. He picked himself up, neither seriously sick nor injured, and went down the alley to the street.

He cleaned up in a restaurant washroom. Then, with three glasses of milk soothing his innards, he returned to his wife's apartment.

Light gleamed under the door. He could hear her stirring about inside. Rapping on the door, he called softly, "It's Mitch, honey."

There was a dead silence for a moment. A very long moment. Then there was a *click* followed shortly by another *click* as she keyed the two locks.

Mitch gripped the doorknob. He turned it simultaneously throwing his weight against the door.

Bette had been waiting behind it. Now, half-stunned—crushed between the wall and the door—she surrendered the section of lead pipe with which she had meant to slug him. Mitch tossed it into a corner.

He released her, then guided her stumbling to a chair despite her profane protests.

She was a nice armful of woman, this Bette. Small, but busty, slender but lusciously curved. Mitch could never look at her—particularly in a nightgown as she was now—without getting steamed up. Unfortunately, he was also unable to look at her for long without playing her for a chump. But that was her own fault, he told himself virtuously. When a dame was so easy to outguess, when she just wouldn't smarten up, what was a hustling man to do?

The dazed look went out of her eyes. She addressed her husband with a kind of surly joy. "Well, go ahead, you lowdown louse. Go on and frisk the joint! Take everything you can find."

"I just came to say goodbye," Mitch said quietly. "I only wish there was some way to make up for all the wrong I've done you."

"Nuts! I know what you came for."

"I don't blame you for feeling that way," Mitch said.

"Goodbye, my sweet. I want you to know that I'll never love another woman."

He planted a chaste kiss on her forehead, swiftly to avoid a punch. Sadly, shoulders sagging, he started for the door. Bette looked at him with worried puzzlement, wondering what the gimmick was this time. Wondering if maybe . . .

He was one hell of a handsome guy. And gosh, he could be a lot of fun.

"Mitch . . ."

He shook his head, spoke without turning. "No, Bette. I think we'd better leave it at goodbye. You're too good for me. I want you to know that I'd never wrong you again, but—"

Gosh, he *must* have changed. If not, why hadn't he robbed her again tonight? Of course, he wouldn't have got anything, but he didn't know that. "Mitch!" she wailed. "Don't go, honey!"

Mitch allowed himself to be persuaded. He went back, and Bette sat on his lap.

He softened her up good. Then, to use a con man's expression, he told her the tale. Not about the chalice; that was too involved. This one concerned a certain Mame Dorset, madam of a parlor house.

Immediately, Bette's suspicions flared up again.

"No, by gosh! My dough's in the bank, and that's right where it's staying."

"All right." Mitch didn't argue with her. "I only wanted the money for you. I'd just as soon forget it myself."

"I won't touch a penny of that money! All the times you've gypped me—"

"I know. So let's drop the subject. After all, what's fifteen hundred dollars? You can draw that much salary in eight or ten weeks."

"Well—" Bette bit her lip. "It's certainly a nice piece of change, Mitch . . ."

"I understand," Mitch said, "it's dishonest. It's very bad of me to think about clipping poor Mame."

"N-no. I don't mind your clipping *other* people, Mitch. After all, a man has to do *something* and you're very good at it. If you'd just let me handle the dough you make instead of—"

"That's what I was going to do," said Mitch. "But as long as you're not interested . . ."

He seemed prepared, practically determined, to drop the subject. Bette gnawed her lip some more, trying to peer inside her husband's larcenous mind, seeking for the trap which might be awaiting her.

"Let me get one thing straight, honey. How do you know you can turn Mame's furniture for fifteen hundred?"

"She's been offered that much. She's been considering selling it for that."

"Yes, but that's legit. How do you know you can—"

Mitch explained. The old-fashioned mahogany furniture was well-known to the underworld. It had been appraised and listed by the thieves' market at fifteen hundred. And the dough was ready and waiting for the guy who could get it away from her.

"Just like that?" Bette frowned. "Mame can't do anything about it?"

"Like screaming to the cops? A madam yelling copper?" Mitch shrugged. "I guess she could sue me if she wanted to."

Bette giggled. "You say the funniest things, honey! Now one other thing, the big thing. I draw the dough out of my bank and give it to you, but I stick with you all the time. You don't get out of my sight for a moment. That's right, isn't it? I mean, I hate to sound suspicious, but—"

"That's the pitch," Mitch nodded firmly. "I deposit the money in another bank, but you'll be waiting right outside the door. And when I come out, I give you my passbook."

"Well . . ." Bette hesitated briefly. "It certainly sounds all right, honey. I have the passbook. I'll have a check for twenty-five hundred made out in the name of Mame Dorset."

Her voice trailed away. She frowned again, but not with suspicion. She looked at Mitch curiously, somehow seeming to look at herself at the same time.

"Mitch," she said, "what's the matter with us? Why do you do these things, and why do I want you to?"

"Come again?"

"Don't you see, honey? It takes brains to think up a deal like this. I'll bet there's presidents of big companies who couldn't do it. So why, if you're that smart—why be a crook? I mean, you could make it easier and bigger on the legit."

Mitch shrugged. The noncommital gesture, seemingly no answer, spoke volumes. This was his element; he had been born to it and he had always lived in it. And he was incapable of visualizing any other way of making a livelihood.

Why was he a crook? Well, why does a shark live in the water? It was that simple, and complex.

The matter slid in and out of Bette's mind; that's the way Bette's mind worked. Her face cleared, and she kissed him lovingly. "I'll need some identification, won't I, Mitch? Something to show I'm Mame?"

"Take out another social security card." He returned the kiss. "Yeah, and maybe you'd better buy a dog license."

"Mmmm..." She wriggled against him luxuriously. "Kinda tired, honey. Mommy's kind of tired..."

5

The following morning he opened a bank account with Bette's money while she waited watchfully outside. He gave her the passbook and a check made out to Mame Dorset, and then they separated. She was to cash the check, closing out the account, at a quarter-of-three. Which meant, although she hadn't thought of it, that she would not have time to redeposit the money in her own bank.

Of course, she could buy a cashier's check with the dough. But Mitch was sure she wouldn't. The kid was a born chump, and she'd never be anything else.

He called on a "right" furniture dealer, arranging for the purchase and transportation of Mame's stuff. While he was there, he got the name of a "good" dealer in art objects, just in case Doc Krug should get contrary.

He had a couple of drinks and a good lunch. At about one-thirty in the afternoon, he rapped on the door of Mame Dorset's house. It was very quiet; at this time of day, the girls would still be asleep. Mitch was starting to knock again when the door opened a few inches, and Mame's maid peering out at him.

"Mister Mitch!" A frightened gasp. "Go 'way from here! Miss Mame's just naturally going to kill you and me both if—"

"Then we'll have a double funeral," Mitch said easily, and he shoved his way past her. "How about it, Rosie? Like to be buried with me?"

The maid blanched. She made a grab for him as he started for the stairs. "Please, Mister Mitch! Puh-lease go 'way! Miss Mame just waked up, and she's taking a bath an'—"

"And about time, too," Mitch said. "I'll give her a hand." He shook off Rosie's restraining hands. As she watched in helpless terror, Mitch mounted the stairs and entered Mame's bedroom.

Mame saw him through the open door of the bath. With a wild yell, she grabbed up a scrubbing brush and hurled it at him. Mitch ducked it. Mame lunged up out of the tub, oblivious to its soapy treacherousness. And feet skidding, letting out another wild yell, she went under with a tremendous splash.

She came up again, spewing soapsuds, her peroxided hair a moplike mess. Mitch handed her a towel, gravely remarking that she seemed upset. "You act like you're sore at me, Mame. What's it all about?"

"*What's it all about!*" Miss Dorset shrieked. "You dirty son of a—You plant a cop on me, and then you've got the nerve to ask me what it's all about!"

"Cop? *I* planted a cop on you!" Mitch appeared horror-struck. "Surely that lovely young creature I brought here wasn't a cop!"

"You're damned right she was, and don't tell me you didn't know it!"

"Now, Mame. Why in the world would I—"

"You think I don't know? To rob me, that's why! You were going to come in after the raid and strip the joint. And the only reason you didn't was because Duke English was gunning for you!"

"Why, Mame, dear!" Mitch shook his head sadly. "You can't believe I'd do a thing like that! Why, what kind of a man would I be to—"

"The kind you are!" Mame shrieked. "Sure, you'd do it! There ain't a damned, lousy rotten thing in the world that you wouldn't do! I'm going to kill you, Mitch! I'll kill you, by God, if it's my last act on earth! I trusted you, and you, you stinking, lowdown, slimy, double-crossing . . ."

Her eyes rolled in her head. There was froth at the corners of her mouth, and her voice rose, grew wilder and wilder. Then, right at the peak of her curses and threats, when they reached a blood-curdling crescendo, she gasped, choked, and burst into tears.

Mitch had been waiting for that. As with many another woman, Mame's tantrums invariably ended this way. Swiftly he went into action, beginning his attack while she was still drained dry emotionally.

Weakly, too breathless to protest, she allowed him to help her out of the tub. He stretched her out on the bed, patted and rubbed her with the towel talked to her in his smooth, soothing voice.

"You have a beautiful figure, Mame. Lovely. I'd never believe you were a day over thirty-five."

"Oh, y-yeah. Sure. You—you really mean it, Mitch?"

"That girl deceived me, Mame. You know how deceitful these young girls are."

"Well . . ."

"She got me to feeling sorry for her. She wanted to get into the business, she said, so I told her I'd start her off right at the top. I said, 'Look, sister, this Mame Dorset is class with a capital C. She's a lady herself, and she'll make one out of you. She'll—"

"And I would have, too, Mitch! I'd have done it if I had to kick the stuffing out of her. Why, I've taken girls in here, really tough bimbos, and inside of three months . . ."

Mitch nodded sympathetically, choking back a laugh. Mame was undoubtedly the toughest, tightest-fisted battle-axe in the trade. Once a bim got in Mame's clutches, she was up the well-known creek. She never got out of debt. She worked for her board and room, and, of course, the exercise. And if she didn't like it, just let her say so. Mame would give her something that she liked even less.

Mitch glanced at the clock; it was two straight up. He swung into the beginning of his patter.

Mame went for the first part, the groundwork. Smooth operator that he was, it was easy too believe that Mitch had made a connection with a movie studio. Why not, anyway? Why shouldn't he have talked himself into a spot where he could tap the till? He'd suckered everyone else, so why not the movies?

"And that's where you come in, Mame. That's how I'm going to put you on the gravy train special. You see, they're doing this story about a parlor house, an old-fashioned one, you know, and . . ."

He gave her the rest of it. Mame stared at him. She didn't look like she was going to sock him, or even like she wanted to. She just seemed kind of weary and a little sad.

"Aaah, Mitch, why do you do it? Why did you have to do it?"

"Do what?"

"You just get through hitting me with one swiftie. Then, just when I'm pulling out of it, startin' to like you again, you bang me with another one. Dammit to hell, I don't know why I—"

"Look," said Mitch. "Fifteen hundred is a good price for that junk. I'm giving you twenty-five. You call that pouring a quick one? Now tell me."

"You're damned right!" Mame nodded emphatically. "Whenever you start writing checks, I start running!"

"Call up the bank," Mitch said. "Get the manager on the phone."

"Nuts!"

"Go on," Mitch said. "I'll talk to him and let you listen."

Mame wavered. She snatched up the phone. "You think I won't, huh? Well, I'll just call your bluff, buddy!"

The manager came on the wire. Mitch took it and spoke to him, holding the receiver slightly away from his ear so that Mame could listen.

"Yes," the man said. "Yes, I remember our conversation this morning. The twenty-five hundred is earmarked for Miss Mamie Dorset. It is to be paid to no one else."

Mame looked bewildered. Then, her eyes narrowed knowingly, and she whispered to Mitch. He nodded and spoke to the manager again.

"One other thing, Mr. Baker. You are not to honor any stop-payment on the check . . . Will you repeat that, please? Miss Dorset is with me, and I want her to hear you confirm it . . . Thank you very much, sir."

Mitch hung up the receiver. Mame shook her head incredulously.

"It's on the level," she said, in an awed tone. "You did something that was actually on the level!"

"Yes?" said Mitch with a trace of stiffness. "That's all you have say to me?"

"Well . . . I guess I owe you an apology, maybe."

He rode back to the store with the moving van. Pocketing fifteen hundred from the furniture dealer, he returned to Bette's apartment.

She was waiting for him. She had been worried, fearful that he might have got himself jammed up. And when he walked in grinning, obviously safe and successful, she was almost tearfully happy.

He kissed her, and scooped her in up in his arms. Smiling down into her face, he walked toward the bed with her.

"How about you, baby? Any trouble at your end?"

"Not a bit, Mitch. That manager was just as nice as he could be."

"Swell. You put the dough back in your own bank?"

"I couldn't, honey. It was too late."

"Was it?" Mitch shifted her in his arms. "And was it too late to buy money orders or a cashier's check."

"Well, no, I guess not. But those things cost money, you know, and—"

Mitch dropped her suddenly, and she fell to the bed with a little scream. He flipped her over on her stomach, sat down on her and took out his roll of tape.

She didn't struggle much. She had learned the futility of struggling with him, if she had learned nothing else. Mitch bound her wrists and ankles, stripped tape across her mouth and stood up.

She rolled over. Tear-filled eyes glared at him as he stripped the money from her purse. He looked down at her with a kind of smile-frown; irritated, but also apologetic.

"Now, what could you expect, Bette? Honest to God, what else could you expect?"

Bette made no answer, naturally. She closed her eyes, and two great tears squeezed beneath the lids, coursed slowly down her cheeks.

Mitch bit his lip. He turned abruptly and headed for the door. He opened it, took one last look at her as he stood on the threshold. What the hell? he thought. She'd be all right. She wasn't hurt any, she had a good job, she could work herself free in an hour. She was okay, and he was okay. And yet, he felt sort of bad.

"Baby..." he spoke awkwardly, hoarsely. "I guess it's pretty hard to believe, but I do love you. I really do love you, honey."

"And I," said a voice behind him, "I love you, too, dear."

Mitch jumped, whirled. Duke English beamed at him. Duke was small, but the gun with the silencer on it was awful big. "A little game, eh?" He nodded toward the door, smirking. "Can I play? I'll let you be It!"

"No, look, Duke," Mitch said hastily. "You paid me off for that whiskey deal. We're all square now."

"Why, lover," Duke pouted. "I'm not twitted with you; truly I'm not. I—but hadn't you better close that door? I'm afraid it's making a draft on the little woman."

Mitch closed it slowly, giving his mind time to catch up with the situation. Duke was calling it quits on the whiskey swindle. It must be, then, that he changed his mind about bankrolling the chalice deal. In that case...

He turned around, faced Duke again, laughing inwardly, outwardly sober and worried. "Can you make it fast, Duke? I've got a lot of hustling to do if I'm going to close on that chalice."

"You're still after it, then?" Duke said. "You're still sure it's a sweet item?"

"Ten thousand sweet items. A ten-G gross."

"And you couldn't promote the little woman? You haven't raised any of the necessary elsewhere?"

"Well," Mitch hesitated cautiously, "I have and I haven't. I've kind of made a start, you know, and uh—"

Duke studied him. He beamed, and patted Mitch's cheek. "Well, your troubles are over, dear boy. I shall be your partner, and provide the cash."

"Swell,' Mitch said, "that's swell, Duke. Now, I can get a train for San Diego in about twenty minutes."

"Train?" Duke pouted. "Oh, you don't want to ride those nasty old trains, honey. I'll let you drive my car."

"*Huh!*" Mitch made a fast recovery. "Well, that'll certainly be a lot better, Duke. I can—"

"And would you mind terribly, darling? You won't mind if I ride along with you?"

6

Mitch gaped. Laughing gaily, Duke giving him a push toward the stairs. "Move, honey," he said. "You'd better get moving!" Mitch moved.

Duke's big black Cadillac was parked at the curb. Mitch slid under the wheel, and Duke climbed into the back seat. He murmured approval as Mitch cautiously moved the car out into the stream of afternoon traffic. "That's fine, darling. I do get nervous so easily, and when I get nervous . . . Even with a silencer, I just simply loathe the sound of a gun."

The warning was unnecessary. Mitch hadn't the slightest notion of pulling anything. After all, he'd gotten a total of four Gs from Mame and Bette, to which add half the profit, at least, from selling the chalice—another four thousand. That was enough for twenty-four hours of hustling. Enough, at least, to prevent his risking a bullet for a few thousand more.

They left the city and hit the highway for San Diego. It passed through some of the most beautiful scenery in America, a semitropical expanse of orange groves and gleaming white-sand beaches. A salt-sweet breeze swept in from the ocean, air that one wanted to gulp down like champagne. And Mitch settled back in the seat, very relaxed and content, feeling that this world he had been born into was indeed a wonderful place to live.

. There was no need, he decided, to feel troubled about Bette. Hell, he'd really been pretty nice to her. Taught her a valuable lesson; relieved her of money which she didn't know how to spend properly and would only worry about. Yes, he'd been very fair and decent to Bette. He wasn't like some guys—this character Duke, for example. Now, there was one for you. Straight out from under the rug. He'd climb a tree to give you trouble when he could stand on the ground and be friends.

Mitch didn't dig the Duke at all. Duke was up to here in the chips; he was so loaded that it was making him stoop-shouldered to carry it around. Still, he went right on grabbing for more, and the nastier he could be about it, the better he liked it.

Take that talk of his. That was meant to rub you against the grain. A kind of defense with him. Uneducated, unable to talk good English, so he made with the dear-dear stuff. It was a cover-up for him. It helped him to get even for the shortchanging which he felt the world had given him. That was probably the source of a lot of Duke's nastiness: a feeling of inferiority. But why the hell didn't he get at the source of it? With his dough, he could . . .

Abruptly, for no reason he was aware of, Mitch's thoughts drifted from Duke to his own pleasant prospects. Eight grand. Between eight and nine grand! The first really big dough he'd ever got his hands on. To hell with a mere stateroom! He'd take a two-room suite on the Super Chief. And when he hit New York—brother! The big town would never be the same again. They'd be cleaning up the red paint for the next century.

It is about one hundred and thirty miles from Los Angeles to San Diego. They got there shortly after dark, and Mitch parked a little below and across the street from the bar. Duke looked at the place, frowning, as they got out of the Cad.

"You can't mean it, dear. A priceless antique is in a flyspecked hole-in-the-wall like *that*?"

"I told you," Mitch shrugged.

"Incredible! And how did yon uncouth creature get it into his possession, dear boy?"

"How do I know? What's the difference as long as he's got it?"

"An interesting question. Pray precede me, sweetheart."

Mitch started across the street, a careful two paces ahead of Duke. He was ever so slightly uneasy as he stepped through the door of the bar, just a little worried by Duke's remarks. Then, his eyes lighted on the whatnot behind the cash register, and his uneasiness vanished.

The chalice was there. It was still what his memory had told him it was; invisibly marked with the imprint of capital-D dough, glowing with the strange beauty which the centuries could not and would never dim.

"Made it, huh?" The proprietor beamed at Mitch. "That dame, the redhead, said you wouldn't, but I knew better."

He got out a piece of newspaper and began wrapping the cup. Mitch watched him, doing a little rapid arithmetic in his head. The girl had a grand in cash. If she'd peddled that junk furniture of hers, put the bite on some of her boyfriends, she might have raised as much as . . .

"How much?" he said.

"Well you know you promised to give me an extra two hundred. Whatever she offered you—"

"I know. How much altogether?"

"Six thousand, two hundred dollars."

"Six thou—" Mitch let out a gasp. His eyes narrowed to angry slits. "What the hell are you trying to hand me, buster? That babe couldn't have—"

"What do you mean, what am I trying to hand you?" The proprietor bristled. "You calling me a liar?"

"But . . . No, of course not—"

The man snatched up the cup and tossed it under the counter. Chin jutting stubbornly, he gestured toward the door.

"Get outta here! No one calls me a liar!"

"I'm sorry," Mitch apologized. "I didn't mean it like it sounded. I was just surprised, you know, I hadn't counted on . . ."

Dammit, Doc Krug must've got to the babe after all!

Only he could have bid the price this high—one so high, he thought, that Mitch couldn't meet it. And even at six grand he was getting a bargain.

"Well, all right," the proprietor grumbled, "as long as you didn't mean it. Just give me sixty-two hundred and we'll get this over with."

Mitch hesitated, shooting an uneasy glance at Duke. This was going to knock hell out of his profit, and it was going to look funny to flash four Gs in front of the Duke. Still, he'd either do it or there'd be no deal.

"Yeah, honey?"

Mitch stammered out an explanation. A couple of other guys had given him some backing. He'd kept quiet about it, for fear that Duke would think he was lying and get sore.

"What a dreadful picture you have of me!" Duke said. "I wouldn't think of cutting in on you, honey."

"But—"

"Huh-uh. There's a distinct odor of frammis about this. The old razza-ma-tazz. When I put money into a tin cup it has a blind guy holding it."

"Tin hell!" Mitch yanked out his wallet and slapped all but a few small bills onto the counter. "There's four grand I'm putting up. Would I do that if this wasn't on the level?"

"Not an unremote possibility, honey. The old clincher, you know. Still . . ." Still the dough had impressed him. It was the one thing that invariably impressed Duke, Mitch knew.

The proprietor scowled at Duke with obvious dislike. In about a minute, Mitch guessed, he'd order them both out of the place.

"Come on, Duke," Mitch pleaded. "Play with me on this. You've made the trip. You've got the dough. Don't back out on it now, just when—"

"You better do somethin'," the proprietor cut in with a growl.

Duke looked from him to Mitch. His eyes remained on Mitch as he reached for his wallet.

"Very well," he said, counting from a sheaf of bills. "Oh, but very well, dear. But this hadn't better be what it might be."

The proprietor shoved his money with Mitch's and gave it a fast recount. He said, "Sixty-two hundred, on the nose," and handed over the cup.

Mitch left the place, still walking in front of Duke. He got behind the wheel again, Duke got back into the rear seat and they headed for Doc Krug's house.

It was near the ocean, a cottage sitting far back from the street and almost hidden by trees and shrubbery. The dense foliage, dank with the night dew, accented the loneliness of the place, gave it a desolate, mournful air. As Doc opened the door for them, Mitch felt like he was entering a tomb rather than a house.

They went down a short hallway, and into a living room. Doc sat down at a table, switched on the brilliant overhead lamp and looked leeringly at his two guests.

"So," he said, "you have a chalice by Cellini. The exact duplicate of an item which is known to be unique. It has no authentic duplicate, and yet—"

"But you were damned hot to buy it," Mitch snapped. "You were ready to pop six grand for it."

"Did I, indeed? And when and where did I do that?"

"Come on!" Mitch said. "Stop bluffing and open it up. Look at it and then tell me it's a fake!"

"Please, dear." Duke gave him a deadly grin. "Don't ask him to tell us that. Think how badly I'll feel if he does."

He slid a hand inside his coat. He jerked his head at Doc, and Doc picked up the cup. Slowly, his fat fingers fumbling, he began to unwrap it.

Mitch watched him, almost forgetting to breathe. A fine cold sweat broke out on his forehead. He chewed his lip, angrily asking himself why the nervousness.

The cup was the McCoy, just like the first one had been. He knew it as well as he knew he was alive. He'd known it last night; he'd known it tonight when he saw it for the second time. It had seemed to call to him from its perch on the whatnot shelf, whisper the magic word, money, to which his ear was ever attuned. And as he watched, the bar owner had lifted it down from its shelf and—and—

Mitch's heart skidded. His stomach did a slow, sickening flip-flop.

The guy had got sore, just as he finished wrapping it. He'd tossed it out of sight, under the counter, and—And there could have been another cup there! A fake, wrapped in exactly the same way as the real Cellini . . .

Mitch shot a swift glance at Duke. The racketeer was leaning forward a little, all his attention riveted on Doc and the object he was unwrapping. Mitch measured the distance between them. He edged sidewise cautiously, every muscle tensed, braced for immediate action.

The last wrapping fell from the cup. Mitch didn't need to be told it was a fake. He yelled unnervingly, swung his stiffened right arm with all his fear-inspired strength. It struck Duke's shoulders like a club, knocking him off balance, pitching him forward across the table.

He bowled into Doc. Doc shot over backwards in his chair and Duke landed on top of him.

Mitch ran; hell, he was already running. There was an ominous *ker-chung* as he hurled himself toward the hall— the sound of Doc's silencer gun. There was another as he clawed open the door, cleared the porch and the steps with one flying leap. Ducking and darting, he fled through the trees toward the street. Racing against the bullets that were certain to follow the first two.

Duke would be on his feet by now. He'd be lunging out the door, plunging through the trees in hot pursuit. He'd never swallow this, the rooking he thought he'd been handed.

Kuh-lunk!

A baseball bat seemed to crash into Mitch's forehead. His racing feet shot from under him, and his body literally soared into the air. He came down flat on his back, all the wind knocked out of him, paralyzed with shock.

He was conscious but he couldn't move. In the dim

moonlight, he looked dazedly upward . . . The thick branch of a tree. That was what had hit him, or rather what he had hit. At the rate he'd been moving, it was a wonder that it hadn't knocked his head off. Drearily, he almost wished that it had. Anything was better than to be like this. To lie here helplessly, waiting for a guy to kill you.

What was holding Duke up, anyway? Why the hell didn't he get it over with?

The minutes dragged by. Mitch's head began to clear, and a little breath came back into his body. He rolled his eyes, squinted through the foliage toward the house. He stopped breathing for a moment, straining his ears to listen.

There was nothing to hear. No sound. A guy couldn't move in this timber without at least a little racket, but there wasn't so much as a cracking twig. Obviously, Duke hadn't followed him, wasn't looking for him. It didn't make sense . . .

Didn't it, though!

He'd been conned. Not Duke. Duke had taken him, and blown him off. Given him the hard scare to keep him running. It was the old double-switch, the reverse play. You let the sucker talk you into a deal you'd set up yourself. When it blew up, you made more than him, and he made for the hills.

Mitch choked back a moan. In the darkness, a shamed flush spread over his face. A chump, no less! He, Mitch Allison, the hustler's hustler, the fastest of the fast boys, had been played for a chump! He pushed himself up, rose to a sitting position. Bitterly, his blood seething to a slow boil, he put questions to his mind, angrily prodding it to answer.

How did Duke know when to close in? . . . Simple, you sap! With his connections, he could tab anyone all over L.A. . . . But how did he know what I was holding? . . . He didn't have to, dammit! The cup's price is put out of your reach. You shell out your dough first, and Duke makes up the difference.

Mitch asked himself one more question, one of several

parts. As the answer spewed back at him, he started crawling toward the driveway . . . *Stop being a jerk, you jerk! This is a going concern, not a one-shot. The hustlers go to Doc—a right guy to see. Doc steers them to the girl. From then on it's the old merry-go-around until Duke blows the chumps off.*

Mitch came out of the trees and onto the driveway. He moved silently toward Duke's car, guessing that the chumps would never talk even if they did wise up. They'd be ashamed to. A deal like this could get them laughed out of their underwear. As for going to the police, that just wasn't done in these circles. You had too much to hide yourself. The law says something about appealing with clean hands, and you—guys like you and Doc and Duke —had to keep your hands in your pockets.

Mitch tested the trunk-lid of Duke's car. It was unlocked. He took out a heavy wrench, lowered the lid again, and quietly opened a rear door. He eased it shut, crouched down on the floor, waiting. It would be okay—he'd still have the big difference—even if Duke spotted him there. He had this wrench, and all Duke had was a gun loaded with blanks.

It was some thirty minutes before the door of the house opened. Doc and Duke lingered on the porch for a moment, their laughter, faint snatches of their conversation, drifting out to Mitch.

". . . still running, doubtless . . . A man of long legs, and little brain . . ."

". . . small bonus for Butch, dear? When he returns from his vacation, that is . . ."

". . . agree. And you will give the seven-fifty to Peg . . ."

"Plus my love, darling. Oodles and loads of my love. Sweet Peggy and I have a date . . ."

The door closed. Duke came through the trees to the car. He slid into the front seat and Mitch slugged him over the head.

There was plenty of muscle in the blow. It chilled Duke like a well-digger's feet. Mitch slugged him again to keep him that way—and because he felt like it—and dragged him over the seat. He threw Duke's gun into the trees, pocketed the roll he was carrying and dropped his body to the floor. He was going to do something really big for Duke, he decided. Something he'd never forget. But he didn't know what it would be at the moment, and there were other matters more pressing.

Mitch got out of the car. He brought his hands down on the horn; then, with the blast echoing through the trees, he raced toward the house.

The door opened. Doc called through the screen. He hesitated, waiting for a reply, and then came out on the porch. "Duke? Is there some trouble with the—?"

Mitch gave him a medium-heavy tap on the noggin. When Doc came to, he was on the floor in the living room, and Mitch was bent over him with an upraised wrench.

"P-please"—Doc's eyes rolled in terror. "I have money, Mitch! T-take—"

"I took it," Mitch said grimly. "Yours *and* mine. Where's the chalice?"

"I—I have already sold it! I—"

"Huh-uh. It was in the bar tonight, the genuine Cellini, the only one there is. The one you've shuffled from place to place to suck me in."

"It is in my store! Locked up in the safe."

"We'll see," Mitch said. "You'll go along with me, and if it isn't there I'll show you what'll happen, Doc. I'll give you a sample."

He started the wrench downward viciously. Doc let out a squeal.

"The girl, Mitch! The redhead! She picked it up at the bar, after—"

Mitch gave him a scalp-splitting blow. He'd found out all that he'd needed to, and he'd been itching to lay a good one on Doc.

He stood up and looked around thoughtfully, wondering how best to dispose of the fat man. After a moment's pondering, he strolled through the house and out the back door. It was an old place; a considerable distance from its nearest neighbor. It should have a cesspool. It did.

Mitch pried up its iron cover; a nauseating stench rolled up into his face. He struck a match and dropped it into the pit, getting a glimpse of brownish bubbling slime. He found a long pole—once used apparently as a clothesline prop—and measured the overall depth of the pit, as well as the depth of its contents. Satisfied with his findings, he reentered the house and took Doc by the heels.

Unconscious, and weighing what he did, Doc was a cumbrous load to drag. But Mitch had his heart in the job. He hauled him down the steps and on out to the cesspool. Mitch swung him around, so that his legs dangled into the pit. Then, he got behind him, hoisted mightily and let go.

Doc sank downward slowly, his body scraping against the cement walls. He went down into the slime, sinking until the stuff was almost up to is neck and his feet touched bottom. The cold filth revived him, and eyes rolling with terror he looked up at Mitch.

"N-no, Mitch! N-n-noo! You are not a murderer."

"I'm not," Mitch agreed. "You'll get out, Doc. You can reach the top, almost. All you have to do is—"

"*Pl-please!* I will die here! I—"

"You can reach the top. Almost," Mitch repeated. "You can jump for it as soon as you thin down your gut. Shouldn't take you more than a day at the outside."

Doc began to curse him. Sliding the iron lid partly over the hole, Mitch walked away laughing. Doc would get out all right, eventually. Guys like him and Duke were too damned ornery to die.

Reaching the car, Mitch found Duke showing signs of reviving. He slugged him again, bound him up with his belt and necktie, and drove away.

The bar-owner—the *supposed* bar-owner—now? Mitch hesitated, and shook his head. No telling where the guy was. Anyway, he was strictly small-time, not worth bothering with. To take care of Doc, Duke and the girl would be enough, Mitch.

He was still wondering what to do with Duke as he turned into the shabby dirt street across from the railroad tracks. Cutting the lights and motor, he glided to a stop in front of the girl's house.

The shades were drawn, but light gleamed around their edges. Mitch turned his head, looked musingly at the railroad right-of-way. Should he dump Duke there in the weeds? Strip his clothes off and dump him? Not good enough. It lacked finesse, and he would be discovered too soon. What, then?

There was a throaty whistle in the distance; a muted grinding and chugging. Then, the beam of a headlight sliding across the windshield, as a train steamed slowly out of the San Diego freight yards. Mitch scrambled out of the car. Scooping Duke up in his arms, he trotted toward the right-of-way.

He dumped him down in the weeds, ripped the clothes from his body. As the locomotive steamed past, he picked him up again and moved up to track-side. He waited there a moment, eyes straining in the darkness. Suddenly, he raised up on his toes, pitched upward and outward. And Duke's body went sailing through the door of an empty boxcar.

It would be morning before he awakened, Mitch surmised, probably in Arizona. If he wanted to get off the train, all he had to do was roll himself out the door.

Mitch went back to the house, mounted the steps silently and opened the screen. He held it with his foot, and knocked.

"Dukie?" A gay trill came from the girl. "Com-ing!"

There was a scurry of slippered feet. Then a delicious, "Duke, honee!" as she flung the door open wide and looked out.

Mitch belted her in the stomach, said, "Hon-ee to you, honey," and went in.

The chalice was on the table in an opened overnight case. Mitch examined it fondly, put it back in the case and snapped the catches on it.

The redhead was staggering around the room, gasping, bent over like a clothespin. Mitch gave her a light tap on the temple, then strolled into the bedroom as she crumpled to the floor.

He frisked that room and all the others. The results were very satisfying. Like Bette, the girl seemed to be a frugal type, for she had wads of bills stashed all over the joint. Mitch returned to the living room some three thousand dollars richer than he had been.

He took a roll of tape from his pocket and squatted over the girl. She was dressed for her date with Duke—or pretty well undressed. Mitch thought this was a very happy coincidence. He had a job in mind for her, and what she was wearing—or wasn't wearing—would do nicely as a uniform.

She waked up as he completed his binding and gagging. She couldn't talk, naturally, but her eyes asked a frightened question.

Mitch gave her a reassuring smile. "Don't worry, babe. You're going for a nice little ride, and then I'm going to drop you off at a friend's house. A very sweet old lady that runs kind of a social club."

For some reason, the girl didn't seem at all reassured. She squirmed wildly, her face reddening as she tried to curse Mitch through her gag.

Mitch shook his head reprovingly. "Why, how ungrateful of you! Just for that you have to go to bed early."

He gave her a tap on the chin. The girl went promptly to sleep. Mitch slung her over his shoulder and stood up.

It was a little before dawn when he dumped her on Mame Dorset's front porch in Los Angeles. He rang the doorbell, trotted back to the Cad and drove away.

He rode around for an hour or so, then ate a leisurely breakfast at a drive-in restaurant. Afterwards he headed for the business section, turning in finally at a used-car dealer's.

He had the registration papers on the car. He also had Duke's driver's license and certain other identification. The dealer offered him three grand for the Cad, then went up to thirty-three hundred. Mitch accepted this last bid and took a cab to the "right" dealer in art objects.

He was a gnomish little old guy, with a twinkling black eyes and a head of thick gray hair. His hands moved over the cup lovingly, patting and caressing it as though it were alive.

"Beautiful, oh, but beautiful! And exactly as Cellini describes it in the Autobiography. He made it for—was it the Doge, or the King of France? Well, no matter." He gave it a final pat, and looked up at Mitch. "Doc Krug, eh? I had heard some rumors—unfounded, I thought—that it was in his possession."

"Doc Krug," Mitch nodded.

"And how is the good doctor?"

"He's got a few lumps," Mitch said. "He's staying in a cesspool for awhile."

"Very shrewd of him," the dealer said gravely. "The cool atmosphere will reduce the swelling. Now as to your price, Mr. Allison—I think ten thousand is a little exorbitant."

"I don't."

"What would you say to the suggestion that you make me a present of it, out of gratitude for my failure to call the police?"

"I'd tell you go to hell," Mitch said.

"We-ll . . ." the dealer shrugged. "One must always try, you know. Do you mind taking a check?"

"Why should I?" Mitch said. "You'll go right along to the bank with me to get it cashed."

There were a number of people waiting to board the Chicago-bound Super Chief. One of the finest trains in the world, the Super Chief is invariably well patronized, despite the somewhat awesome prices on its deluxe accommodations.

Mitch stood a little to the rear of the well-dressed crowd, tired from much rushing around but still very happy. There was a thousand-dollar watch on his wrist. He was wearing five hundred dollars in clothes, and there was another five hundred bucks' worth in his two new suitcases. He looked more prosperous, better turned out, than anybody here. And still, despite his expenditures, he had almost twenty thousand dollars in cash.

He was set, loaded. He could burn it up for the next year, without turning a lick. He could—but he wouldn't. Already his eyes were roving the crowd, searching, seeking, hunting. He did it unconsciously. Because he was a hustler, and a hustler must always hustle.

His gaze roved. It ceased to rove. His eyes narrowed, held on the target. Then they shifted casually and he looked in another direction.

Those were his marks—an elderly couple in good but ill-fitting clothes. Probably retired farmers, Mitch guessed. People who'd knocked themselves out all their lives and had saved every penny they'd made. They'd have money, all right. If they didn't, they wouldn't be riding the Super Chief.

Mitch looked their way again. His eyes caught theirs, and he smiled. They smiled back at him timidly, then put their heads together and began to whisper.

Mitch grinned to himself. They'd be talking about him, now. Wondering if they'd be able to get themselves acquainted with him. As a matter of fact, the couple was doing exactly that:

"A chump, Papa?"

"The best kind, Mama. A hustler with a load."

"I figure, too. The more they got, the hungrier they look. The retired farmer routine?"

"Uh-huh. Don't trust banks. Never had time to learn none of those hyar-now card games."

"Papa!" The woman snickered softly. "How do we tie into him?"

"We don't. He'll tie into us. Watch!"

A warm smile on his face, Mitch Allison was coming toward them.

The Frightening Frammis

A MITCH ALLISON ESCAPADE

For perhaps the hundredth time that day, Mitch Allison squared his shoulders, wreathed his face with an engaging grin and swung his thumb in a gesture as old as hitchhiking. And for perhaps the hundredth time his appeal was rudely ignored. The oncoming car roared down on him and past him, wiping the forced grin from his face with the nauseous blast of its exhausts.

Mitch cursed it hideously as he continued walking, damning the car's manufacturer, its owner and finally, and most fulsomely, himself.

"Just couldn't be satisfied, could you?" he grumbled bitterly. "Sitting right up on top of the world, and it wasn't good enough for you. Well, how do you like this, you stupid dull-witted moronic blankety-blank-blank!"

Mitch Allison was not the crying kind. He had grown up in a world where tears were more apt to inspire annoyance than sympathy, and a sob was likely to get you a punch in the throat. Still, he was very close to weeping now. If there had been any tears in him, he would have bawled with sheer shame and self-exasperation.

Less than a day ago, he had possessed almost twenty thousand dollars, the proceeds from robbing his wife, swindling the madam of a parlor house and pulling an intricate double double-cross on several "business" associates. Moreover, since it had been imperative for him to clear out of Los Angeles, his home town, he had had a deluxe stateroom on the eastbound Super Chief. Then . . .

Well, there was this elderly couple. Retired farmers, ostensibly, who had just sold their orange grove for a five-figure sum. So Mitch had tied into them, as the con man's saying is, suggesting a friendly little card game. What happened then was figuratively murder.

The nice old couple had taken him like Grant took Richmond. Their apparently palsied hands had made the cards perform in a manner which even Mitch, with all his years of suckering chumps, would have declared impossible. He couldn't believe his own eyes, his own senses. His twenty grand was gone and the supposed suckers were giving him the merry ha-ha in a matter of two hours.

Mitch had threatened to beat them into hamburger if they didn't return his dough. And that, of course, was a mistake, the compounding of one serious error with another. For the elderly couple—far more practiced in the con than he—had impeccable references and identification, while Mitch's were both scanty and lousy.

He couldn't establish legitimate ownership to twenty cents, let alone twenty grand. Certainly, he was in no position to explain how he had come by that twenty grand. His attempts to do so, when the old couple summoned the conductor, had led him into one palpable lie after another. In the end, he had had to jump the train, sans baggage and ceremony, to avoid arrest.

So now, here he was. Broke, disgusted, footsore, hungry, hitchhiking his way back to Los Angeles, where he probably would get killed as soon as he was spotted. Even if no one else cared to murder him, his wife Bette would be itching to do so. Still, a guy had to go some place, didn't he? And having softened up Bette before, perhaps he could do it again. It was a chance—his only chance.

A hustling man needs a good front. Right now, Mitch looked like the king of the tramps.

Brushing the sweat from his eyes, he paused to stare at a sign attached to a roadside tree: Los Angeles—125 Miles. He looked past the sign into the inviting shade of the trees beyond it . . . The ocean would be over there somewhere, not too far from the highway. If he could wash up a little, rinse out his shirt and underwear . . .

He sighed, shook his head and walked on. It wasn't safe. The way his luck was running, he'd probably wade into a school of sharks.

In the distance, he heard another car approaching. Wearily, knowing he had to try, Mitch turned and swung his thumb.

It was a Cadillac, a big black covertible. As it began to slow down, Mitch had a feeling that no woman had ever given him such a going over and seemed to like so well what she saw as the one sitting next to the Cad's driver.

The car came on, slower and slower. It came even with him, and the woman asked, "How far to El Ciudad?"

"El Ciudad?"—the car was creeping past him; Mitch had to trot along at its side to answer the question. "You mean, the resort? About fifty miles, I think."

"I see." The woman stared at him searchingly. "Would you like a ride?" she asked.

"Would I!"

She winked at Mitch, spoke to the man behind the wheel. "All right, stupid. Stop. We're giving this guy a ride."

The man grunted a dispirited curse. The car stopped, then spurted forward savagely as Mitch clambered into the back seat.

"What a jerk!" The woman stared disgustedly at her companion. "Can't even give a guy a ride without trying to break his neck!"

"Dry up," the man said wearily. "Drop dead."

"So damned tight you squeak! If I'd only known what you were like before I married you!"

"Ditto. Double you in spades."

The woman took a pint of whiskey from the compartment, drank from it and casually handed it back to Mitch. He took a long thirsty drink and started to pass the bottle back. But she had turned away again, become engrossed in nagging at her husband.

Mitch was just a little embarrassed by the quarrel, but only a little. Mitch Allison was not a guy to be easily or seriously embarrassed. He took another drink, then another. Gratefully, he settled down into the deeply upholstered seat, listening disinterestedly to the woman's brittle voice and her husband's retorts.

"Jerk! Stingy! Selfish . . . ," she was saying.

"Aw, Babe, lay off, will you? It's our honeymoon, and I'm taking you to one of the nicest places in the country."

"Oh sure! Taking me there during the off-season! Because you're just too cheap and jealous to live it up a little. Because you don't want anyone to see me!"

"Now that isn't so, Babe. I just want to be alone with you, that's all."

"Well, I don't want to be alone with you! One week in a lifetime is enough for me . . ."

Mitch wondered what kid of chump he could be to take that sort of guff from a dame. In his own case, if Bette had ever talked that way to him—*pow!* She'd be spitting out teeth for the next year.

The woman's voice grew louder, sharper. The slump to her husband's shoulders became more pronounced. Incuriously, Mitch tried to determine what he looked like without those outsized sunglasses and the pulled-low motoring cap. But he didn't figure long. The guy straightened suddenly, swerved the car off into a grass-grown trail, and slammed on the brakes.

Mitch was almost thrown from the seat. The husband leapt from the car and went stomping off into the trees. She called after him angrily—profanely. Without turning, he disappeared from view.

The woman shrugged and looked humorously at Mitch.

"Some fun, huh, mister? Guess I rode hubby a little too hard."

"Yeah," said Mitch. "Seems that you did."

"Well, he'll be back in a few minutes. Just has to sulk a little first."

She was red-haired, beautiful in a somewhat hard-faced way. But there was nothing hard-looking about her figure. She had the kind of shape a guy dreams about, but seldom sees.

Mitch's eyes lingered on her. She noticed his gaze.

"Like me, mister?" she said softly. "Like to stay with me?"

"Huh?" Mitch licked his lips. "Now, look, lady——"

"Like to have this car? Like to have half of fifty thousand dollars?"

Mitch always had been a fast guy on the uptake, but this babe was pitching right past him.

"Now look," he repeated shakily. "I-I-"

"You look," she said. "Take a good look."

There was a briefcase on the front seat. She opened it and handed it back to Mitch. And Mitch looked. He reached inside, took out a handful of its contents.

The briefcase was filled, or at least half-filled, with travler's checks of one-hundred-dollar bills. They would have to be countersigned, of course, but that was——

"——a cinch," the woman said intently. "Look at the signature. No curly-cues, no fancy stuff. All you have to to do is sign it plain and simple—and we're in."

"But——" Mitch shook his head. "But I'm not——"

"But you could be Martin Lonsdale—you could be my husband. If you were dressed up, if you had his identification." Her voice faded at the look Mitch gave her, then resumed again, sulkily.

"Why not, anyway? I've got a few rights, haven't I? He promised me the world with a ring around it if I'd marry him, and now I can't get a nickel out of him. I can't even tap his wallet because he keeps all of his dough out of my hands with tricks like this."

"Tough," said Mitch. "That's really tough, that is."

He returned the checks to the briefcase, snapped the lock on it and tossed it back into the front seat. "How could I use his identification unless he was dead? Think he'd just go to sleep somewhere until I cashed the checks and made a getaway?"

The girl flounced around in the seat. Then she shrugged and got out. "Well," she said, "as long as that's the way you feel . . ."

"We'll get hubby, right?" Mitch also got out of the car. "Sure, we will—you and me together. We'll see that he gets back safe and sound, won't we?"

She whirled angrily, and stomped off ahead of him. Grinning, Mitch followed her through the trees and underbrush. There was an enticing roll to her hips—a deliberately exaggerated roll. She drew her skirt up a little, on the pretext of quickening her stride, and her long, perfectly shaped legs gleamed alluringly in the shade-dappled sunlight. Mitch admired the display dispassionately. Admired it, without being in the least tempted by it.

She was throwing everything she had at him, and what she had was plenty. And he, Mitch Allison, would be the first guy to admit that she had it. Still, she was a bum, a hundred and ten pounds of pure poison. Mitch grimaced distastefully. He wished she would back-talk him a little, give him some reason to put the slug on her, and he knew she was too smart to do it.

They emerged from the trees, came out on the face of a cliff overlooking the ocean. The man's trail clearly led here, but he was nowhere in sight. Mitch shot an inquiring glance at the girl. She shrugged, but her face had paled. Mitch stepped cautiously to the edge of the cliff and looked down.

Far below—a good one hundred feet at least—was the ocean: roiled, oily-looking, surging thunderously with the great foam-flecked waves of the incoming tide. It was an almost straight up-and-down drop to the water. About halfway down, snagged on a bush which sprouted from the cliff face, was a man's motoring cap.

Mitch's stomach turned sickishly. Then he jumped and whirled as a wild scream rent the air.

It was the girl. She was kneeling, sobbing hysterically, at the base of a tree. Her husband's coat was there, suspended from a broken off branch, and she was holding a slip of paper in her hands.

"I didn't mean it!" she wept. "I wouldn't have done it! I was just sore, and—"

Mitch told her curtly to shut up. He took the note from her and read it, his lips pursed with a mixture of disdain and regret.

It was too bad, certainly. Death was always regrettable, whether brought on by one's own hand or another's. Still, a guy who would end his life over a dame like this one— well, the world hadn't lost much by the action and neither had he.

Mitch wadded the note and tossed it after the cliff. He frisked the coat and tossed it after the note. Then, briskly, he examined the wallet and personal papers of the late Martin Lonsdale.

There was a telegram, confirming reservations at El Ciudad Hotel and Country Club. There was a driver's license, and a photostat of Martin Lonsdale's discharge from the army. Mitch examined the last two items with particular care.

Brown hair, gray eyes—yep, that was all right; that matched the description of his own eyes and hair. Weight one hundred and eighty—right on the nose again. Complexion fair—okay, also. Height six feet one inch . . .

Mitch frowned slightly. Lonsdale hadn't looked to be over five eight or nine, so—So? So nothing. Lonsdale's shoulders had been slumped; he, Mitch, had only seen the man on his feet for a few seconds. At any rate, the height on these papers matched his own and that was all that mattered.

The girl was still on her knees, weeping. Mitch told her

to knock it off, for God's sake, and when she persisted he kicked her lightly in the stomach. That stopped the tears, but it pulled the stopper on some of the dirtiest language he had ever heard.

Mitch listened to it for a moment, then gave her a stinging slap on the jaw. "You've just passed the first plateau," he advised her pleasantly. "From now on, you won't get less than a handful of knuckles. Like to try for it, or will you settle for what you have?"

"You dirty, lousy, two-bit tinhorn." She glared at him. "I just lost my husband, and—"

"Which was just what you wanted," Mitch nodded, "so cut out the fake sob stuff. You wanted him dead. Okay, you got your wish, and with no help from me. So now let's see if we can't do a little business together."

"Why the hell should I do business with you? I'm his widow. I've got a legal claim on the car and dough."

"Uh-huh," Mitch nodded judiciously. "And maybe you can collect, too, if you care to wait long enough—and if there aren't any other claims against the estate. And if, of course, you're still alive."

"Alive? What do you—"

"I mean you might be executed. For murder, you know. A certain tall and handsome young man might tell the cops you pushed Martin off of that cliff."

He grinned at her. The girl's eyes blazed, then dulled in surrender.

"All right," she mumbled. "All right. But do you have to be so—so nasty, so cold-blooded? Can't you act like—uh—"

Mitch hesitated. He had less than no use for her, and it was difficult to conceal the fact. Still, when you had to do business with a person, it was best to maintain the appearance of friendliness.

"We'll get along all right, Babe." He smiled boyishly, giving her a wink. "This El Ciudad place. Is Martin known there?"

"He was never even in California before."

"Swell. That strengthens my identification. Gives us a high-class base of operations while we're cashing the checks. There's one more thing, though—" Mitch looked down at the telegram. "This only confirms a reservation for Martin Lonsdale."

"Well? It wouldn't necessarily have to mention his wife, would it? They have plenty of room at this time of year."

Mitch nodded. "Now, about the clothes. Maybe I'm wrong, but Marty looked quite a bit smaller than—"

"They'll fit you," the girl said firmly. "Marty bought his clothes a little large. Thought they wore longer that way, you know."

She proved to be right. Except for his shoes, the dead man's clothes fitted Mitch perfectly.

Mitch retained only his own shoes and socks, and threw his other clothes into the ocean. Redressed in clean underwear, an expensive white shirt and tie and a conservative-looking blue serge suit, he climbed behind the wheel of his car. The girl, Babe, snuggled close to him. He backed out onto the highway and headed for El Ciudad.

"Mmmm..." Babe laid her head against his shoulder. "This is nice, isn't it, honey? And it's going to be a lot nicer, isn't it, when we get to the hotel?"

She shivered deliciously. Mitch suppressed a shudder.

"We'll cash the checks," she murmured, "and split on that. We'll divide everything, even-stephen, won't we, honey?... Well, won't we?"

"Oh, sure. Naturally," Mitch said hastily. "You just bet we will!"

And he added silently: *Like hell!*

2

El Ciudad is just a few miles beyond the outer outskirts of Los Angeles. A truly magnificent establishment during the tourist season, it was now, in midsummer, anything but. The great lawns were brown, tinder-dry. The long rows of palm trees were as unappetizing as banana stalks. The tennis courts were half-hidden by weeds. Emptied of water and drifted almost full of dried leaves and rubble, the swimming pool looked like some mammoth compost pit. The only spots of brightness were the red and white mailbox at the head of the driveway and a green telephone booth at the first tee of the golf course.

Briefly, the exterior of the place was a depressing mess; and inside it was even less prepossessing. The furniture was draped with dust covers. Painter's dropcloths, lumber and sacks of plaster were strewn about the marble floor. Scaffolds reared toward the ceiling, and ladders were propped along the walls.

There was only a skeleton staff on duty; they were as dejected-looking as the establishment itself. The manager, also doubling as clerk, was unshaven and obviously suffering from a hangover. He apologized curtly for the disarray, explaining that the workmen who were refurbishing the place had gone on strike.

"Not that it makes much difference," he added. "Of course, we regret the inconvenience to you"—he didn't appear to regret it—"but you're our only guests."

He cashed one of the hundred-dollar checks for Mitch, his fingers lingering hungrily over the money. A bellboy in a baggy uniform showed "Mr. and Mrs. Lonsdale" to their suite. It consisted of two rooms and a connecting bath. Mitch looked it over, dismissed the bellboy with a dollar tip and dropped into a chair in front of the air-conditioning vent.

"You know," he told Babe, "I'm beginning to understand your irritation with Marty. If this is a sample of his behavior, going to a winter resort in the middle of summer—"

"A double-distilled jerk," Babe agreed. "Scared to death that someone might make a play for me."

"Mmm-hmmm," Mitch frowned thoughtfully. "You're sure that was his only reason? No matter how scared he was of competition, this deal just doesn't seem to make sense."

"Well—" the girl hesitated. "Of course, he probably didn't know it would be this bad."

The kitchens and dining room of El Ciudad were not in operation, but the bellboy made and served them soggy sandwiches and muddy coffee. He also supplied them with a bottle of whiskey at double the retail price. They had a few drinks and ate. Then, with another drink before him, Mitch sat down at the desk and began practicing the signature of Martin Lonsdale.

For the one check—the one cashed by the manager—he had done all right. There was only a hundred dollars involved, and the manager had no reason to suspect the signature. But it would be a different story tomorrow when he began hitting the banks. Then, he would be cashing them with people whose business it was to be suspicious. His forgeries would have to be perfect, or else.

So he practiced and continued to practice, pausing occasionally to massage his hand or to exchange a word with the girl. When, finally, he achieved perfection, he started to work on the checks. Babe stopped him, immediately wary and alarmed.

"Why are you doing that? Aren't they supposed to be countersigned where they're cashed?"

Mitch shrugged. "Not necessarily. I can write my name in front of the person who does the cashing. Just establish, you know, that my signature is the same as the one on the checks."

"Yes, but why—"

"To save time, dammit! This is a forgery job, remember? We hold all the cards, but it is forgery. Which means we have to hit and get—cash in and disappear. Because sooner or later, there's going to be a rumble. Now, if you're afraid I'm going to lam out with these things—"

"Oh, now, of course I'm not, honey." But she stuck right with him until he had finished countersigning the checks. She was quite prepared, in fact, to spend the rest of the night. Mitch didn't want that. He shoved the checks back into the briefcase, locked it and thrust it into her hands.

"Keep it," he said. "Put it under your pillow. And now get out of here so I can get some sleep."

He began to undress. The girl looked at him, poutingly.

"But, honey. I thought we were going to—uh—"

"We're both worn out," Mitch pointed out, "and there's another night coming."

He climbed into bed and turned on his side. Babe left, reluctantly. She took the briefcase with her, and she locked the connecting door on her side of the bathroom.

Mitch rolled over on his back. Wide-eyed, staring into the darkness, he pondered the problem of giving Babe a well-deserved rooking. It was simple enough. After—and *if* he successfully cashed the checks tomorrow, he had only to catch her off guard and put her on ice for the night. Bind and gag her, and lock her up in one of the clothes closets. From that point on, however, he wasn't sure what to do. Or, rather, he knew what to do, but he didn't know how the hell he was going to do it.

He couldn't scram in the Cad. A wagon like that would leave a trail a blind man could follow. For similar reasons, he couldn't zoom away in a taxi—if, that is, it was possible to get taxi service this far from the city.

How was he going to do it, then? Equally important, where would he hide out if he was able to do it? For he would sure as hell have to hide out fast after this caper. Babe would squawk bloody murder. It wouldn't make her anything, but she'd sure squawk. Her body was soft and lush but one look at that cast-iron mug of hers, and you knew she would.

So . . . ?

Mitch scowled in the darkness. Now Bette, his wife, had a nondescript car. She could get him away from here, and she could—but it was preposterous to think that she would. Not after that last stunt he'd pulled on her.

Yes, he'd planned on pleading for forgiveness before his meeting with Martin and Babe Lonsdale. But the situation had been different then. There wasn't any fifty grand at stake. There wasn't the risk of a long prison stretch. If he appealed to Bette, he'd have to give her the full pitch on this deal. Which meant, naturally, that he'd be completely at her mercy. And if she wasn't feeling merciful, if he couldn't fast-talk her into giving him a break, well, that would be the end of the sleigh ride.

Enter the cops. Exit Mitch Allison and fifty grand.

I'm going to have to stop crooking everyone, Mitch thought. *From now on I'm going to be honest, with at least one person.*

He fell asleep on this pious thought. Almost immediately, it seemed, it was morning and Babe was shaking him awake.

They headed into Los Angeles, stopping at a roadside diner for breakfast. As they ate, Mitch consulted the classified telephone directory, organizing an itinerary for the day's operations. Because of the time factor, his targets — the banks — had to be separated by a discreet distance, lest he be spotted in going from one to another. Needless to say, it was also essential that he tackle only independent banks. The branch banks, with their central refer system, would nail a paper-pusher on his second try.

Babe watched Mitch work, admiration in her eyes — and increasing caution. Here was one sharp cookie, she thought. As sharp as she was tough. A lot sharper than she'd ever be. Being the kind of dame she was, she'd contemplated throwing a curve to win. Now she knew that wouldn't do it: she'd have to put the blocks to him before he could do it to her.

She was lingering in the background when he approached the teller's cage at the first bank. She was never more than a few feet away from him throughout the day, one of the most nerve-wracking in Mitch Allison's career.

He began by pushing ten of the traveler's checks, a thousand bucks at a time. A lead-pipe cinch with his appearance and identification. Usually a teller would do it on his own, or, if not, an executive's okay was a mere formality. Unfortunately, as Mitch soon realized, these thousand-dollar strikes couldn't get the job done. He was too short on time. He'd run out of banks before he ran out of checks. So he upped the ante to two grand, and finally to three, and things really tightened up.

Tellers automatically referred him to executives. The executives passed him up the line to their superiors. He was questioned, quizzed, studied narrowly. Again and again, his credentials were examined—the description on them checked off, item by item, with his own appearance. By ten minutes of three, when he disposed of the last check, his nerves were in knots.

He and Babe drove to a nearby bar where he tossed down a few quick ones. Considerably calmer, then, he headed the car toward El Ciudad.

"Look, honey," Babe turned suddenly in the seat and faced him. "Why are we going to that joint, anyway? We've got the dough. Why not just dump this car for a price and beat it?"

"Just go off and leave our baggage? Start a lot of inquiries?" Mitch shook his head firmly.

"Well, no, I guess that wouldn't be so good, would it? But you said we ought to disappear fast. When are we going to do it?"

Mitch slanted a glance at her, deliberating over his reply. "I can get a guy here in L.A. to shoot me a come-quick telegram. It'll give us a legitimate excuse for pulling out tomorrow morning."

Babe nodded dubiously. She suggested that Mitch phone his friend now, instead of calling through El Ciudad's switchboard. Mitch said that he couldn't.

"The guy works late, see? He wouldn't be home yet. I'll call him from that phone booth out on the golf course. That'll keep anyone from listening in."

"I see," Babe repeated. "You think of everything, don't you, darling?"

They had dinner at a highway drive-in. Around dusk, Mitch brought the car to a stop on El Ciudad's parking lot. Babe reached hesitantly for the briefcase. Mitch told her to go right ahead and take it with her.

"Just don't forget, sweetheart. I can see both entrances to the joint, and I've got the keys to this buggy."

"Now, don't you worry one bit," Babe smiled at him brightly. "I'll be right inside waiting for you."

She headed for the hotel, waving to him gaily as she passed through the entrance. Mitch sauntered out to the phone booth and placed a call to Bette. Rather, since she hung up on him the first two times, he placed three calls.

At last she stayed on the wire and he was able to give her the pitch. The result was anything but reassuring. She said she'd be seeing him—she'd be out just as fast as she could make it. And he could depend on it. But there was an ominous quality to her voice, a distinctly unwifely tone. Before he could say anything more, she slammed up the receiver for the third and last time.

Considerably disturbed, Mitch walked back across the dead and dying grass and entered the hotel. The manager-clerk's eyes shied away from him. The elevator-bellboy was similarly furtive. Absorbed in his worry over Bette, Mitch didn't notice. He got off at his floor and started down the hall, ducking around scaffolding, wending his way through a littered jungle of paint cans, plaster and wallpaper.

He came to the door of his room. He turned the knob, and entered.

And something crashed down on his head.

3

It was dark when Mitch regained consciousness. He sat up, massaging his aching head, staring dizzily at the shattered glass on the floor—the remains of a broken whiskey bottle. Then he remembered; realization came to him. Ripping out a curse, he ran to the window.

The Cad was still there on the parking lot. Yes, and the keys were still in his pocket. Mitch whirled, ran through the bath and kicked open the door to the other room.

It was empty, in an immaculate order, sans Babe and sans baggage. There was nothing to indicate that it had ever been tenanted. Mitch tottered back into his own room, and there was a knock on the door and he flung it open.

A man walked in and closed it behind him. He looked at Mitch. He looked down at the broken bottle. He shook his head in mild disapproval.

"So you are supposedly a sick man, Marty," he said gutturally. "So you have a great deal of money—my money. So drunk you should not get."

"H-huh? W-what?" Mitch said. "Who the hell are you?"

"So I am The Pig," the man said. "Who else?"

The name suited him. Place a pecan on top of a hen's egg and you've got a good idea of his appearance. He was perhaps five feet tall and he probably weighed three hundred pounds. His arms were short almost to the point of deformity. He had a size six head and a size sixty waistline.

Mitch started at him blankly, silently. The Pig apparently misunderstood his attitude.

"So you are not sure of me," he said. "So I will take it from the top and give you proof. So you are The Man's good and faithful servant through all his difficulties. So The Man passes the word that you are to pay me fifty thousand dollars for services rendered. So you are a very sick man anyway, and have little to lose if detected while on the errand—"

"Wait a minute!" Mitch said. "I—I'm not—"

"So you are to transport the money in small traveler's checks. So you cannot be robbed. So they can be easily cashed without attracting unwanted attention. So you have had a day to cash them. So"—The Pig concluded firmly—"you will give me the fifty thousand."

Mitch's mouth was very dry. Slowly, the various pieces of a puzzle were beginning to add up. And what they added up to was curtains—for him. He'd really stepped into something this time: a Grade A jam, an honest-tohannah, double-distilled frammis. The Pig's next words were proof of the fact.

"So you know how I earned the fifty G's, Marty. So you would not like me to give you a demonstration. It is better to die a natural death."

"N-now-now, listen!" Mitch stammered. "You've got the wrong guy. I'm not Martin Lonsdale. I'm—I'm . . . Look, I'll show you." He started to reach for his wallet. And groaned silently, remembering. He had thrown it away. There was a risk of being caught with two sets of identification, so—

"So?" The Pig said.

"I! Look! Call this Man whoever he is. Let me talk to him. He can tell you I'm not—"

"So," The Pig grunted, "Who can call Alcatraz? So—" he added, "I will have the money, Marty."

"I don't have it! My wife—I mean the dame I registered in with—has it. She had the room next to mine, and—"

"So, but no. So I checked the registry myself. So there has been no woman with you."

"I tell you there was! These people here—they're hungry as hell, see, and she had plenty of dough to bribe them . . ." He broke off, realizing how true his words were. He resumed again, desperately: "Let me give you the whole pitch, tell you just what happened right from the beginning! I was trying to thumb a ride, see, and this big Cadillac stopped for me. And . . ."

Mitch told him the tale.

The Pig was completely unimpressed.

"So that is a fifty-grand story? So a better one I could buy for a nickel."

"But it's true! Would I make up a yarn like that? Would I come here, knowing that you'd show up to collect?"

"So people do stupid things." The Pig shrugged. "So, also, I am a day early."

"But, dammit!—" There was a discreet rap on the door. Then it opened and Bette came in.

This Bette was a honey, a little skimpy in the chin department, perhaps, but she had plenty everywhere else. A burlesque house stripteaser, her mannerisms and dress sometimes caused her to be mistaken for a member of a far older profession.

Mitch greeted her with almost hysterical gladness. "Tell this guy, honey! For God's sake, tell him who I am!"

"Tell him . . . ?" Bette hesitated, her eyes flickering. "Why, you're Martin Lonsdale, I guess. If this is your room. Didn't you send for me to—"

"N-nno!" Mitch burbled. "Don't do this to me, honey! Tell him who I really am. Please!—"

One of The Pig's fat arms moved casually. The fist at the end of it smashed into Mitch's face. It was like being slugged with a brick. Mitch stumbled and fell flat across the bed. Dully, as from a distance, he heard a murmur of conversation . . .

". . . had a date with him, a hundred-dollar date. And I came all the way out here from Los Angeles . . ."

"So Marty has another date. So I will pay the hundred dollars myself . . ."

There was a crisp rustle, then a dulcet, "Oh, aren't you nice!" Then the door opened and closed, and Bette was gone. And The Pig slowly approached the bed. He had a hand in his pocket. There was a much bigger bulge in the pocket than a hand should make.

Mitch feigned unconsciousness until The Pig's hand started coming out of his pocket. Then Mitch's legs whipped up in a blur of motion. He went over backwards in a full somersault, landed on the other side of the bed, gripped and jerked it upward.

Speed simply wasn't The Pig's forte. He just wasn't built for it. He tried to get out of the way, and succeeded only in tripping over his own feet. The bed came down on him, pinning him to the floor. Mitch set him to sleep with a vicious kick in the head.

Mitch realized he had been moving in a blur. But now his mind was crystal clear, sharper than it ever had been. Where was Babe? Simple. Since she couldn't have rid-den away from the place, she must have walked. And Mitch knew where she had walked to.

What to do with The Pig? Also simple. The materials for taking care of him were readily at hand.

Mitch turned on the water in the bathtub. He went out into the hall and returned with two sacks full of quick-drying plaster . . .

He left The Pig very well taken care of, sitting in plaster up to his chin. Then, guessing that it would be faster, he ran down the stairs and out to the Cadillac. Wheels spinning, he whipped it down the horseshoe driveway and out onto the highway.

He slowed down after a mile or two, peering off to his right at the weed-grown fields which lay opposite the ocean. Suddenly, he jerked the car onto the shoulder and braked it to a stop. He got out; his eyes narrowed with grim satisfaction.

He was approximately parallel now with the place where he had assumed the identity of Martin Lonsdale. The place where Martin Lonsdale had supposedly committed suicide. And out there in this fallow field was an abandoned produce shed.

From the highway, it appeared to be utterly dark, deserted. But as Mitch leaped the ditch and approached it, he caught a faint flicker of light. He came up on the building silently. He peered through a crack in the sagging door.

There was a small stack of groceries in one corner of the room, also a large desert-type water bag. Blankets were spread out in another corner. Well back from the door, a can of beans was warming over a Sterno stove. A man stood over it, looking impatiently at the food.

Mitch knew who he was, even without the sunglasses and cap. He also knew who he was *not*—for this man was bald and well under six feet tall.

Mitch kicked open the door and went in. The guy let out a startled "Gah!" as he flung himself forward, swinging.

He shouldn't have done it, of course. Mitch was sore enough at him, as it was. A full uppercut, and the guy

soared toward the roof. Her came down, horizontal, landing amidst the groceries.

Mitch snatched him to his feet, and slapped him back
into consciousness. "All right. Let's have the story. All of
it and straight, get me? And don't ask me what story or
I'll—"

"I w-won't—I mean, I'll tell you!" the man babbled
frantically.

"We—tied into Lonsdale at a motor-court. Figured he
was carrying heavy, so Babe pulled the tears for a ride. We
was just going to hold him up, you know. Honest to Gawd,
that's all! But—but—"

"But he put up a fight and you had to bump him."

"Naw! No!" the man protested. "He dropped dead on us!
I swear he did! I'd just pulled a knife on him—hadn't
touched him at all—when he keeled over! Went out like a
light. I guess maybe he must have had a bad ticker or
something, but anyway. . ."

Mitch nodded judiciously. The Pig had indicated that
Lonsdale was in bad health. "So okay. Keep singing."

"W-well, he didn't have hardly any dough in cash like
we thought he would. Just that mess of checks. But we'd
pumped him for a lot of info, and we figured if we could
find the right kind of chump—excuse me, Mister—I
mean, a guy that could pass for Lonsdale—"

"So you did a little riding up and down the highway until
you found him. And you just damned near got him killed!"

He gave the guy an irritated shake. The man whimpered
apologetically. "We didn't mean to, Mister. We really figured we was doing you a favor. Giving you a chance to
make a piece of change."

"I'll bet. But skip it. Where's Babe?"

"At the hotel."

"Nuts!" Mitch slapped him. "You were going to hole up
here until the heat was off! Now, where the hell is she?"

The man began to babble again. Babe hadn't known how
soon she could scram. There'd been no set time for joining

him here. She had to be at the hotel. If she wasn't, he didn't know where she was.

"Maybe run out on me," he added bitterly. "Never could trust her around the corner, I don't see how she could get away, but—"

Mitch jerked a fist swiftly upward.

When the guy came to, he was naked and the room had been stripped of its food, water and other supplies. His clothes and everything else were bundled into one of the blankets, which Mitch was just lugging out the door.

"Wait!" The man looked at him fearfully. "What are you going to do?"

He departed. A mile or so back up the road, he threw the stuff into the ditch. He arrived at the hotel, parked and indulged in some very deep thinking.

Babe had to be inside the joint. This money-hungry outfit was hiding her for a price. But exactly where she might be—in which of its numerous rooms, the countless nooks and crannies, cellars and subcellars that a place like this had—there was no way of telling. Or finding out. The employees would know nothing. They'd simply hide themselves if they saw him coming. And naturally he couldn't search the place from top to bottom. It would take too long. Deliverymen—possibly other guests—would be showing up. And then there was The Pig to contend with. Someone must have driven him out here, and he would not have planned to stay later than morning. So someone would be calling for him, and—

Well, never mind. He had to find Babe. He had to do it fast. And since he had no way of learning her hiding-place, there was only one thing to do. Force her out of it.

Leaving the hotel, Mitch walked around to the rear and located a rubbish pile. With no great difficulty, he found a five-gallon lard can and a quantity of rags. He returned to the parking lot. He shoved the can under the car's gas tank and opened the petcock. While it was filling he knotted the rags into a rope. Then, having shut off the flow of gasoline, he went to the telephone booth and called the hotel's switchboard.

The clerk-manager answered. He advised Mitch to beat it before he called the cops. "I know you're not Lonsdale, understand? I know you're a crook. And if you're not gone from the premises in five minutes—"

"Look who's talking!" Mitch jeered. "Go ahead and call the cops! I'd like to see you do it, you liver-lipped, yellow-bellied—"

The manager hung up on him. Mitch called him back.

"Now get this," he said harshly. "You said I was a crook. All right, I am one and I'm dangerous. I'm a crib man, an explosives expert. I've got plenty of stuff to work with. So send that dame out here and do it fast, or I'll blow your damned shack apart!"

"Really? My, my!" The man laughed sneeringly, but somewhat shakily. "Just think of that!"

"I'm telling you," Mitch said. "And this is the last time I'll tell you. Get that dame out of the woodwork, or there won't be any left."

"You wouldn't dare! If you think you can bluff—"

"In exactly five minutes," Mitch cut in, "the first charge will be set off, outside. If the dame doesn't come out, your building goes up."

He replaced the receiver, went back to the car. He picked up the rags and gasoline, moved down the hall to the red-and-white mailbox. It stood in the deep shadows of the *porte-cochere* and he was not observed. Also, the hotel employees apparently were keeping far back from the entrance.

Mitch soaked the rag rope in the gasoline and tucked a length of it down inside the mail box. Then he lifted the can and trickled its entire contents through the letter slot. It practically filled the box to the brim. The fluid oozed through its seams and dripped down upon the ground.

Mitch carefully scrubbed his hands with his handkerchief. Then, he ignited a book of matches, dropped them on the end of the rope. And ran.

His flight was unnecessary. For the "bomb" was an almost embarrassing failure. There was a weak rumble, a kind of a growl—a hungry man's stomach, Mitch thought bitterly, would make a louder one. A few blasts of smoke, and the box jiggled a bit on its moorings. But that was the size of it. That was the "explosion." It wouldn't have startled a nervous baby. As for scaring those rats inside the joint, hell, they were probably laughing themselves sick.

Oh, sure, the box burned; it practically melted. And that would give them some trouble. But that didn't help Mitch Allison any.

From far down the lawn, he looked dejectedly at the dying flames, wondering what to do now. He gasped, his eyes widening suddenly as two women burst through the entrance of El Ciudad.

One—the one in front—was Babe, barelegged, barefooted, dressed only in her bra and panties. She screamed as she ran, slapping and clawing wildly at her posterior. And it was easy to see why. For the woman chasing her was Bette, and Bette was clutching a blazing blowtorch.

She was holding it in front of her, its long blue flame aimed straight at the brassy blonde's flanks. Babe increased her speed. But Bette stayed right with her.

They came racing down the lawn toward him. Then, Bette tripped and stumbled, the torch flying from her hands. And at practically the same instant, Babe collided head-on with the steel flagpole. The impact knocked her senseless. Leaving her to listen to the birdies. Mitch sat down by Bette and drew her onto his lap. Bette threw her arms around him, hugging him frantically.

"You're all right, honey? I was so worried about you! You didn't really think I meant the way I acted, did you?"

"I wouldn't have blamed you if you had," Mitch said.

"Well, I didn't. Of course I was awfully mad at you, but you *are* my husband. I feel like murdering you myself lots of times, but I'm certainly not going to let anyone else do it!"

"That's my girl." Mitch kissed her fondly. "But—"

"I thought it was the best thing to do, honey. Just play dumb and then go get some help. Well—"

"Just a minute," Mitch interrupted. "Where's your car?"

"Over by the ocean," Bette pointed, continued. "Like I was saying, I found her listening out in the hall. I mean, she ducked away real fast, but I knew she had been listening. So I figured you'd probably be all right for a little while, and I'd better see about her."

"Right," Mitch nodded. "You did exactly right, honey."

"Well, she had a room just a few doors away, Mitch. I guess they had to move her nearby because they didn't have much time. Anyway, she went in and I went right in with her..."

She had asked Babe the score. Babe had told her to go jump, and Bette had gone to work on her, ripping off her clothes in the process. Babe had spilled, after a time. Bette had learned, consequently, that there would be no help for Mitch unless she provided it.

"So I locked her in and went back to your room. But you were gone, and I guessed you must be all right from the looks of things. That guy in the bathtub, I mean." Bette burst into giggles, remembering. "He looked so funny, Mitch! How in the world do you ever think of those stunts?"

"Just comes natural, I guess," Mitch murmured modestly. "Go on, precious."

"Well, I went back to her room, and the clerk called and said you were threatening to blow up the place. But she wouldn't go for it. She said she was going to stay right there, no matter what, and anyway you were just bluffing. Well, I was pretty sure you were, too, but I knew you wanted to get her outside. So I went out in the hall again and dug up that big cigar lighter—"

Mitch chuckled and kissed her again. "You did fine, baby. I'm really proud of you. You gave her a good frisk, I suppose? Searched her baggage?"

Bette nodded, biting her lip. "Yes, Mitch. She doesn't have the money."

"Don't look so down about it—" he gave her a little pat. "I didn't figure she'd keep it with her. She's ditched it outside somewhere."

"But, Mitch, you don't understand. I talked to her, and—"

"I know. She's a very stubborn girl." Mitch got to his feet. "But I'll fix that."

"But, Mitch—she told me where she put the money. When I was chasing her with the torch.

"Told you! Why didn't you say so? Where is it, for Pete's sake?"

"It isn't," Bette said miserably. "But it was." She pointed toward the hotel. "It was up there."

"Huh? What are you talking about?"

"She . . . she mailed it to herself."

4

Sick with self-disgust, Mitch climbed behind the wheel of Bette's car and turned it onto the highway. Bette studied his dark face. She patted him comfortingly on the knee.

"Now, don't take it so hard, honey. It wasn't your fault."

"Whose was it, then? How a guy can be so stupid and live so long! Fifty grand, and I do myself out of it! I do it to myself, that's what kills me!"

"But you can't expect to be perfect, Mitch. No one can be smart all the time."

"Nuts!" Mitch grunted bitterly. "When was I ever smart?"

Bette declared stoutly that he had been smart lots of times. Lots and lots of times. "You know you have, honey! Just look at all the capers you've pulled! Just think of all the people who are trying to find you! I guess they wouldn't be, would they, if you hadn't outsmarted them."

"Well . . ." Mitch's shoulders straightened a little.

Bette increased her praise.

"Why, I'll bet you're the best hustler that ever was! I'll

bet you could steal the socks off a guy with sore feet, without taking off his shoes!"

"You-uh-you really mean that, honey?"

"I most certainly do!" Bette nodded vigorously. "They just don't make 'em any sneakier than my Mitch. Why— why, I'll bet you're the biggest heel in the world!"

Mitch sighed on a note of contentment. Bette snuggled close to him. They rode on through the night, moving, inappropriately enough, toward the City of Angels.

Pay as You Exit

Celeste saw the inner tube on the highway, its spike-like valve-stem reared menacingly upward; but at precisely the same moment she saw the hitchhiker. He seemed to dart in front of the car, monstrously magnified in the glare of the headlights. A threatening hulk of a man who shook his fist and shouted curses at her.

Celeste tugged wildly at the steering wheel, reflexes trying to maneuver her safely between two dreadful hazards —killing the man or being forced to stop in his proximity. But the car was almost new, and she wasn't yet used to driving it. So she only managed to miss him, the right front wheel rolling squarely over the valve-stem.

There was a dull *pow*. A *whish-whish-whish* of escaping air as the wheel revolved. Then, a swiftly diminishing series of heavy *thumps*—the uncushioned rim of the wheel slugging the pavement. And finally, a split-second eternity later, a shivery last *thump*; and the car was stopped.

Celeste raised her eyes to the rear-view mirror. Dully watched him approach in the glow of the taillights. *I should have killed him!* she thought. *I WILL kill him, if I get a chance!*

But the wish, the thought, was hardly in her mind before she was denying it.

Kill someone? Needlessly take another's life? She had no proof positive so far that there was a need—any reason at all. And until and unless she did have a reason . . .

He opened the door of the car, reached in and appropriated the keys. Then, his hand closed over her arm, and he yanked her out to the pavement.

"Uh-*huh*," he said, on a maliciously aggrieved note. "Gonna go right on past me, wasn't you? Got a big car with plenty of room, but you wasn't gonna stop, was you?"

He towered over her, his stubbled face pouting, accusatory. Celeste stifled a wild desire to laugh, fury suddenly overriding her fear.

"Why, you—you overgrown oaf! I almost wreck my car, almost kill myself to keep from killing you, and you —you—"

"Yeah? So what's that got to do with me?"

"What's that got to do with *you*? Why, you planted that old inner tube in the road, that's what! And don't tell me you didn't! You put it there and then forced me to swerve into it."

"So?" he dismissed her complaint with a shrug. "Only way I could stop you, wasn't it?"

"But—" Celeste stared at him incredulously. "But you had no right to stop me!"

"Now, there you go," he said aggrievedly. "Talking about your rights! What about my rights, huh? I got as much right to ride in fancy cars as you have. I s'pose you think it's just fine an' dandy for you to ride, an' for me to walk. A poor, sick fella that never really had a chance in life' an' . . . an' . . ."

He snuffled, his lower lip stuck out self-pityingly. Then he gestured for her to precede him to the rear of the car. Kept a venomously watchful eye on her as he took tools and a spare tire from the trunk.

He had seen her kind before, he declared. People that was always thinkin' of themselves and not givin' a hang about poor folks like him. He'd seen 'em, and he knew just what to do about 'em.

"Now, you get around there!" he grunted, pointing with a tire iron. "Stand there in front of them headlights while I'm changing the tire!"

Celeste obeyed.

He jacked up the car. Scowling and muttering to himself, he removed the ruined tire and discarded it, then began fitting the spare tire to the rim. His hands were huge. He used them with delicate distaste, mumbling grimly of people who didn't care how much trouble they caused other people.

He tightened the last of the lugs. Lowering the jack, he shot her a challenging look. "Well?" he said. "You *don't* care, do you? You don't think I got any rights?"

"No, I don't think that," Celeste murmured, telling herself that the man was unbalanced, that it was best to be reasonable and placatory. "I know you have rights. The same rights I have. But—"

"But nothin'! I got 'em, an' I mean to use 'em. An' don't give me no guff about me interferin' with your rights when I'm just doin' what I have to."

"But it's not guff," Celeste said. "It's the law. You're breaking the law when you interfere with the rights of another person."

"The *law!*" He laughed angrily and stood up. "The law! Well, you keep that law, baby. I don't want no part of it."

"But you should," Celeste persisted gently. "It's simply a matter of common sense. If you don't respect my rights, then I—"

"*Hold it!*"

He sprang, almost bowling her over backwards. Yanking the purse from her hands before she could get it open.

Panting heavily, he took out the gun, motioning for her to move away from him. Then he took out the wallet, his eyes gleaming as he noted its bulging contents.

"Uh-*huh!!*" he grunted, as though a question in his mind had at last been resolved. "I might of knowed it! Now, don't you make a move, lady! Don't you make one little move, or..."

Cautiously, he laid the gun down on the fender of the car and reached a hand into his hip pocket. It came out with a huge roll of bills, to which he transferred the bills from her wallet. He returned the roll to his pocket, tossed her wallet into the ditch. He picked up the gun again, his face ludicrously stern with its look of virtue offended.

"Reckon you better answer some questions, little lady. Where did you get all the money you was carryin'—as if I didn't know."

"Where did you get all the money you were carrying?" Celeste said, "as if I didn't know."

"You're a holdup artist, right? That's why you're packin' a gun."

"Why else?" Celeste said wearily. "Surely, a woman traveling alone at night on a lonely road wouldn't carry a gun for protection."

The man nodded again; said that, yes, sir, he might of knowed it. These people that talked so nicey-nice about the law an' right an' wrong was usually the worst kind of crooks.

"Why, I'll bet this ain't even your car! Someone gave you a lift an' you stole it off of 'em."

"Which would justify your stealing it off of me," Celeste sighed. "Oh, for Pete's sake!" she added explosively. "The registration slip is in the car. If you'll check it with the identification in my wallet, you'll see that it belongs to me."

"Huh-uh. Wouldn't prove a thing. You could've stole the car an' wallet both. Reckon you did just that, too."

He shook his head gravely, a man steeling himself for an unpleasant duty. "Well, sir," he said, "I reckon they's only one thing t'do under the circumstances. I was only meanin' to catch a ride into town with you. But you turnin' out like you did—a gun-packin' hijacker an' car thief—well, you can see how it makes a difference."

"So does this," Celeste said, and she drew a gun from

her coat pocket. "This one is loaded. Yours is empty. Or maybe you'd like to try it?"

He tried it. The slapping of hammer against chamber echoed hollowly in the night.

"Y-You"—he stammered fearfully. "What are you gonna do to me?"

"What were you going to do to me?"

"B-But—but, looky here, now. . ." He gulped; paused. He looked into her eyes and saw that any entreaty was useless. Now there was only one thing to cling to . . . poor thing that it was. "Well, anyways," he said, voice strident with bravado. "I had you figured right, didn't I? Well, didn't I? You're a thievin' killer just like I thought, ain't you?"

Celeste didn't answer him. Merely smiled enigmatically as she triggered the gun.

The Flaw
in the System

I watched him as he came up the mezzanine steps to the Credit Department, studying his worn suit, his frayed necktie, his scuffed shoes. Knowing, even as I waved him to a new-account booth—with the very first question I asked him—that he was strictly on the sour side. And feeling a kind of surly happiness in the knowledge.

For an installment house—a dollar-down-the-rest-of-your-life outfit—we didn't catch many sour ones. They knew they couldn't beat us—how can you fast-talk a machine?—so they left us alone. But here was this guy, an n.g. from the word go, with a hundred and seventy-five bucks in sales slips! I wondered what the hell was wrong with our clerks, why they hadn't sent him up for an okay in the beginning instead of wasting their time on him.

I looked up from the slips, sharply, all set to read him off. I looked into his eyes—the warmest, friendliest eyes I had ever seen, in the kindliest face I had ever seen. And all I could think of was that somehow, in some way acceptable to the home office, I had to let him have the stuff. I spoke to him, asked a question, in a tone that was almost pleading and apologetic. He shook his head.

"No," he said pleasantly. "I cannot make a fifty percent

down payment. The fact of the matter is, I cannot make any down payment at all."

"Well," I said regretfully, "I'm awfully sorry, sir, but I don't think——"

I broke off, unable to tell him, however politely, that the deal was no soap. I had a feeling that if the friendly warmth in those eyes died out, something very necessary to me would die with it.

So I filled out a sales contract—just writing down the answers he gave me without comment or further discussion. When I was through, I made a few telephone calls and then I took the contract in to Dan Murrow's office. Dan was our credit manager.

He scanned the contract swiftly, mumbling to himself: "One seventy five with no d.p. Unemployed. N.G. from credit bureau. N.G. from two other accounts. No property. Hotel-resident—no permanent address. No—*GET OUTTA HERE!*" Dan yelled suddenly. "What are you bothering me with this for?"

"I'm sorry," I said. "Handle it for me, will you, Dan?"

"What the hell's there to handle?" he snarled. "What's wrong with you?" But he snatched up the contract and headed outside. I stayed where I was, listening.

I heard Dan say, "Now, look Mister. I don't know what you're trying to pull, see, but——" And then his voice changed. Suddenly it became the same way mine had been, soft and humble and apologetic. Begging for the good will of a man who was not only a total stranger, but an out-and-out deadbeat to boot.

Well . . .

The guy left. Dan came back into his office, gave me a thousand-watt glare, and jerked his thumb toward the door. He didn't say anything. It didn't look like a good time for me to say anything, so I went back to my desk and made out a duplicate on the contract.

All our records were made in duplicate, the dupes going to the home-office store and to Mr. Dorrance, the head credit manager. Mr. Dorrance trusted no one. He left nothing to chance. As long as you did exactly as you were instructed to do, you were all right. If you didn't—well, however sharp and tough you were, Dorrance was a lot sharper and a lot tougher. He had his eyes on you all the time, and he made sure you knew it.

It was a good system. You might get sore at the whole blasted world, or you might get to where you just didn't give a damn, or you might even quit. But the system rocked right along, permitting no errors, working perfectly.

At least, it always had worked perfectly until now.

Dan Murrow didn't speak to me the rest of the afternoon. But by quitting time he had straightened out a little, and we went to a place for a few beers. He was still kind of on the belligerent side. Sheepishly belligerent. He knew the account was sour—that it just couldn't be anything else—but he tried to pretend it wasn't.

"A hundred and seventy-five bucks," he said. "With our markup, that's around ninety dollars profit. What kind of credit manager would I be if I chased away that kind of dough?"

"Yeah," I said. "I guess that's right."

"So maybe he's a toughie," Murrow went on. "We got a legal department, ain't we? We've got collectors—boys that know how to make the tough ones soft. Sooner or later we'll catch that cookie on a job, and when we do . . ."

His voice trailed away. He looked at me, his eyes strangely bewildered.

Obviously we weren't going to catch the guy on a job. We weren't going to catch him with any attachable assets. This would be the way he made his living—by gypping stores and hocking or selling the merchandise. And there wasn't a thing we could do about it.

It wasn't fraud, because there'd been no misrepresentation. He was a deadbeat, but legally speaking he wasn't a crook.

His first payment fell due on the following Saturday. Naturally he didn't meet it, so Murrow put a collector onto him. The collector reported back that the guy had skipped town. Whether he was lying or not, I don't know. Murrow had an idea he was, but he couldn't see that it mattered much.

"*If* we collect," he said, "*if*—which we can't—it wouldn't help us any with Dorrance. We broke the rules, see? Like drawing to an inside straight, only ten times worse. Maybe a miracle might happen and we'd fill the straight. But it's still all wrong. We could pay this account ourselves, but Dorrance wouldn't like it one jot better."

We sweated out the weekend, wondering what Dorrance would do and knowing that whatever it was, it wouldn't be nice. Late Monday afternoon Murrow came to the door of his office and motioned for me to come inside. He looked a little pale. His hand shook as he closed the door behind me.

"Dorrance," I said.

"Yeah. His secretary, I mean." Murrow grinned sickishly, trying to make his voice sound satirical. "Mr. Dorrance wants a full report on that very peculiar account," he recited. "A detailed report, setting forth any reasons we have—*if* we have any—for opening such an account."

"Yeah?" I said. "Well . . ."

"We got to think of something, Joe." He leaned across the desk, desperately. "Some way we got to get ourselves off the hook. It means our jobs if we don't. It might mean even more than that. Yeah," he nodded, as I looked at him startled. "We had no good reason to okay that guy, so could be we had a bad one. But then again maybe we were in cahoots with him, splitting the take."

"Well . . ." I spread my hands helplessly.

"Let's start at the beginning," Murrow said. "Why did you do what you did, anyway? Why didn't you just turn this character down yourself instead of passing him onto me?"

"I—well, I just didn't want to," I said. "It wasn't as if he was compelling me, or hypnotizing me, or anything like that. And it wasn't because I felt sorry for him. It was just—well, it doesn't make any sense—it sounds crazy now. But—but—"

"I know," Murrow murmured. And then he brought himself up sharp. "Go on and spill it! Maybe we can come up with something."

"Well," I hesitated. "It was like I had to do it to prove something. That I was a person—a human being, not just part of a system. That there wasn't any system big enough to keep me from making a mistake, just like there wasn't any big enough to keep me from doing the right thing. So—well, I guess that's why I did it. Because it was the only way, it seemed, that this guy would go on liking me. And I was afraid that if he ever stopped liking me, I—I just wouldn't be any more. I'd have moved off into a world I could never come back from."

Murrow looked at me silently. After a moment he let out a scornful grunt—rather, he tried to. "Brother!" he snorted. "Are you a big help!"

"How about you?" I said. "Why didn't you give him a turn-down?"

"Never mind about me!" he snapped. "Because I'm stupid, that's why. Because I got so many dumb clucks working for me, I'm getting dumb myself . . . Well, you got anything else to say?"

I shook my head. "Nothing that would make any sense."

"Let's have it," Murrow said wearily. "You haven't *been* making any sense, so why should you begin now?"

"I was just wondering," I said. "I mean, I wasn't wondering exactly, but—He stuck two other stores in town besides ours. He could have made a clean sweep, yet he only took two. But those two are the same kind of outfits we are."

"So?" Murrow frowned. "So he plays the installment houses. What about it?"

"Not just the installment houses. A certain *type* of installment house," I said. "The hard-boiled kind. The iron-clad system houses. Places where every contingency is provided for by the system, where the human element is

ruled out . . . The system says no sales to the unemployed.
No sales to transients. It says that if a risk looks very bad,
we must insist on a down payment that practically covers
the wholesale cost of the merchandise. It allows for *no*
exceptions under *any* circumstances. It doesn't allow us to
think or feel—to do anything but apply our own special
yardstick and throw out anyone who doesn't measure up to
each and every one of the rules. Why, one of the saints
themselves could walk in here and if he didn't—"

"Chop it off," Murrow said. "Get to the point."

"I've already got to it," I said. "This guy knows exactly
how we operate—yet he chooses us. He deliberately
makes things tough on himself. Why did he do it?—if he
was just after the merchandise. If, I mean, he was doing it
just for himself instead of—uh—"

"Yeah?" Murrow said grimly. "Yeah?"

"Nothing." I turned toward the door. "I guess I'd better
be getting back to work."

I had just sat down at my desk when Murrow came out.
He asked me for a description of the guy, adding roughly
that at least I could help him that much.

"Well"—I tried to remember. "He seemed awfully
friendly. Really friendly and kind, you know. The way he
smiled at me, it was like he'd known me for a long time—
as if he knew me better than I knew myself."

"Nuts!" Murrow yelled. "Do you or don't you remember
what he looked like?"

"What about you?" I said. "You talked to him longer
than I did."

Murrow wheeled around, stamped into his office and
slammed the door behind him.

Naturally he didn't send any report to Dorrance—how
could he? There was nothing to report. And there was
nothing we could do but wait until Dorrance called again
. . . demanding an explanation for the unexplainable.

But Dorrance didn't call.

A week passed.

Two weeks.

And there wasn't a single peep from the home store.

I suggested to Morrow hopefully that maybe there had been a slip-up, that the matter had got buried somewhere and was now in the process of being forgotten. But Murrow said there wasn't a chance—not with our system.

"That's what they want us to think—that we got away with something. We think that, see, so maybe we'll try something else. And when we do . . ."

"But we aren't going to! We haven't tried anything yet, have we? We made this one mistake—kind of a mistake— but from now on—"

"I'll tell you what," Murrow said. "If you've borrowed anything against your petty cash, you'd better pay it back. Check the collectors—make sure they don't hold dough over from one day to the next. Keep your accounts posted right up to the minute. Have everything in perfect order, understand? Because if it isn't—if there's anything wrong at all—we'll be in the soup. A hell of a lot deeper than we are right now."

I did what he told me to.

Four days later Dorrance showed up.

It was on a Saturday, a few minutes before closing time. He lingered near the entrance until the last of our customers had left; then he came up the stairs, a big man with a flabby face and eyes that were like two chunks of ice.

He answered our nervous greetings with the merest of nods. He cleared off a desk—waving me away when I started to help him—and started laying out the contents of two heavy briefcases.

"All right," he said, spreading out his records—picking one contract, *the* contract from among them and placing it deliberately to one side. "You know why I'm here. If I want to know anything I'll ask you. If I want you to do anything I'll tell you. Got that? Good. Now open the safe, unlock the cash drawer, and bring your account files over here."

It was almost midnight when he finished checking us. Almost five hours—with Murrow and me hanging around red-faced and embarrassed. Feeling unaccountably guilty and looking a hell of a lot guiltier. Hardly speaking unless we were spoken to or moving unless we were ordered to.

Five solid hours of waiting and watching—while Dorrance did his damnedest to spot something crooked.

Then, at last, he was through. He leaned back in his chair, massaged his eyes briefly with a thumb and forefinger and gave us another of those infinitesimal nods.

"That does it," he said. "You boys are okay."

Something inside of me snapped. Before I could stop myself I blurted out an angry, "Thanks. I'll bet that disappoints you, doesn't it?"

"Now, now," Murrow said quickly. "Mr. Dorrance is just doing his job."

"Then it's one hell of a job!" I said. "He comes in here late at night and—"

"Yes," said Dorrance quietly. "Yes, it's one hell of a job, son. I'll be glad to see the day when it isn't necessary—which unfortunately, it seems to be at present. This is the tenth store I've hit in the past three weeks. Four of them didn't check."

"Well," I said. "I didn't mean to say that—that—"

"It gave me quite a start," Dorrance went on. "Of course there's always bound to be a little gypping—one-shot, off-and-on stuff. But these birds had been doing it regularly. They'd invented a system for beating our system . . . I wonder"—he hesitated, then his eyes strayed to that laid-aside contract. "I've been wondering why I didn't foresee that it would happen. We've discouraged individuality, anything in the way of original thinking. All decisions were made at the top and passed down. Honesty, loyalty—we didn't feel that we had to worry about those things. The system would take care of them. The way the system worked—supposedly—a man simply *had* to be loyal and honest.

"Well, obviously, we were all wet; we found those four stores I mentioned, and God knows how many others there are like them. And about all I can say is we were asking for it. If you won't let a man think for you, he'll think against you. If you don't have any feeling for *him*, you can't expect him to have any for *you*."

He paused, picking up that lone contract and glanced at us questioningly. Murrow and I didn't say anything. Dorrance shrugged.

"Now let's face it," he said. "This man has stuck store after store in our chain. He's hit us for thousands of dollars. How he got away with it, we don't know. None of our men have been able to explain. But there *is* an explanation —several of 'em, in fact . . . Perhaps he worked for an outfit like ours at one time. He knew you people had been pushed to the top of the arc in one direction and that you were all set to swing the other way—out of resentment, frustration anger. The desire to do something for once that *didn't* make any sense. All he had to do was catch you at the right time, and you'd let him walk off with the store.

"Or it could be that he's simply a damned clever con man operating in a new field. A good con man would know that the easiest people to take are those who've never been taken—people who supposedly know all the angles, who are so sure that no one would even try to beat them that they're a cinch for the first man who does." Dorrance paused, then went on.

"He's a very dangerous man. He did us a good turn, indirectly, by starting this investigation, but that doesn't change the situation. He's a menace—as dangerous as they come—and if we ever spot him again he's got to be treated as one. Just grab him, understand? Latch onto him, and we'll figure out a legal charge later. Why, a man like that —he could wreck us if he took a notion to! He could wreck our entire economy!"

Murrow glanced uneasily at the contract, wondering, as I did, what Dorrance intended to do about it. And about us. Then Murrow said nervously that he didn't imagine the guy would be back. "Do you, Mr. Dorrance?"

"Why not?" Dorrance snapped. "Why don't you think he'll be back?"

"Well"—Murrow looked at me uncomfortably. "I'm not sure, of course. It was just an idea. But—"

"Dan means it wouldn't be smart for him to come back," I said. "He'd know that we'd be on the lookout for him."

"Oh," said Dorrance. After a long moment he pushed himself up from his chair and reached for his coat. "That wraps it up, I guess. Now let's get out of here. You boys have to work tomorrow, and I have to travel. As for that contract, throw it in your p-and-l's. Can't collect on it, so it might as well go into profit-and-loss."

Murrow and I didn't move; we just weren't up to moving yet. And we couldn't think of anything to say either. But there was an unspoken question in the air. Dorrance answered it snappishly, as he packed his briefcases.

"What's the matter with you?" he said, not looking at us. "You can't put two and two together? Do I have to draw you a diagram? That fellow hit the home store hard too— hit us the hardest of all. I personally okayed him for four hundred dollars . . ."

He sounded sore, but he didn't look it. Somehow he looked kind of happy.

Sunrise at Midnight

1

The place was on the Sunset Strip, a second-floor outfit with several big-lettered banners declaring that twenty beautiful girls were on duty to massage gentlemen in private. Judging by the stream of guys that went up and down the steps there were a hell of a lot more gentlemen in L.A. than I would have imagined. But, anyway. Johnny was almost two hours late getting off, and her face was so pale with weariness that her freckles stood out like brown-chalk dots.

A city detective named Narz was with her. He gave her butt a little pinch and a slap as she slid into the seat next to me, then thrust his head into the window before I could drive away.

"Gonna borrow your wife for a while tonight, Brad," he said. "Okay by you?"

I said it damned well wasn't okay. "Joanna's going to bed tonight just as soon as she has some dinner."

"Aah, come off it. She's been in bed all day."

I stepped on the gas hard. He jerked his head back out of the window, but not quite fast enough. It grazed him as the car shot out onto Sunset Strip; sent him reeling backwards, almost losing his balance.

Johnny gave me a doubtful look. "He's going to be awfully mad, honey. We can't have him mad at us."

"Forget it," I said.

"I can't go to jail, Brad! I j-just couldn't stand it!"

"Forget it," I said again. "Narz isn't going to cause you any trouble. Never, ever again."

The worry went out of her eyes, and she sighed, relieved. Cuddled close to me, her head resting against my shoulder.

She was an easy person to lie to, almost childlike in her unquestioning faith in me. But I wasn't lying about Narz.

He *wasn't* going to make trouble for her or me or anyone else. He was through making trouble. Permanently.

2

The Strip used to be one of the showplaces of Southern California, with some of the world's swankest nightclubs, shops, restaurants and so on. It still wasn't a complete mess, by any means, because too much money was invested in it, and money fights hard. But it had gone a long way downhill. Riding it down were the massage parlors and the topless bars and the bottomless bars and the nudie bars, because sex fights hard, too, and it fights dirty.

I've never fully understood how the joints were able to operate so openly. No one seemed to understand. But there were a lot of contributing factors. For one thing, the Strip and portions of the streets leading off of it were in an unincorporated area—in the county rather than the city of Los Angeles. Which meant that the sheriff's department had to police it, and the sheriff's department was spread far too thin as it was.

Another thing: The state had preempted certain policing functions normally handled by local authorities. It had taken them over, that is, but without the money to enforce them. Then there were conflicting laws—a growing number of them—as to what was legal and what was not.

And there were batteries of highly paid lawyers to advise the proprietors of pornographic shows and houses of prostitution on exactly how to operate so as to avoid arrest, or if arrested, to get the case dismissed on grounds of entrapment or violation of constitutional rights.

The joints did get busted and raided. But the chances were they'd go right back into business, and the public—burdened with one of the nation's highest tax rates—just didn't give a damn. Why not go after real criminals?—that was the attitude of the public. Why bother with vice when people were being murdered and robbed and raped in broad daylight? When there was no safety in a man's home or outside of it?

I turned off the Strip, and started down the hill toward the city's "basin." On the way, I noticed that a cocktail lounge featuring "live entertainment" was operating again after a two-day closing by the cops. The live entertainment consisted of a naked man and woman having sexual intercourse. Drinks were five bucks each.

"Almost home, Johnny," I said, as we neared Wilshire Boulevard. "How about a nice dry martini, while I draw you a warm bath and scare up some dinner?"

She didn't answer. I said, "Johnny? . . . *Joanna!*" Then I saw that she was asleep, dead to the world with exhaustion, and I didn't say anything more. Suddenly, there was a great lump in my throat, and I couldn't have spoken to save my life.

I coasted gently into our driveway and stopped in the garage. I got my arms under Johnny, opened the side door of our apartment and carried her inside, passing through the kitchen-dining area and into the living room. I lowered her softly to the massive lounge and took the telephone off the hook. She still showed no signs of awakening, and I hoped to God nothing disturbed her. She was so very, very tired, so helpless, and it was my fault; and letting her sleep was all I could do for her.

We lived on the ground floor of a duplex. In addition to the kitchen-dining room and this, the living room, there was a den, two bedrooms, two baths and a powder room. There was also a wet bar set in an alcove of the living room. The upstairs apartment, a duplicate of ours, was un-occupied and probably would be indefinitely. Prospective tenants came to look at it occasionally but lost interest fast when they heard what the rent was.

I fixed myself a stiff drink at the bar, being very quiet so as not to disturb Johnny. I finished the drink and mixed a second one, wondering what I'd better do about getting Johnny's dinner. It didn't matter about me. I could eat a can of something or some of the delicatessen stuff which I always kept on hand. But Johnny needed a good hot din-ner, a taste-tempting meal as well as a nourishing one, since she was apt not to have much appetite when she be-came very tired.

I fretted about it, worrying as I worried about everything where Johnny was concerned. I finished my second drink, standing at the bar, then went back to the lounge and knelt down on the floor beside her. Color had come back into her face, and her scattering of freckles had faded away to their normal near-invisibility. I lowered my head until my ear almost touched her breast, and I found her heart beating strong and steadily.

I straightened again, relieved but still worried about the matter of her dinner. Then, I broke into a smile, suddenly realizing that there was nothing to worry about. She'd probably bathed half-dozen times already today; and she was certainly relaxed enough without taking another bath. As for food, she could dispense with that tonight, too, her prime need being rest, and tomorrow was Saturday, one of her Saturdays off. In fact, she had the whole week-end off. Saturday and Sunday both—she and the other girls had rotating schedules—so she could rest and sleep as late as she liked and eat when she had the appetite for it.

I went into the master bedroom, turned down the covers of the king-size bed. Then, I carried her in from the lounge, laid her down on the bed and removed her shoes.

She wasn't wearing stockings, and her skimpy little dress was fastened by a single zipper, extending its brief length.

I unfastened the zipper and slid its short sleeves off her arms. There were no undergarments beneath it—no bra or panties. Why underclothes, the way she earned her living, *our* living? So now she was nude, and the room was cool, and I should have pulled the covers up over her. But I didn't. I couldn't. My pulse was pounding, a hot flush spreading over my face. And, of course, I wouldn't have disturbed her for the world. But I couldn't help looking at her. I mean, I really couldn't . . . For here was such beauty revealed to me that it almost brought tears to my eyes.

Despite what she was, what she had gone through for days and weeks and months, there was a flowerlike daintiness about her.

Her full breasts were without a sign of a bruise—completely unabused. Women are instinctively careful of their breasts. The flesh below them, the clean flat pane of her abdomen and belly, was also unmarked. But below that, her cleanshaven crotch with its ultimate hallmark of femininity, well . . .

There, *there* was the bar sinister of sexual excess. Of excess piled upon excess.

There she could *not* be careful, for it ceased to be hers during the period of its employment. It was the man, the men, who owned it, with the unrestricted right to plunge and lunge and thrust; and she was the slave to those men until the explosion of their seed released her.

That delicate delicacy of womanhood could not be protected. And it was so swollen tonight as to resemble half of a small fruit; a peach, say. So swollen that the tiny opening at its center was all but sealed shut, a pinline fissure barely discernible.

I closed my eyes, sickishly.

I opened them again, startled, at the sound of her voice.

"It's all right, Brad." She was smiling softly, her voice throaty with love and understanding. "Come on to bed."

"No!" I said. "I'll sleep in the other room tonight."

"Why, honey?" Her smile began to fade. "Don't you want me?"

"No," I said. "Not tonight, anyway."

"Oh," she said, her smile vanishing completely. "Well, I guess I can't blame you. I guess if y-you'd been with w-women all day"—her voice trembling now. "Even if it w-wasn't your fault, and you r-really didn't w-want t-to—"

"Oh, my God, baby!" I gave her a fierce kiss, then gently kissed away the tears in her eyes. "I love you for that. Sacrificing yourself for a slob like me. But—"

"You are not a slob! Anyway, you're not responsible. It was Narz who forced me into it."

"I know," I said, "but I'm still responsible for you, and you've—you've, uh, given yourself so much today . . ."

"I never give myself *any* day," she said. "Not ever. Myself . . . You're the only one I give myself to, and I've saved up a lot to give you, and I want to give it—I've just *got* to, honey!—and—an'—"

And . . .

It was two hours before I arose from the bed. She had saved so much for me and given it with such passionate eagerness. There had been pain at the presentation of the first of her savings—there were three such presentations, in all—so greatly had the approach to it been tightened by swelling. A great shudder ran through her entire body, and she gasped, choking back a groan. After that, however, the gasp came only as the gift was given to me, and the convulsive tightening that accompanied it was a joyous one.

She was sound asleep, almost before I could tuck the covers up around her. Sleeping on her side, her hands under her face, palm to palm, as though she were praying. She always slept in that position. I once asked her why, and she gave me a playfully sharp slap.

"Silly. You know why."

"If I did, I wouldn't have asked."

"Well, I can't very well sleep on my stomach, can I?"

I didn't suppose she could, I decided. With breasts as full and firm as hers, her head would have been hanging down. I asked her what happened if she changed sides in her sleep, and she said nothing happened. Her hands automatically resumed their praying position, holding her off of her stomach.

"Don't you ever sleep on your back?" I asked.

"No, I don't!" she said. "Not if I can help it!"

She didn't talk much in those days, back when we first came together. The most innocent question was apt to annoy or embarrass her—as my last one apparently had—so I didn't press the point. Later on, however, when the ice of her inhibitions had been thoroughly thawed, I got the answer to my question. Bit by bit.

"It's because I get to thinking," she said, "and it's hard to go back to sleep."

"Thinking?" I said. "About what?"

"You know," she said, blushing furiously. "About what I might be doing. On my back, I mean."

I finished dressing, turned off the light and left the bedroom, leaving the door just a little ajar. Fixing another stiff drink, I carried it over to the lounge and sat down, then returned the telephone receiver to its cradle. A couple of minutes later, after I'd gulped down half of the drink, the phone rang. Narz, of course. He'd been trying to call for more than an hour. Frustrated and impatient, he'd begun throwing down the booze, just as I'd known he would, and his words were slurred and angry.

"What the hell you tryin' to pull?" he snarled. "Where's Johnny?"

"Now, Ken"—I put an appeasing whine in my voice. "The poor girl simply had to get some rest. She's worn out, and—"

"Knock it off, an' get her over here! She ain't in my 'partment inside of an hour, s'gonna be too damn bad. Know what I mean?"

"Now, Ken," I whined, "be reasonable, Ken."

"One hour!" His voice rose. "She gets here in one hour, or you'll—hic!—be the sorriest sonabitch in the world!"

I said, well, all right, if that was the way it had to be.

"Now you're gettin' smart," he said, and he slammed down the phone.

I also hung up.

I had my fourth drink of the night, taking my time with it. Then, I left the apartment and drove toward Ken Narz's place. I was running a risk, I knew, and I'd been months in coming to the decision I meant to carry out tonight. But I couldn't let things go on like they were, and I figured the odds were on my side. He couldn't use his authority as a cop in a situation like this; he'd gotten too much mud on his badge. It would simply be man against man—me against him. And a guy that had done what he'd done had to be a coward.

All I had to do was make him know I meant business. Then, Johnny and I would be rid of him for good.

Or so I thought . . .

3

I was working as sports editor of the *Chronicle* when I first met Johnny. One thing about not being too much of a much yourself is that it makes you sympathetic to other people with the problem, and Johnny certainly had it in spades.

She was a waitress in a little restaurant across the street from the paper. I'm kind of finicky about the sort of place I eat in—the type of guy that will skip two of the day's meals so that he can sort of splurge on the third one—and ordinarily I wouldn't have been caught dead in a joint like that. But it was convenient to the paper, so I dropped in one day when I was rushed for time.

It didn't have any tables, just a right-angle-shaped triangle with one portion of it extending along the rear. The front and longest section of the counter was covered by a brassy-voiced, henna-haired type, a real pro at hashslinging. She was waiting on about a dozen customers, with the skill that comes from long practice, working with unhurried haste and managing to kid around with them as she served their orders.

The waitress at the rear was Johnny. She had only one customer—one of the *Chronicle's* machinists, wearing a cap of folded newsprint. Just as I came in the door, he leaped from his stool with a yowl, scattering dishes and silverware right and left, as he tried to brush the day's blue-plate special from his clothes.

"Jesus Christ, girl!" he yelled. "What the hell's the matter with you?"

"Now, Pete," I said, giving Johnny a reassuring smile, "Why all the fuss? Anyone can make a mistake."

"But, goddammit, Brad! She—"

"Easy," I whispered, giving his arm a warning squeeze. "Play along with me, and you get a couple of tickets to tonight's fight."

The proprietor came out of the kitchen, preceded by a dishwasher with a mop. While the dishwasher began cleaning up the mess, the proprietor—a Greek, I think—scowled and blustered at Johnny.

"Wossa matter you, Jo'na? You no do nothing right?" Then, to Pete, "I bring you 'nother lunch."

"All my fault," the machinist mumbled unwillingly. "Let the girl wait on me."

The Greek jerked his head at Johnny, giving her a severe look. She managed to snap out of her terror-stricken freeze and scampered through the door to the kitchen. The Greek sighed heavily, rolling his eyes.

"That Jo'na! No need job so bad, I fire long ago. I sure fire, anyway, she work here full time."

I asked what she did the rest of the time, and he explained that she was attending business college. Adding gratuitously, and doubtless sincerely, that he admired anyone who tried to improve themselves.

"'Scuse, please. I take your order, Mr. Maxwell?"

"No hurry," I said. "I'll wait for Joanna. By the way, can't her folks help her?"

"No got. Raiseed in—how you say?—orph'nage."

He went off up front to take charge of the cash register. Johnny returned with Pete's lunch, only spilling part of it as she served it to him. She didn't do so well with my pie and coffee, slopping most of the coffee into the saucer and skidding the pie off its plate and onto the counter.

Pete grinned at me maliciously. I put the pie back onto the plate, poured the coffee back into the cup and began to eat. Johnny turned away with the hopeless expression of one beyond hope.

I don't think I'd ever seen such a frump. The white wraparound uniform she wore, probably supplied by the restaurant, was about six sizes too large for her, and she appeared to be trying to fight her way out of it when she moved. Her hair was done up in what I can only describe as a wad. She wore a pair of tiny dime-store glasses which squeezed her eyes to the size of beans. Her severe little face was shiny, utterly free of so much as a little powder. Worst of all was her body, or perhaps her posture. She was a short girl, no more than five feet, if that, but she kept her shoulders slumped, actually stooping. So everything about her physique seemed out of kilter, as though it had been thrown in unmeasured as an afterthought.

I've said I was a not-so-much myself. Compared to her I was a combination of Prince Charming and Einstein, but still, we were members of the same family, though very, very distantly related. So I was drawn to her, moved to do something for her. Simply because she was as she was.

Or possibly I had another reason, without knowing that I did. Or being willing to admit it. I've always sympathized with people who've gotten a bad shake from life, and I've helped them whenever I could.

But usually—not always, but usually—I've gotten far more back than I gave. I didn't plan it that way; I don't think I'm capable of that kind of thinking, but that's the way it worked out.

I started going to the restaurant every day, always insisting that Johnny serve me. Then, one day when I went in she was gone, and the Greek almost took my head off when I asked about her. Jo'na was a bum, he declared. Just no 'tam good. Alla time make big mess, foul up ever'ting. Was no use try to help such a girl. Even the school—the business college—

The college had finally given up on her, too. In all honesty, they could no longer allow her to waste her time and money.

"Is no good bum," he repeated. "I try help, Mr. Maxwell. I try, but—" He nodded toward the street, his scowl deepening. "How you gonna help somet'ing like her?"

I turned and looked out the window. Johnny was just passing by. Apparently, she'd gone out the rear door of the restaurant and come around front through the alley. She looked even worse in her own clothes—Goodwill Store stuff, I suspected—than she had in the waitress uniform. But she still tugged at me like a magnet, and my hunch about her was stronger than ever.

I ran out of the restaurant and caught up with her. I told her she'd gotten a big break in being canned and tossed out of business college. The biggest break she'd ever had, and if she'd play along with me—do exactly as I said—I'd prove it to her.

"How about it, Johnny? Will you do it?"

"Uh-huh." She nodded firmly, without a second's hesitation. "Of course, I will, Bra—Mr. Maxwell."

"Brad," I said. "Now, wait right here while I make a phone call."

I stepped into a sidewalk telephone booth and closed the door. I called a girl I'd bumped into when she was down and given a hand-up to. Part of it was pulling a few strings at the Press Club and getting them to take her on as a cashier. They'd had to let her go after a few months—she came on a little too strong even for the Club—but by then she was off and running.

"Brad, darling,"—a sultry, beddy-bye voice. "I just this minute called your office. I've got that two hundred I owe you, and—"

"That's not why I was calling," I said. "Not exactly.

There's something I want done, but it won't take two bills. We'll call it square on the rest, if you'll do it for me."

"You know I will, honey. What do I do?"

"I'm sending a girl over to your apartment. I want you to take care of her."

"Take care of a *girl*? You've got the wrong number, pal."

"Oh, for God's sake, Rose!" I said.

"Now, now," she laughed. "You know me and my jokes. But just what do I do for this babe?"

"You'll know when you see her," I said. "Wiggle your pretty pink little can, and you should be able to have her at my apartment by the time I wrap up the day. Still have a key, don't you?"

"The key, yes. But your love"—she sighed dramatically. "Your love I seem to have lost."

"Don't cry, little girl," I said. "I'll always think of you as a sister."

"Why, you incestuous bastard!" she said.

And she laughed and I laughed, and we hung up.

I wrote down Rose's address and gave it to Johnny. I said I'd see her after I got off work, and that meanwhile she was to do whatever Rose suggested.

"And, now, let's get rid of these," I said, and I took off the dime-store glasses and dropped them in the gutter. They were just a cop-out, you see. She couldn't explain— probably didn't know—that her constant bungling and unceasing failures were rooted in giant economy-size feelings of inferiority and insecurity. So she used can't-see as an excuse. If there'd actually been anything wrong with her sight, she wouldn't have been wearing glasses like those.

She didn't say anything when I threw them away. Simply looked at me out of eyes that suddenly seemed ten times larger in a face that was ten times softer. And seeing my approval, my obvious pleasure at her transformation, she was pleased and approving also.

I gave her some money and helped her into a cab, a little startled at the way her shoulders had straightened and her body had gained shape inside the shapeless, rummage-store clothes. But like the man said, I hadn't seen nothin' yet.

Rose was watching for my arrival that night, and she met me on the apartment stoop, closing the door behind her.

"I think I've changed my mind," she said. "Now if you ever want *that* girl taken care of, you should excuse the expression . . ."

"Here, here," I said severely. "You go right straight home, you bad girl!"

"Oh, all right," she said. "Did I bid you sweet dreams?"

"No, you didn't."

"Well, good for me," she said. "A guy should have *everything*?"

I waved her on her way. Then, I locked the door from the inside and went down the foyer to the living room.

Johnny was there, one cobweb-hosed leg crossed over the other, an arm draped carelessly over the back of the chair. The position automatically thrust out her breasts, and provided a generous glimpse of upper thigh. *How had Rose had time to coach her so thoroughly, along with everything else?* Johnny looked at me silently out of shadowed eyes, her rose-tinted lips parted slightly, letting that, the she in her, say it all. Then, she stood up, and I sat down. Or maybe fell down would be more accurate.

Rose believed in getting off to a fast start, a knockout punch on the first swing, and she'd done a solid job of selling her philosophy to Johnny.

Her dress was one of those simple "fun" things (to borrow an adjective from *Vogue, Bazaar,* et al.), which philanthropists like I. Magnin and Saks Fifth Avenue magnanimously peddle to the underprivileged at a mere one hundred and fifty dollars or so. Staunchly matching the *Yanquees* in generosity, La Pueda, or possibly I. Pina, had provided spike-heeled wisps of leather called shoes, priced at no more than a big night in Vegas.

What the outfit did for Johnny was what God would doubtless do for all lovely girls disguised as frumps, except for His preoccupation with fallen sparrows and visiting disaster upon the nonbeliever. But, of course, He'd given her plenty in natural estate, even though He had neglected its gardening.

Sassoon wouldn't have been available on short notice, but some equally talented kinsman had to be responsible for her hair, the exquisite simplicity of its fashioning. As for the rest, the facial and its various components—the brow-arching and all the other—well, maybe Factor had tired of counting his Cadillacs and resumed the practice of his own unique magic.

What Rose had wrought—its embellishment, at least—had cost twice two hundred dollars. She was very generous, very grateful, as the people I favor almost always are.

And now, staring at Johnny, unable to take my eyes off of her, I knew I'd again pulled the old hat trick. That I'd jabbed the program with a pin and landed a longshot. And I knew I was going to land in hell if I didn't call a halt.

Those long thighs with the full-flaring hips; those rich, high-hinged breasts, crowding against each other in their lushness; the short, flat-bellied waist that I could have circled with my hands; that... All that in a package of minus-five feet and ninety-eight pounds. I knew I'd die if I didn't have her, but there are good and bad ways to die.

As I'd sat staring at her, obviously overwhelmed, her own confidence had grown, and she now actually became bold. Edging closer and closer to me she displayed her new and delicious self. Giving me sassy, teasing looks over her shoulder, while she slowly turned this way and that, hand on hip; at last, frankly waggling her svelte little butt.

Finally, she paused frowning in puzzlement; obviously wondering what she was doing wrong. But the pause was a brief one. Rose had given her a cram session during their several hours together, doubtless telling her that a gal had to keep throwing it if the guy was slow on the catch and that I sometimes acted "awful funny." So, now, mustering up all her daring, she leaned down and whispered that she'd like to see the bedroom.

I looked at her coldly. Then, I grabbed her by the arm, and slammed her down on the lounge beside me.

"You've seen the whole apartment," I said. "Rose would have shown it to you while you were waiting for me. So why the bedroom bit?"

"W-Well"—nervously. "I j-just thought that—"

"Wrong date, baby," I said. "I only take virgins on the thirty-first of February, and I'd rather not take them at all. They're always getting big bellies, because they don't know how to take care of themselves, and—"

"They do not! I do too know! Rose told me—!" She broke off, her face flaming. Then, bewilderedly, "W-why, Brad? If you didn't like me, why—"

"I felt sorry for you," I said. "I've felt sorry for a lot of people and it's been too bad for them. Here"—I took a hundred dollars from my wallet and tossed it in her lap. "That'll give you a start. You can come back for more if you need it, but I don't think you will. Because you'll find thousands of jobs waiting for you now. Receptionist, hostess, clerk—all kinds of jobs that you can handle, and—*What the hell are you doing?*"

She had kicked off her shoes and was now rolling down her stockings. She finished removing them, while I again asked her what the hell she was doing.

She didn't answer me. Simply stood up and pulled the dress off over her head.

The bra and panties were bikini type. Mere strips of lace that only fractionally served the purpose for which they were theoretically made. I grabbed her hands and pulled her back down on the lounge.

"The proud and haughty act, huh?" I said grimly. "I won't have you, so you won't have the clothes."

"No, I won't! I won't wear them another minute! I'll call Rose, and borrow something from—" She broke off, choking back a sob. "Rose likes m-me—at least s-she l-likes me, a-and—"

"Baby, dammit, listen to me, baby!" I turned my head away. "Liking doesn't begin to describe the way I feel about you. But we'll have to button it up right there. I didn't intend to and I don't want to, but that's the way it's going to be, the way it has to be . . ."

I laid it on the line for her, or as much as I could force myself to: the fact that tying up with me was taking the steps going down. I was pure phony, I said, and she was solid gold; and she'd better realize when she was well off.

"So take off. Just beat it, and don't come back," I said, making it as rough-tough as I could. For I was on the point of breaking up, and I couldn't let her see me that way. "Find a dairy and mix in with the other cows. Or show your ass at a riding stable. Make like a pony, see, and they'll never know the difference. Or do whatever you damn please, as long as I'm not part of it. Anyway—"

I told her I was going to lie down a while, and I got up and started for the bedroom: spoke to her without turning around. "When I get up, I don't want to find you here. If I do, I'll throw you out, and baby, I'll throw you hard!"

I got into the bedroom and slammed the door. I managed to strip off my clothes, and I started to get into some pajamas. But I couldn't make it. The Thing inside of me that gnawed ceaselessly at my guts chomped down a little too hard, and I was suddenly blind with tears. And, blindly, I fell into bed and buried my face in the pillows.

I didn't hear her when she came in. And small as she was, so exquisitely small, there was no sagging of the bed to announce her presence. I was just alone, and then I was no longer alone. She was just there, lying a little high on the pillows, a breast cupped delicately in one hand as she gently urged my head downward to receive it.

"There . . ." an uxorious sigh. "Isn't that better, mmm? Mama's baby feel better?"

Mama's baby! Jesus! I was at least twice her age.

"Look!" I said desperately. "You've got to—You just don't understand!"

"I don't have to," she said. "I love you."

It is written that for each thing there is a season, and a time for everything under the heavens. Thus, the season for comforting and cuddling soon passed, and there was harvest to be reaped. An abundance that seemed to grow with each taking of it.

I had no sweet dreams that night. Only her, the dream that needed no sleep to be realized; that needed none and allowed none.

Around daylight, she went to the bathroom for the last time; and she was asleep almost as soon as she returned to bed. On her side, her palm to palm hands under her face in an attitude of prayer. She looked younger than ever; refreshed rather than depleted by our long night of love.

I got cautiously out of bed and entered the bathroom. Reluctantly glanced in the mirror and hastily looked away. Almost groaning at the haggardness I had seen.

I sat down on the stool and smoked a cigarette, hashing things over in my mind. Trying to see a way out of the hopeless situation I'd dragged Johnny into; trying and knowing that there was none.

We'd talked some during the night, and she'd told me she was twenty-five. Which had to be a lie, of course, told to ease any guilt feelings I felt. She couldn't be much over twenty-two, and quite possibly she wasn't even that old. I'd said that I was thirty-eight—also a lie, needless to say. But a cosmetic surgeon and a skillful dentist can take years off a man's appearance. So I didn't look forty-five.

Ordinarily, that is . . .

Fortunately, she slept very late that day, a Saturday. I was up well ahead of her, and by the time she arose, I was pretty much my old self again. Or, should I say, my younger self.

We had breakfast, which she prepared and served flawlessly—such wonders can love and its concomitant, self-confidence, accomplish. After eating we went to her rooming-house and picked up her clothes, all of which I firmly discarded after a brief examination.

Obviously, the outfit Rose had gotten her wouldn't suffice as a wardrobe, so I said we'd just have to hit the old bargain basement again; i.e., Saks, Magnins and similarly cheap little places. She looked at me seriously, her sweet-severe little face wrinkling with a frown.

"But Brad, honey, those places aren't cheap."

"Well, gee whiz! Gosh darn," I said. "But maybe they'll go easy on us when they hear you're a blushing bride-to-be. You do blush, don't you?"

She started to nod, then gulped and stared at me, stunned. "You m-mean — you mean y-you really want t-to —"

She suddenly grabbed me around the neck, showered my face with a dozen or so quick kisses. She drew back for a moment, then repeated the process; concluded with her lips against my ear, daringly whispering, *Just wait until to-night. Just you wait and see what you're gonna get!*

As a matter of fact, I didn't get anything that night, since it was occupied with getting to Arizona, the nearest place to get a quick marriage, sans the preliminaries demanded in California. And what with the heavy Sunday traffic, it was so late when we got back to L.A. that we were both too pooped for anything but sleep.

The following day, all the *Chronicle's* employees were assembled in the expanses of the city room, and the publisher addressed us. For once apologetic, instead of snappish and sharp as he normally was.

He did hope we'd understand, he said. There'd been rumors for months that the *Chronicle* was about to fold, and he'd flatly denied them all. But he'd had to—didn't we see? Otherwise, advertisers would start pulling the chain, since no one likes to ride a dying horse. And how could you maintain life in a paper, bring new money into it, once you admitted its illness was terminal?

It was damnably unfair to us, he confessed. If we'd known the truth, we might have been able to find other jobs. Or at least we could have been more careful about spending or assuming obligations which could not be met without a regular income. Still and nonetheless . . .

I remained for the bottom line of his speech. But I didn't listen to it; I didn't have to. I'd heard it almost verbatim before, from San Diego to New York, from Texas to the Dakotas:

"As of today, this paper will suspend publication."

4

They say that Los Angeles is seventy-five suburbs connected by barbecue sauce. That no matter how hot it gets in the daytime, there's never anything to do at night. That its whores are reasonably priced, but you have to pay extra for cream and sugar. That it's one large hamburger smothered in smog. That it's a long way to to picalilli, but there's always a Lilly to tickle your pickle. That—

Well, hell, why go on? We'll wrap it up with just one more, one not so pointed, perhaps, but certainly much to the point: Los Angeles is a place where old Iowans go to die, and young ones come to *LIVE*. Or to live it up, to coin a cliché. The retirement hotels, homes and communities are equaled in number only by their opposite number. Domiciles of one kind or another devoted exclusively to the young—the "swinging singles," so called.

City Detective Ken Narz lived in one of the latter places; one of the tackier ones, since it bordered on L.A.'s inner city. An apartment house, its exterior was an architect's nightmare in its extravagant attempt to appear smart; and its interior should have been a nightmare to any knowledgeable building inspector. But a lot of very peculiar things happen in Los Angeles—for example, temporary idiocy and blindness among the powerful and highly placed. And they continue to happen, even as they are under investigation and the outcry against them grows deafening.

I parked in the block below the apartment house. Sat in the car smoking and thinking. Hashing over the alleged man that was Ken Narz.

I'd only been on the *Chronicle* a few months when I got on the horn to him and suggested that he drop by my office. He said he'd been planning to do just that—in fact, was just starting out the door when I called. And he was there, facing me, not five minutes later, his coat not-so-carelessly open to reveal the belt-holstered gun.

The standard garb of an L.A. dick is blue serge suit, white shirt and black tie. I don't believe it's demanded, a regulation; merely a "suggestion" which has filtered down from on high, and it's seldom ignored—more than once. Ken, however, was wearing a Bill Blass plaid and a pink shirt, and he had a polka-dot scarf draped around his neck as a surrogate for a tie.

I gave him a raised-brow look, then remarked that I regretted his leaving the force, but I was sure he'd find circus life pleasant. He stared at me flat-eyed, took a deep drag on his cigarette and spewed the smoke into my face. "Don't like the threads, huh?" he grunted. "Well, I don't like snoops, so pull in your nose or I'll step on it."

I turned to my typewriter for a moment and wrote down what he'd said. Then, I asked him about the Gwaltney-Rico fight. "My information is that you have a piece of Gwaltney and he pulled an el floppo on orders from you."

"Try and prove it, you son-of-a-bitch!"

"I doubt that I can," I said, "but that's pretty snappy dialogue." And I wrote it down, also. "Now, a funny thing happened on the way to the office the other day. A rather charming young lady—charming but just a wee bit drunky—"

"A funny thing happened to her, too," he said, "and that book she told you she worked for. It ain't around no more, and neither is she. They got lost." He snapped his fingers under my nose. "Just like that."

"Beautiful, beautiful," I said, rattling the keys of the typewriter again. "I wonder if you'd have some equally interesting comment on that third race at Hollywood park ten days ago. I understand that the owner of the favorite, the nag that ran backwards, is pretty chummy with you—"

"I never seen him in my life," he said evenly, "and we'll both swear to it."

I laughed, and started to turn back to the typewriter. He put a hand on my arm.

"Now, looky, Mr. Maxwell," he said, his voice suddenly wheedling and humble. "This is no place to talk. How's about dropping by my pad tonight, and I'll tell you plenty of stuff you ought to know."

"Well"—I hesitated. "I'll have a pretty good story right here after I shape it up a little."

"Naah," he said, "that's no good. You don't want to print that." He pulled the sheet out of the typewriter, wadded it up and put it in his pocket. Then he winked at me and stood up. "Around eight o'clock tonight, okay?"

"Why not?" I said.

He lived in the same place then that he presently occupied, and I almost laughed out loud when I saw his apartment. The living room was senselessly sunken; you had to descend to it by three steps. The bath was a shower, and so small that one would have to tuck his legs behind him to sit on the toilet. There were no other rooms. Merely two alcoves, one for a bed and the other for a kitchenette.

He met me at the door wearing black silk pajamas and a red silk robe—both monogrammed. I said I was glad to see he was ready for bed, and I'd tuck him in as soon as I heard his prayers.

He laughed and said he had a babe to do that. She was a secretary, and if anything came up during the night, she took it down for him. "Jesus, the tail in this joint! I don't know when these kids find time to work."

"When do *you* find time to work?" I said. "And aren't you a little advanced in years for the romper set?"

He said, "Oh, shit!" and made a brushing motion with his hand, dismissing the question. Then he wheeled up a portable bar and mixed drinks for us from an assortment of very good booze.

"Gettin' down to business," he said as he sat down, "you were bluffing me today. You couldn't have printed that stuff with nothing to back it up."

"Oh, yes, I could," I said. "I could write it up as rumors which you had declined to deny, and what you'd told me instead of denying them." I took a sip of my drink and settled back in my chair. "Now newspapers, or their attorneys, rather, are leery of that type of story, and you can't get away with too many. But it wouldn't take many to do a job on you."

"Oh, yeah?" He grinned wisely. "So why didn't you run the story instead of coming here?"

"I thought you had something important to tell me. Of course, if you haven't . . ."

"Well . . ." He hesitated. "That's a nice dog-bed you're wearin'. What'd you pay for it?"

"The suit? The price was three hundred and fifty dollars."

"Hell, I could've got it for you for half that!"

"I got it as a gift," I said, "from a party named Anon—anonymous, that is. A small remembrance for favors rendered."

"No kid?" He wet his lips, again hesitating, then nodded toward a blanket-covered pile in the corner. "I'll get a flunky to load up your car when you leave. Scotch, bourbon, vodka; just take your pick."

"No need," I said. "I must have a year's supply at my apartment."

"Huh!" he grunted. "And you talk about me bein' on the make!"

"Not the same difference." I shook my head. "I don't slant sports stories or allow them to be slanted, and my good will isn't for sale. But a guy in my job, well, the stuff just comes to him. It does to almost every sports editor. Or anyone of any prominence, whoever he is."

"Uh-huh. Well, maybe. But what about them favors rendered?"

"That's just what they were—with no strings attached. Say you lend a couple of bills to a guy in a squeeze. He's grateful, naturally, so he adds on something extra when he pays back the loan." I finished my drink and set the glass on the bar. "Now what's your story?"

He refilled my glass and poured another drink for himself. He sat silently for a time, staring down at the floor, taking an occasional sip of his booze. Then, he slowly raised his eyes, frowning with troubled puzzlement.

"Looky, pal. L.A.'s got just about the world's cleanest police force, and probably the toughest to get on and stay on. Am I right or Amarillo?"

"Right," I said. "Indubitably."

"So how you think I made it, and keep making it? It ain't no secret that I'm a bastard. The greenest rookies on the force know it. But I keep right on doing business at the same old corner. So how you think I swing it?"

"I give up," I said. "How?"

"Because of something I lucked into a long time ago. I don't know," he said, his eyes growing absent. "I just don't know. My old lady was married twice, and my stepfather was an all-right guy and so were his kids. They all did their damnedest to help me. But some guys you can't help, and I guess I was one of them. Jesus"—shaking his head—"It still kinda bugs me."

"But?" I said.

"What? Oh yeah. I was working for a private dick at the time; couldn't get a license myself. So one day I had to lay a subpoena on a real big shot, probably the biggest. His house had about forty rooms, and he had maybe as many servants. But none of the hired hands was workin' that day. He'd given 'em the time off, see? I thought that added up to something funny, and I didn't knock very loud. I just sort of pushed the door open, went on in, and started prowling around. And—"

"You caught him in bed with another guy's wife," I said. "Am I right, or ami amas ama?"

Ken Narz groaned and slapped his forehead. "Oh brother. He could have had sixteen broads in the sack, and it wouldn't have meant anything. Not in this town. What he was sacked up with was two other guys—both big shots like he was. They'd been having a party, and they'd passed out that way. Well, I had this little self-developing camera I always carried. Just in case I ran into a worm chasing an eagle or somethin'. You know . . ."

"I get the picture," I said. "And I get the boys in the bed got one, too."

"I should be stingy?" He shrugged. "I'd shot ten others. Sure, I left 'em a picture, with my phone number written on it. I sealed the others up in a thick envelope and turned them over to a guy I knew I could trust . . ."

The man had promised not to open the envelope unless "something kinda oddball happened to Narz," like waking up dead or suddenly disappearing. "He knew the kind of character I was, an' he was just the opposite, and he didn't want any part of the frammis he figured I was pulling. But he felt sort of an obligation to me. He'd always come through when I needed him"—Narz shook his head fondly. "What a guy! There never was no one else like him."

He was silent for a moment, smiling reminiscently over some happy memory of the man. Then, he sighed and returned to the present.

"Well, that's about it. That's how I got to be a cop, and how I moved up from uniform to plainclothes. With all the records showing. I did it legit."

"I don't believe it," I said. "I just don't believe it."

"Listen, pal." He leaned forward and tapped me on the knee. "These three characters were *big*. Mucho grande. An' you can do anything you're big enough to do, in this town or anywheres else."

"That part I'll buy," I said. "But settling for being a cop when you could have milked your pigeons for a fortune— huh-uh. That just doesn't figure."

"Why the hell not?" he bristled. "My family, my stepdad's family, was respectable. Why wouldn't I do something to make 'em proud of me, instead of always being ashamed?"

"And *were* they proud of you?" I said.

"Sure, they were! Bein' a cop is about as respectable as you can get."

I laughed, and he glared at me indignantly. Then, his eyes shifted and dropped; and he mumbled that at least the family was proud of him for a little while. "At least, I tried to be on the up-and-up, even if I couldn't make it. That's better than never tryin' at all, ain't it?"

"Look, Narz—Ken," I said. "You never expected or wanted to be a straight cop. How could you, when you got on the force by blackmail? With a start like that, you could only go one way. And that's the way you went."

"Well..." He hesitated. "Well, hell," he sighed. "All that easy money layin' around, and me with practically a license to steal. Me, I guess I'm the only guy I ever kidded, Brad."

"Not quite. I'd say you did a pretty good job kidding those highly placed homos."

"Huh? You mean, you think I'm still squeezing 'em?" He shuddered in a way that couldn't be make-believe. "I made a deal with those guys and I kept it. Because they—I mean certain people they sent around to see me—made me know I'd better. No, siree, pal! I never tried for another touch, and I ain't going to neither!"

"But what about protection? Your trusted friend who's holding the envelope with the other—"

"Forget it! Hear me? Just forget it!"

He lifted his glass half-full of straight whiskey and took it down at a swallow. Even with a jolt like that, he remained shaken for several minutes. At last, color came back into his face, and he became a reasonable facsimile of his normal self.

"Well, that's the way things stand, Brad, gettin' back to where I started from. I'm in solid in the force, and nothin' can shake me out. You can make trouble, sure, an' trouble I don't like. But why make it when it won't get you nowheres?"

"Why, indeed?" I said.

I hadn't done anything for him; it was just a case of not

doing anything against him. But he regarded the two as identical, as perhaps they were, and I received substantial reminders of the fact.

For example: Five two-dollar win paramutual tickets that paid off at two hundred and forty dollars per.

And a one-thousand-dollar wristwatch (with a sales slip, so that I could exchange it for cash).

And a week's stay (American plan) at a Las Vegas hotel-casino, also redeemable in cast at its face value.

And various other tokens of appreciation.

I wasn't absolutely positive that the stuff came from him, but I wasn't meant to be. It's a delicate business—this giving and receiving of ultragenerous gifts—and one always haunted by the possibility of investigation. And if the recipient doesn't know who gave him something, how can it be traced to the donor?

Of course, he knows who might be inclined to be grateful to him—and *how* grateful—and the person's ability to show his gratitude. But that's no evidence. Merely a guess, legally speaking, and one is under no compulsion to guess.

I doubt that Ken Narz put out a nickel in expressing his gratitude to me. He may have put on a little more pressure where it was convenient to do so or found new sources of income to squeeze, with resultant benefit to me. But personally he was very tight-fisted.

I found that out during the several parties I attended at his apartment.

He had innumerable cases of the very best booze, but none was available to his young, determinedly "swinging" guests. They got beer and wine, the cheapest and worst, and no vast amount of that.

Hell, he didn't owe them nothin'. Anyways, they wouldn't know good stuff if they had it.

I wondered why the youngsters kept coming to his parties; why, particularly, the girls were willing to go to bed with him. Ken said absently that they must appreciate all the things he'd done for them. Like keepin' quiet when they done things they could be jailed for—smokin' pot or "taking a loan" from a guy before they'd put out. Or like seein' that they got bail money, if they were pinched. Or gettin' the loan sharks not to bust them up if they fell behind in their repayment of the bail money—plus interest, plus interest upon interest plus late charges, plus this that and the other, all of which contrived to stretch a loan of one hundred dollars into a debt of one thousand.

"I take care of these kids good," he declared solemnly. "Real good."·

One night I overheard a girl ask him for help. She was pregnant and she simply had to have some money. "So go peddle your ass," Narz told her coldly. "You're already knocked up, so what's to worry?"

When she had gone, stumbling as she went up the steps to the door, I asked Narz if that was an example of how he took care of his kids.

He replied with a question of his own.

"You an' me are kind of in the same position, pal. We both know lots of people, and practically none of 'em are standing still. They're going up or down, right? So how long can you lay out for losers without going down yourself?"

"I've helped a great many people," I said, "and not gotten anything back."

"So you swung at a few wild ones," he shrugged. "But I'd say you scored eight out of ten times at bat. That's better than I do, an' with me it's a business."

He grinned and nudged me in the ribs. I moved back, looking at him coldly, and the grin went off his face.

"Looky," he whined, "I really couldn't give that gal any dough. I just ain't got it to give. I got myself in a hell of a bind in the market an' they're on me day and night for margin."

"Forget it," I said. "I'll help her myself."

"I mean it, pal. I'm really in over my head."

"Never mind. Just give me her name and apartment number."

He did so, still mumbling apologies. I turned and left, taking a backward glance at him as I went out the door.

He looked puzzled, thoughtful, calculating. Like a man who suspects he has overlooked a very good bet.

I left my car and walked up the block to the swinging singles apartment house. I pressed the elevator button, and when the car descended several people got out. Youngsters I'd seen and been seen by at Ken Narz's parties. But that was all right. He wasn't going to make any fuss about what happened to him tonight. He'd been very far out of line in what he'd done to Johnny, and he couldn't and wouldn't holler copper on me. When, that is, he recovered sufficiently to do any calling at all. Which could be quite some time.

When you grow up as I did, when the only parent you remember having is a tramp newspaperman and a dipso, when you are out of school as much as you're in; in your almost incessant traveling from city to city, when you are always ill-fed, ill-housed, ill-clothed; when that is the way things are—you make a lot of mistakes.

Then, someone comes to you during the night—God or the Devil, both like to latch onto you while you're young —and He says, Jesus Christ, kid, what the hell *is* the matter with you? You don't have time to study books, even if you did feel like it. Anyway, you'll have different books next month—a different school, different teachers—and studying won't make you any more than it did in the last town you were in and all the towns before that. So let's get it all together, baby, and grab that ring for a free ride. (I remember now: It was the Devil talking. God was conferring that night with the Four Horsemen.)

I wasn't any smarter (not academically) after the Old Fellow's lecture; but my grades proclaimed me a budding genius. And my rise to that status was both swiftly and simply accomplished. Being the cleanest kid that ever was, was a big part of the miracle. Being the neatest kid that ever was—and this despite my runover shoes and frayed garments. *(The poor, brave little man! Practically nothing to do with it, but doing so much with it. Oh, I think I'm going to c-cry! Sniffle-sniffle.)* Met with general admiration and approval, I lost my shyness and the curse of mumbling and bumbling and became eagerly vocal and fluid of speech. My hand was the first to shoot up when a question was asked—regardless of my ignorance of the answer. For I could talk interminably—by turns smiling or serious, but always with a mystically charming air of brightness—about nothing whatsoever.

Virtually the only studying I did was that of popular public figures—picture stars to politicans; people who were overwhelmingly attractive to others. I studied their mannerisms; the way they spoke and smiled and gestured and used their eyes—the multitudinous elements of personality with a capital *P*. And I aped those mannerisms, they became mine, and I could use them as naturally as had their original owners.

So, ultimately, along with being the cleanest, neatest and smartest, I became the most popular kid in whatever class, or classes, I attended. Regretfully, I was not popular among the brooding, overgrown element, who were detained in the same grade year after year. Regretfully, since any of them could whip a spindling sprout like me in a fair fight with one hand tied behind him, and were increasingly insistent upon demonstrating the fact.

As always, however, when I was in need and cried out to Him, my Mentor popped up with the answer to the problem:

Fight, shmite (He jeered), and forget about that fair stuff. You don't fight, *period*. Fighting can make your clothes lousier than they already are. It can spoil your looks—an you got none to spare, kid. It can hurt your snow-wh reputation, no matter whose fault it is. It is *o-u-t*, an shitting you not. What you do is get the guy alone since he thinks you're a pushover). Then, jump o and scratch and claw and bite and make with until he's crying for Momma. Contingen him in the belly, or give it to him in the nuts, and when he goes down, *stomp him!*

Clobber the guy: That's what you do, baby. Clobber the living crap out of him. And if he's stupid enough to whine about not fighting fair, join the crowd that laughs at him. A loser is a loser is a loser—that's all that matters, in the end—and no one will want what he got. And he won't want a rematch. Because, baby, when you really give it to a guy, when you really clobber the crap out of him, you fill the void with something very special. The stuff that won the world for all the smart boys, from the first Fascists, the Syrians, on up to modern times. The good stuff. The stuff that makes men into mites . . .

Terror, baby. Terror.

I walked down the corridor toward Ken Narz's apartment, mentally measuring the amount of the stuff I should give him. Measuring very, very carefully until I hit upon exactly the right dosage. Enough to make him believe that he'd almost been killed, without bringing him within miles of that admirable but thoroughly impractical end. Killing was not to be thought of (although I had thought of it, even threatened it, in moments of extravagant anger). Killing was unnecessary. Killing was stupid, and I was simply incapable of it.

I paused before his apartment, looked down at the base of the poorly fitted door. Only a sick-firefly glow of light shone through the opening. I judged that he had only one table-lamp going, and it turned down very low. *Oh we're gonna shuffle, shuffle off to—*

Shuffle off! Don't even think it, hear me? That's bad stuff, and you've got the good. *All you need is a brown shirt, and that can wait a while.*

He was very close to the door and seemingly coming closer. Not for any reason, of course. Simply because he was drunk and wandering about willy-nilly, grunting incoherent curses when he stumbled or bumped against something.

Cheers for my side, I thought. Just the way I want him. Sufficiently aware to know what he was getting and who was giving it to him. But completely defenseless and relaxed; unable to put up a fight or suffer serious injury. Bless you, Mr. Barleycorn. Blessings from all the liver-limp drunks, whose stiffness is nonstiffening, an impenetrable shield unshared by those who know not the Demon and are therefore endemic incubators of the fatal *stifficus neckus*.

I rattled my fingernails against the door, as a woman might. He lurched forward, his body striking the panels with a thud. Then the knob turned lazily, and the door suddenly swung open, and—

I got him with two swifties, a quick one-two with my knees. Both hit him square in the mush, the second one landing right on top of the first, so that he got the full impact of both. I had the door and closed and was following him as he sailed across the room, skimming and skidding against the furniture until his head struck a marble-topped coffee table with a dull, exploding-pumpkin sound. I turned on several lamps, adjusting them just so, taking my time about it because I didn't want to look at him. Then, I heard sounds coming from him, and sounds meant life. I crossed to where he was and bent down close. And—

Death also makes sounds. *Mingled blood and brains washing from the cleft-wide skull. And the broken bones and crushed cartilage, uneasily settling themselves in the smashed face—*

Face? THAT was a face?

THAT WAS A FACE?

very quietly now we are here to bulge our eyes and gaze upon the dishonored dead and to shit in our pants while we do so at the terror that has been turned back upon us and it will matter little if we do for the mark of cain (ain't it sweet) is already on us practically every fucking inch of us is smeared with the blood of this cop we have killed and hang down your head and cry brad maxwell for soon you too will die

5

Nnnnnnnnnyaaaaahhhh. . . .

Try that number again please.

Nnnnnnnaahh........

Once more please, and omit the aspirate *h* which is frigging the frammis.

Nnnnnaahoo. . . .

Close but no cigar. Once more with feeling.

Nnnnnnn. Nnnnoooo. Nnn-no. . . .

Now, you've got it. Try it *fortissimo*.

NNNO NNO NO NO NO NO NO NONONONONO . . . NO! NO! NO! It is not true. It cannot be true.

You do not kill cops. It violates the unwritten law. It is against scripture. See? It says right here, Thou shalt not kill cops. Hmmm. A misprint. The word *cops* seems to have been dropped. But no matter. As every schoolboy knows, the Bible is allegory. *Yes, Bradley, you dear sweet boy. Can you give us an example?* Now, any one of us who has achieved the age of puberty can cite cases of people being talked to death by goddamned fools. And this is the true meaning of being slain by the jawbone of an ass. Similarly, then, although the proscription against killing may seem to be a general one, it applies, in fact, only to cops. If we see anything at all—a moot point—we see the proof of this daily. To give an instance, let us say that a graduate student who is working on her doctorate in baton-twirling discovers that there is little demand for such truly relevant skills; and skidded out of her skull by this hideous fact of life—plus speed, *LSD*, and a few joints of pot—she bludgeons your Aunt Fanny into the hereafter (Aunt Fanny having stupidly ventured out of her house after four in the afternoon). The murderess promptly surrenders to the police—after they catch up with her in Algiers—and they praise her, publicly and officially, for her spirit of cooperation and her obvious anxiety to strengthen the cause of Justice. Subsequently, she is tried and convicted of improperly twirling a baton (the murder weapon), and receives a three-day suspended sentence. She appeals the verdict on the grounds of judicial prejudice, for she had been diddling since the fourth-grade of grammar school, whereas the maidenlady judge has openly confessed that she still cherishes her cherry. Naturally, the case is dismissed, and the police department wangles a job for the defendant as their official baton-twirler. Whether the title is a cop-out for cop-*in*, and the "batons" she twirls are invariably attached to a man with a badge, deponent sayeth not. He will swear on his Momma's favorite thimble, however, that enrollments for the force have increased so greatly that there are now more cops than there are civilians. And the official b.t. is greeted with thunderous huzzahs as she begins her daily stint by defecating on the American flag and addressing the boys as fascist pigs.

Well, let's see. Where was I?

> *Never mind where you was, ol' boy, an' start thinking about where you is. Sitting here smeared with the blood of the cop you have killed, and so scared that you could piss and puke endlessly. No good running. Too many people can place you here at the approximate time of death. And the fact that you had plenty of motive for killing the son-of-a-bitch will be promptly uncovered. So—*

Ah, yes. I was about to contrast the conduct of the cops when a garden-variety of citizen gets killed with that which obtains when one of their own is a victim. Now—

> *We know, goddamn it! And so do you. They never let up until they nail you. No matter that they hated the dead cop's guts and would have liked to kill him themselves. That won't make*

things any easier for you. In fact it may make them harder; for you have chosen to intrude into the sacrosanct world of the cop, and for that there is no forgiveness.

It was obviously time for some heavy thinking. Not for the composing of more or less entertaining but basically meatless chit-chat—the daily, weekly, monthly and yearly special at Maxwell's Market. In fact, I must think for two, even as an expectant mother must eat for two, since Johnny was obviously incapable of real thinking, or she would not have joined her life to mine.

Thus, having no palatable alternative, I thought; and soon found myself on the phone to Johnny. Telling her exacty what to say and what not to say when the cops called on her, which they indubitably would and very shortly.

Then, I called Central Police and notified them of Karl Narz's death and promised to remain where I was until police arrived on the scene. Which I did, and they did.

6

When the *Chronicle* folded and I ceased to be an influential sports editor, practically everyone I knew and who knew me promptly forgot the fact. None was interested in drinks or lunch or getting together at the Press Club to cut up old touches. They were *busy,* see? They had *jobs* to do. Anyway, what ever gave me the idea that I had any call on them?

I was a stranger.

I say it was that way with practically everyone I had known, because it wasn't with all of them. A few, surprisingly those who had never owed me anything or who long ago had overpaid their obligation, remained interested in my welfare.

Sue Crystola wired a thousand dollars from Baltimore

with the message, *More where this came from, soul brother*. Rose called twice a day with persistent proffers of help. Musso-Frank's, the oldest restaurant in Hollywood, notified me that the customary limits on charge accounts had been removed in my case and that there would not be the slightest hurry or worry about payment. A girl named Francine—But that's getting ahead of the story.

One of those who remained acively interested in me— and this was truly surprising—was Ken Narz. He was by the apartment almost every day, usually when Johnny was there, if I hadn't managed to get her out. And I was pleased and touched, at first, but I eventually became pretty damned annoyed.

"So where's Johnny today?" he said on his final visit to the apartment. "Out blowing in more dough that you ain't got and can't get?"

"Ken," I said, "what my wife does with my money is none of your business. As a matter of fact, however, she's seeing about a job today."

"Receptionist or some crap like that? Maybe seventy-five a week? Hell, you let her throw away three times that much."

It was true that Johnny was running a little wild with money. I'd always been pretty fast with a buck myself; and she was starved for more of the good life, which I'd introduced her to. And why should she be careful, when I persisted in telling her—out of pride—that there was no need to be?

"Pal," Ken was saying, "face the facts, pal. There's only two papers in town now, and one of 'em's on strike, so that leaves only one where you could work—if they'd hire you. And what chance have you got with all the guys from the struck paper and the *Chronicle* over there looking for jobs?"

"I'll get something," I said firmly. "And the job that Johnny's seeing about pays very, very well. I can't say that it's the kind of thing I like to see her do, but I guess there's really nothing wrong with it. Uh—it's a place up on the Strip. La Casa de Dance, I believe it's called—"

"Yeah," Ken snorted. "They oughta call it La Palace de Dry Screw. Jesus, Brad, are you out of your mind?"

"I understand that it's perfectly respectable," I said stiffly. "They don't sell drinks and no drunks or rough stuff are allowed. As I say, it's not exactly the kind of—"

"Hold it," Narz said. "Just hold it, and let me give you the straight poop. Tickets are two-bits a dance, the girl gets half, and a dance lasts a minute. So a guy just about has to spring for five bucks, or forget it, and he knows he'd better pop for ten if he wants a real workout. Which is what it's all about, natch. Those gals don't fool around with no stupid crud like bras or girdles, nor panties neither probably. And what a guy can't feel, ain't worth—"

"That's enough," I said. "Johnny will not be going to work there."

"Let me get to the point, will you? Let me tell you why the joint is really a bummer."

"You already have. I'm thoroughly convinced that it's a bummer."

"Listen. Just listen, godammit. In a good week, a girl can maybe make two and a half bills. But she's probably worn out a couple pairs of shoes, plus ruining a dress or two, in doing it, so she's lucky to have a hundred and fifty clear. And what's the sense in a deal like that?"

"Ken," I said wearily. "I've already told you that—"

"Wait a minute! I ain't finished yet," he said. "The gal puts out dry all week for peanuts, and that's stupid. What she ought to do—what Johnny ought to do—"

"Don't tell me," I said. "Not if you want to keep your teeth."

"Aah, you don't mean that." He gestured, brushing aside the threat. "That's what it's for, ain't it? And with a box of candy like hers, who's gonna miss a few pieces? Hell, she could put out by the shovelful and still have plenty left for—"

He broke off as I got to my feet. Then, he jumped up

and put his chair between us. Began edging backward toward the door.

"Don't be like that, Brad," he pleaded. "I guess we don't look at things the same way, but I sure didn't mean to insult you."

"All right." I stopped moving toward him. "Now, just get out, and don't come back."

"And we're still pals, huh? You still like me?"

"Pals?" I spluttered. "Like you?" And it was all so damned preposterous, that I suddenly burst out laughing. "Oh, God, go on, get out of here. And I mean it, Ken, don't ever come here again!"

He said okay, if I didn't want him here. But I was welcome any time at his apartment. "Any old time at all, Brad. You can give me a ring first, in case I got something cookin' on the mattress—How about makin' it tomorrow night, huh? Well, the day after, then?"

"Ken," I said slowly. "Ken, if I have to tell you to beat it JUST ONE MORE TIME, I'M GONNA—"

"I'm goin', I'm goin'! But you call me now, hear?"

And at last he was gone.

About ten minutes later, when I and a tall drink were communing with one another and deciding that nothing was worth getting that shaken up about, whether one came in a handsome bottle or a degenerating carcass, the phone rang.

I let it ring about eight times, and then disgustedly surrendered. Rose's beddy-bye voice came over the wire.

"Boo, you pretty man. Guess who's coming to see you?"

"No one," I said, "because I'm not here. I'm out and my wife is out, and if I even glimpse you approaching in the distance—"

"Mr. Nice Guy," she sighed. "Small wonder that we all love him. But I'm glad Johnny's out. Francine's about to come down on you like a wolf on the fold."

"That did it," I said. "When lovely lady stoops to the folly of paraphrasing Byron, it is time to rise up and take arms against her."

She giggled. "Now don't tell me you've forgotten Francine. She was that chick who got herself preggy in one of those jumping-juniors joints. I had to move out of your pad while you were getting her fixed up."

I said, oh, yeah. I did remember Francine. "Didn't she marry that ancient but anxious character with the big racing stable? Stud-hoss, I believe they called him."

"Of course, she married him! You introduced them, and the hot-blooded S. Hoss took it from there! God," Rose groaned. "What *am* I going to do with you? You don't even remember setting up a deal like that!"

"I don't dig. Francine must be Mrs. Midas now. Why does she want to see me?"

"Because," said a husky but distinctly feminine voice, immediately behind me, "Stud-hoss has gone to that great big pasture in the sky. The Head Wrangler spotted him when we were in Switzerland and decided that the Stud had done his duty by the fillies and it was time for the last round-up."

Rose snickered and hung up. I turned around, wondering what the hell, then remembering that I had not relocked the door after Ken Narz's departure.

"Well?" said Francine, pertly tapping the floor with her foot. "Don't you know it's not polite to stare at a girl? Even if she is wearing fifteen thou' in Chinchilla and an original from one of the hautest *haute couturiers* in—"

"—Dallas," I said. "Neiman-Marcus. Where the hautest *haute couturiers* go before creating their originals. Something in the water, I guess."

She pouted crossly that how could I expect her to remember things when she hadn't even been kissed? So I kissed her—the equivalent of shaking hands in these parts, though probably less stimulating—and sat her down on the lounge. And sat down a discreet distance away.

"That's it," I said. "I am thoroughly and happily married, and for us the days of wine and roses are *finis*."

She said, oh, all right. "But why did you make me forget your address, hmm? And why weren't you keeping track of me all this time?"

"So soddy," I murmured humbly. "Or awful offal, as they say in Juan les Pins."

She nodded, satisfied with the apology. Then, she opened her purse, plucked six five-hundred-dollar bills from it and shoved them into my pocket. "And don't you say you can't take it!" she warned sternly. "I'm loaded, and you certainly did plenty for me when I needed it!"

"Well, gee, Mom, thanks," I said. "And thanks. Oh, yes, and just in case I didn't mention it, thanks."

She smiled at me in a certain way, a very dear and well-remembered way. As she had smiled when it was still necessary for me to carry her from bedroom to bathroom and back again. Or when I was giving her her daily bath . . .

She smiled that smile at me, and squeezed my hand. When I opened it, there were three one-thousand-dollar bills in it. I shook my head firmly and held them out to her.

"Huh-uh, Francine, my oversexed pet. But definitely not. You were repaying something the first time. Very generously, to be sure, but I could accept it as a repayment. But this—Now, you're trying to buy something, and I'll have to ring this up a no-sale."

"Aahh, Brad, don't be nasty. A friend can't give a friend a gift?"

"No," I said. "Not under these circumstances."

"Why not, darling?" She leaned toward me. "I'll tell you the truth, Brad, the God's truth. I haven't been able to make it since we split. Not even once! Now, wait—wait a minute, dammit. The three *G's* are yours. I'm not buying *anything!* I'm going to leave right now."

She made motions of getting up. "Well," I said. "If you want to put it that way"—I paused, raising a brow at her. "Did you say you were leaving?"

"I did, and I am. But I thought you'd want to kiss me goodbye first. Of course, if you don't want to . . ."

"Of course, I want to!" I said warmly, and I kissed her.

"Now, that's it, lambie. You run along and be sweet and— Let loose now, Francine!"

"Mmm?" She clung to me. "Mmm, Brad?"

"You know I'm married, damn you! I love my wife more than anything in the world, and if you think for a moment that—"

"Oh, shit on your wife!"

"Wh-aat?" I grabbed her by the shoulders and held her away from me. "What did you say about my wife?"

"I said, shit on her."

"Now, goddamn you!" I gave her a hard shake. "You want to dirty-talk me, that's one thing. But you ever pop off about my wife, and by God, I'll—!"

"Shit on her, and piss on the pile."

"I'm warning you, Francine! Any more of that, an' I'll make a washboard out of your ass!"

"Fuck your wife." She made a jabbing motion with one finger. "Up her rosy red."

It was a game, of course. A game that I could play, without doffing my shiny armor. She had always had a strong streak of masochism, which, I suspected, had been nourished by her late husband. Stud-hoss would never hit one of the so-called lower animals. But rumor rumored that he had an extensive collection of dog whips. In his-and-hers bedroom . . .

But what the hell, anyway? She was an old and very dear friend, and friends owe each other something. And if she could be made content with no more than a game— well, how could I deny the poor child so little?

I grabbed and held her wrists with one hand. With the other, I jerked her dress up and her pants down, yanked her across my knees and proceeded to wallop her bare backside.

Obviously, there was no need to imprison her wrists. So I moved that hand down until I had a large handful of breast; and on about the sixth or seventh smack to her tail, I squeezed the breast hard. Almost instantly, her buttocks drew tightly together and her breast leaped from my hand,

and a tremendous, earth-quaky shudder shook her entire body. It was followed by a series of aftershocks (or aftershakes) of gradually decreasing force, until they ceased entirely and she lay quietly across my knees. Except for one impatient little twitch.

So I bent down quickly and brushed my lips against one buttock then the other. Expunging any tingles of pain and making them well again. For this is the only known way to make a spanked bottom well.

She sat up quite sedately, drew her panties into their original position and readjusted her dress.

She arose from the lounge, took a loose turn around her neck with the Chinchilla stole and saw to it that its remaining length of about eight feet were draped down her front and rear in approximately equal parts. Then, studying herself in a nearby mirror, she addressed me matter-of-factly.

"The girl thought it was very good," she said. "Not as good as when the giving is mutual, but still good. What does the boy think?"

"He's too busy blushing to speak," I said. "But I think I'm safe in saying that he accomplished as much for himself as he did for the girl. Unless, of course, someone busted an egg in his shorts."

She laughed unwillingly. "So what did you gain by playing 'I love you truly, Your Devoted Husband'?"

"*You* gained," I said. "I saved you a trip to the privy."

She frowned and said that it was just such distinctions as that which would surely lead me to the old hog-wallow, and I said hog-wallow, where is thy sting. I got a very severe scowl for that crack, but one intermingled with concern.

Then, strange and mysterious child that she was, she did one of the strangest and mysteriousest things I had ever witnessed. She squinched her eyes shut and extended her arms in front of her as though searching or feeling for something and rocked back and forth from one foot to the other, always bringing her feet down in the same place. And she intoned in shivery appeal.

"Mmmmmm-mmmm, ahhhhh-ahhh. I am told that: I am a beautiful baby bitch, and that tiny Hairy-ette who rests so cozily between my thighs is the most wondrous of kitty-kats (though given to snapping in the fashion of turtles); and the twins, Bub-Bub, seem to tug me forward into naughtiness (and so amply that I can touch them with my chin), and my Bumbum sticks out behind, counterbalancing the twins, and it is not only adorable and sweet to fondle, but capable of delightful wickedness, namely the deed that caused the death knell to be sounded over the city of Sodom; and I heat up quickly (and am more than ready to serve) to one hundred degrees centigrade. And I cry out for help. Help, help the beautiful baby bitch."

I sat staring at her, mumbed and more than a little shocked, and I thought, Shit, mother, I can't dance, and what the hell is this, anyway? At last I found my voice, and said:

"You are truly a beautiful baby bitch. And your body is a temple of unspeakable delights, curving marvelously and generously (in exactly the right places) and with the treasure it contains. So why art thou—thou of all people—in need of help?"

"Mmmmmm-mmmm, ahhhhhh-ahhhh," she moaned, continuing her curious antics. "Because I am a beautiful but poor baby bitch, poor in all the things that matter, and I am also blind, in the only way that counts, and I have lost my sense of smell, being unable to smell shit when my nose is clogged with it. And I am lost in a wilderness and must be guided from it ere I perish. Help, O, help, the poor blind beautiful baby bitch whose nose no longer differentiates between the stinky stuff and wild honey and who is lost in a wilderness."

I jumped up and stood beside her. Extending my arms in front of me tremulously and rocking back and forth from foot to foot.

"Ugggggg-glugg, Pull the plug," I groaned. "This is *literally* poor, broken-down Brad Maxwell, who is poor any damned way you figure it, and who *is* blind, except for his

contact lenses, and who has caught so much shit as to ac-
quire a taste for it and would welcome an invitation to eat a
plateful in Macy's window at high noon; and whose mouth
contains so much bridgework that it is often confused with
the Golden Gate. Hell-up, hell-up for the poor, blind, broken Brad Maxwell, who emerged from his mother's dead
womb into a wilderness. As do all men—but not with his
near-hysterical eagerness—he still yearns for the snug har-
bor from which he emerged and seeks his way back to it
constantly, and all to no avail. For he is invariably detoured
into the uteri of beautiful baby bitches, and—"

"You bastard!" snarled Francine. "Come along, goddamn you!"

She grabbed me by the arm, yanked me across the room
and up the foyer and out to the stoop. I opened my eyes
and said wonderingly, well, gosh, the blind have led the
blind; and she said, who the hell else would bother?

"Aahh, shaddup," she continued, not looking at me
since she was searching for something in her handbag.
"Not that you ever say anything. Not that you ever talk. I
don't know whether you're actually contemptuous of
women, and possibly everyone, but I know you're not stupid and you don't need to be a center-stage horse's ass
umpteen hours a day. You could talk intelligently, but you
never do. You just string words together, a lousy imitation
of talk. I know, I know. I came here wanting action talk;
that's what I and all the others always want, don't you see,
Brad? You're such a sweet, likeable, good-hearted bastard
in spite of anything I've said—that we're actually dying to
give you our all and do it in a way that won't disturb your
idle mind or demand any real effort from you, for God's
sake. And—and you make us *want* to, you son-of-a-bitch
—this is best accomplished by whistling for Sex to rear its
lovely head. Well, screw you. I love you enough to tell you
that you're killing yourself with flatulence; and you're not
going to see me again ever. You probably *will* get around
to eating it in Macy's window. But I'm not going to watch

you." She looked up from searching her handbag. "What's the matter? Didn't make you mad, did I?"

"Not at all," I said, almost strangling over the words. "And I hope it won't make you mad when I shove your six grand up your ass."

"Well"—she glanced at the red Ferrari, standing at the curb—"I might have trouble squeezing it into the seat of yon firewagon. But perhaps if you put it in my coin-purse —See if you can find it, will you, darling? I think I must have dropped it on the lounge."

I slammed into the house and began searching the lounge, throwing the cushions this way and that. I practically tore the damned thing apart, but the coin purse was not to be found. I looked under the lounge and made a thorough search of the surrounding area. And at last I spotted it. It was lying right out in the open on a small lamp table, and it was bulging with currency. I snatched it up and hurried out to the stoop. But Francine was gone, of course, and the red Ferrari was gone from the curb.

I went slowly back into the house. After a stiff drink, I sat down and began counting the money in the purse . . . four five-hundred-dollar bills and twenty one-hundreds. Four thousand dollars in all. Or a total of ten thousand, counting the six she had given me originally.

TEN THOUSAND DOLLARS!

Ah, Francine, you strange, loveable, hateful darling! Francine, my beautiful baby bitch . . .

7

Some two weeks later, I was having an after-lunch liqueur in Musso-Frank's when I saw Rose. She was standing in the doorway between the dining room and the more intimate lounge-grille where I was; frowning rather crossly as her eyes roved over the tables and the open leather-upholstered booths. I caught the head waiter's eye and nodded toward her. He brought her over to my booth, and saw to her seating. She glared at me, her breast rising and falling. And I looked away diffidently.

"You've been to a convention," I said, "and you just came in from L.A. International Airport. Better known to us jet-setters as LAX."

Rose said something that sounded like ship but wasn't. Then, she said of course she'd been to a convention; did I think she looked that way *all* the time?

"And don't ask me what kind of convention it was," she continued bitterly. "Can you tell what guys do for a living when they've got their pants off? Well, can you?"

"Shh," I said. "That drink you need is practically here."

She said she wouldn't *shh,* and never mind where the convention wás either. Because how the hell would a girl know when she hardly got out of bed for almost two weeks?

"Fort Worth or Detroit or Miami Beach," she murmured wearily, taking a big slug of her double martini, rocks. "And I think the guys were bankers or snake-charmers, or—*wuff!*" She gasped. "What is in this toddy?"

"Imported Russian Vodka," I said. "The one-hundred-proof."

"Oh," she said slowly. "And just where the dickens is my Black Sea Caviar?"

"I'm sorry," I said, glancing around for a waiter. "If you'll wait just a minute—"

"Stop it!" she hissed. "Damn you, stop it or I'll scream!"

"Oh? But I thought you wanted—"

"Just get me another one of these"—she jiggled her glass. "I think I'm going to need it."

I got her a second drink and silently signaled the waiter to start a third our way. She drank in silence for a couple of minutes, studying me with dark and baleful eyes.

"What's the matter, Rose?" I said at last. "What are you sore about?"

"I'm not sure of the details," she said, "but I know damned well you've been up to something, and I mean to find out what, I called your apartment today, the minute the plane landed. There wasn't any answer, of course, so I had the cab driver take me by there and I couldn't raise either you or Johnny, and I was so g-goddamned worried and s-s-scared. A-And—" She broke off, brushing angrily at her eyes. "That Johnny! I'd like to stick her head in a johnny. You didn't have any sense to begin with, and she's made you ten times worse!"

"Now, Rose," I said uncomfortably. "Now, Rose."

"Don't you Rose me, Brad Maxwell! I tried to call you the night of the day Francine visited you. I tried to call you all the next day and the next one—right up until the time I had to catch my plane. Now, just what have you been up to?"

"Well . . ." I hesitated. "Francine saw you that day after she saw me?" I asked. "Do you know where she went to after that?"

"Outer space, probably. I hear there was a hell of a disturbance in the Van Allen Belt. But never you mind about Francine. Just—"

"But I have to mind," I said. "I'm really concerned about her, Rose."

"So are her bankers. They don't know what to do with the interest on the three million old Stud-hoss left her. Now"—Rose took a deep breath. "I know that Francine laid ten grand on you. I know, because I threatened to beat the pee out of her if she didn't come clean with me. What I want to know is what you did with the dough?"

"Well . . ." I hesitated again. "What makes you think I don't have it?"

Rose simply sat and looked at me. But I didn't like the way she looked or the color her complexion was assuming. So I explained that Johnny had needed some new shoes and a bag to go with them and a new dress to go with *them*.

"What the hell, Rose?" I continued uneasily. "A girl has to have a new dress when she has a new bag and shoes. Those things are particularly important when you're a little down on your luck. You've got to keep up your prestige."

Rose said, rather glumly, that this was a matter of common knowledge. And naturally a guy who didn't have anything but his tail and his hat, both of which contained holes, wouldn't dare drive around in a car that was almost two years old. So what kind of new one had I bought?

"I didn't buy a new one," I said. "My God, I wouldn't do anything foolish like buying a new Bentley."

"Uh-huh. Of course, not. You wouldn't—*whaat?*" Her eyes popped wide. "Does that mean you bought a *used* Bentley?"

"It was a steal," I said. "And they allowed me three thousand trade-in on my car, so I only had to put up two more for the down payment."

Rose moaned softly. She said she knew she wouldn't be able to bear it, but she wanted to hear the rest of the story. *Pronto!*

"Well, Johnny and I had never had a honeymoon," I said, "and everyone's entitled to a honeymoon. Hell, you know that, Rose. A marriage isn't really consummated until you've had your honeymoon. So, well, it was only a few hours' drive to Las Vegas . . ."

Rose put her head down on the table and began to cry.

"Hell,"
from IRONSIDE

The piano player, that unreasonable facsimile thereof, was doing all right tonight. When you suddenly jump a six-bag habit to eight, you *have* to do all right. Man, you just have to! For time at least. You do it without doing it. Simply by opening a vein and letting the whole wondrous world rush in and take over, doing everything that needs doing for you. Wiping your chin or combing your hair or arguing with the fuzz or playing the piano. The world is you, and you're it and everything is as smooth an' as easy as *di-wah-didy*. Like now, when the world-you is making the ol' eighty-eighty rise right up in meetin' an' declare itself, a-weavin' and a-rockin' with the glorious tidings that "It Must Be Jelly, 'Cause Jam Don't Shake Like That."

Want a little backin', a little helpin'-out? Well, just send up a signal... "Yaka Hula"... "Chong... "Limehouse" ... "Jada"... "Dardanella"... "Toot, Toot, Toosie"... an' you got it, the very beat that ever was. The truly great ones. Euday Bowman. (Got a big fifty bucks for writin' "Twelfth Street Rag.") Kenny Martin. (Who says you can't play with a skinful of booze?) Wingy Mangnone. (Baby, you play more trumpet with one arm than the top men with two.) Blue Steele . . .

You go into "Beale Street," all of you, you go right there to Beale an' the street's just like it used to be. All the sights an' sounds an' smells, with everyone fat an' sassy an' busy, or actin' busy 'cause young Boss Crump, he don't like no easy riders (*Easy Ridin' Man*), Mr. Crump. An' when one of them long, limber gals rolls her hips at you, why you just vamp till you find the beat, an' then you move in real lowdown, diggin' the sugar out of the bottom of the cup, an' when you got it all you just steps right up an' pops the question, "Is You Is, or Is You Ain't My Baby?"

Figures moved out of the smoky, stinking, stinging fog which passed for air in the place. Slowly, they clustered around the piano player. A senselessly grinning Ape. A perpetually, silently cackling Witch. A horned Devil, with a tail draped over his shoulder. A chalk-faced, scarlet-mouthed vampire.

Demons, monsters, goblins . . .

They gathered around the piano player, arms fraternally draped around one another's shoulders, swaying and beating time to the sound of the music. And he, the piano player, looked up, looked around him and began to scream.

The scream was all but inaudible. A muted, gasping burble; the counterpart of the scream in a nightmare, the terrified shriek for help which no one ever hears. Staggering up from his bench, the piano player lunged through the hideous creatures, scattering them left and right; then, at a stumbling half-run, fled blindly into the rest room.

He braced his body against the door, trying to hold it shut. But something, someone, pressed firmly against it, and he heard a familiar voice; rather, he heard words that were familiar—soothing and explanatory—for the voice itself was strained of identity by its owner's disguise.

The piano player stepped away from the door. It opened, and God came in. No other than God, self-appointed. For it follows, as night follows day, that one who elects to kill assumes the role of Deity.

The Killer was a Skeleton tonight—a phosphorous-paint skeleton etched upon a black shroud. He took the piano player by the elbow, turned him around facing the wavery mirror of the rest room and pointed.

"Remember?" he said. "It's a very special party, a masquerade. There's nothing to be afraid of."

The piano player looked into the mirror. He saw a ridiculously dished-in mask of a face, with a bulbous nose. He saw the velvet cap, its belled peak crumpled to hang over his forehead. He looked down the length of his tight-fitting velvet costume to the cloth-covered slippers with their long pointed toes, tinily-belled and curling up at the ends.

The piano player slowly nodded, relieved. He said, "Ohhh," drawing the word out, letting God know that he understood. Then:

> For a cap and bells our lives we pay,
> Bubbles we buy with the whole soul's tasking.

"Very good," the Killer said approvingly. "Very good," and concluded the stanza:

> Heaven alone is given away,
> Only God may be had for the asking.

The piano player nodded again. "A Fool, naturally. What else would I be but a Fool?"

"Now, now," the Killer said. "It's a compliment. Fools are among our very finest people. Why, there is no place in the world today where great decisions are being made, where men are in trouble or conflict, where you won't find a Fool."

The piano player sighed blearily. Wearily, resigned. He mumbled that there was a time for sowing and a time for reaping; to take cash and let the credit go, nor heed the thunder of a distant drum.

"Now, that's better," the Killer said heartily. "Got your kit with you? Well, go ahead and shoot up, then. There's plenty of time. Our guest isn't arriving for well over an hour—almost an hour and a half."

The piano player's heart took a little jump. Fingers clumsy with eagerness, he started to reach inside his costume, to bring out the needle and the spoon with the hooked handle. Then, with a tremendous effort he made himself stop; looking silently at the Killer, hinting, lying to him with his hesitation. Or, perhaps, not lying in the larger sense. For no one actually ever has *enough;* he cannot have something that has never been defined. He may have less than enough and he may have more than enough, but he can never have enough.

The Killer took note of him. He decided it was time, the piano player's time, to have the never-defined enough.

"Go ahead," he urged quietly. "Go right ahead and shoot. I'll give you another cap to take after the party. Straight stuff. A fix like you never had before."

"W-well . . ." The piano player looked at him. After a time, he nodded slowly. "All right," he said. "All right."

He shot up. The Killer clapped him on the back and gave him the promised cap. The one that would finally be enough. Then he left the rest room, telling himself that it had had to be done. An imperfect machine had slipped past the Inspector, and its imperfection had grown to such dimensions that it was no longer safe to operate.

Destroy it? Oh, no. The Killer didn't kill; God didn't destroy. He simply decided that certain of his creations needed to be recalled to the Factory, there to be repaired, if in his opinion repairing rather than scrapping seemed indicated.

As for the Fool, the piano player, he was resigned to God's will. The desire and the will and all reason to resist it had gone out of him as the heroin had gone into him. He would at last have enough. That was enough.

"And the world so loved the god," he told the wavery mirror, "that it gave him its only son; and thereafter he was driven from the Garden. And Judas wept, saying, Yea, verily, I abominate onions, yet I can never leave them alone."

Eve tugged open the door of the place and stepped hesitantly inside. Then, as the incredible stench struck her like a blow—the thick smog of stale smoke and stale bodies and stale drinks—she almost fall back. Held herself where she was only by a tremendous exertion of willpower.

She stood blinking, trying to penetrate the stinking and clouded dimness. Gradually, her eyes accustomed themselves to the dimness, and she was able to see a little. And that little brought a gasp of horror to her lips. Why it looked like . . . *like Hell!* A madman's concept of Hell!

She, Eve Whitfield, had come off a twisting San Francisco street and stepped into Hell.

She couldn't see what she was looking for, the rear table with a magazine lying open on it and a cigarette tray sitting on top of the magazine. The smog was too thick; there were too many monstrously masked and garbed figures in the way. Staggering and swaying in lunatic simulation of a dance.

Gingerly, she started to make her way through them toward the rear. Cringing a little as they brushed against her. Then, an apelike figure suddenly grabbed her and drew her close to him, grinning into her face as he violently jigged her up and down. She jerked away from him, taking a half-stumbling step backward. She bumped into a Devil, and he, the Devil, twirled her around with drunken gracefulness and brought her face to face with a Frog. The Frog grasped her other wrist. Dipping and swaying, dragging Eve up and down with him, they began to dance.

A dance like no other had ever been. A quadrille, a waltz, a tango, rock'n'roll—everything and nothing. A dance to fit the preposterous music of the piano.

There was beauty in the music, or more accurately, the memory of beauty, now as lost as a lost love; something that lay buried in an unknown dimension like the final decimal of pi. Now, as though avenging itself upon an evil and uncaring world, it had sprouted into hideousness—a seed gone mad. And its terrible blossoms of sound hinted at a greater terror to come. Here, said the music, was a taste of Armageddon. Here, the Ultima Thule. Here, the inevitable destination of a planet whose mass of six sextillion, four hundred and fifty quintillion short tons was turned into a slaughterhouse instead of a garden. Here, the fruit of neglect, that socially approved form of murder. Here, the basic lie in its final extension.

A whole *was* greater than the sum of its parts . . . or was there no Bomb, no minute amalgam of neutrons and protons? Add three billion to the planet's mass, and subtract kindness and caring, and you were left not with an unkindly, uncaring three billion, but death. So said the seed, the music, now sunk in the morass of a wilderness from which it had vainly cried out. There would be no refuge from the coming terror. No place to hide. No familiar thing to cling to. Something would become nothing, robbed of its intrinsic beauty and safety and all else. There would be only a smoking, steaming, blown-apart, crushed-together mishmash where brother was himself eaten by brother while eating brother, ad nauseum, ad infinitum. Even so:

> *"Deutschland Uber," "Mississippi Mud," "Internationale Funeral March," "Stars Fell on," "The Star-spangled," "Sheik of Araby," "I Left My Heart in," "Black Bottom," "Rhapsody in," "Saber Dance," "Spring Song," "At Sundown," "How You Gonna Keep 'Em," "Down on the Levee," "Boo-Hoo," "Mammy," "Fire Dance," "Over There," "Toot, Toot, Tootsie," "Goodbye, Forever" . . .*

A Witch with thick ankles motioned curtly to the Devil and the Frog. They released their grasp on Eve Whitfield, and the Witch took her by the arm, guided her through the crowd to a rear table with an opened magazine on it and an ashtray on top of the magazine.

Eve sank gratefully down at the table, nearly breathless, a little weak from her enforced dancing. The Witch sat down near her, informed her that the party she wished to see would be along shortly.

"Now, what'll you have to drink, dear?"

"Nothing," Eve said. "I don't care for a thing, thanks."

"Got to have something. House rule," the Witch said firmly. Then, leaning closer for confidential speech, "Know how y'feel, honey. Tell you what I always do in this place. Order somethin' that ain't dolled up, y'know? Somethin' clear that you can see through, like vodka an' soda."

"But I—"

"I'll have one with you, if you'll buy. About all I got these days is the habit."

"Oh, well, of course," said Eve, and she put money into the Witch's gloved hand.

The latter went away, returned shortly with the drinks. Eve stalled, fumbling with a cigarette, until the Witch had taken a long, thirsty drink. Then, she took a tiny sip of her own drink.

It seemed all right—chloral hydrate is colorless, tasteless, odorless. Eve told herself that it would have to be all right. As Belle Larabee, she represented money to the blackmailer. He would have no reason to harm her, at least until he had collected.

So, as the Witch greedily drained her glass, Eve took a long drink from hers. She needed one after what she had been through, and with the ordeal she had still to face.

The Witch mumbled a "Drink hearty," and arose from the table. She said she would just find Eve's party herself, see to it that he came to the table right away. Eve nodded her thanks, and the Witch disappeared in the crowd. But she did not immediately summon the Killer.

She meant to. More importantly, she had been ordered to by none other than the Skeleton, the Deity, himself.

But even as she hurried to obey that order, she collided with a rail-thin Demon. So she stopped to talk to him, to plead with him, for what was to be only a moment. But the Demon shook his head, shaking it more and more firmly the more urgently she pleaded. And the intended moment became a minute. Minutes.

In the weed-grown patio behind the place, the Killer paced back and forth, occasionally smacking one gloved fist into the palm of his other hand, occasionally swinging his arm in a gesture of emphasis, or snorting out a curt laugh of triumph as he scored in the debate within himself.

In the darkness, against the black background of the shroud, the phosphorous Skeleton moved eerily to and fro, every move exaggeratedly jerky, seeming to flop and fling itself about like a thing animated by a string.

Tonight was a very special night for the Killer. So special that he had worked himself into a fever pitch of excitement, at last crashing through the hard shell of reserve and inhibition in which he had always been contained. For tonight—the woman who was to die tonight was someone he knew. Knew as he had known no other woman. And his other victims had been strangers to him.

He knew them, naturally. He had watched them, studied them over a considerable period of time. Taking note of each of their transgressions, carefully keeping score on them, withholding his awful judgment until the score reached a certain total and they had proved themselves in need of recalling to the Factory. For he, the Killer, was a just and forbearing Deity.

They had not known him, but he had known them. Finally and regretfully (or so he told himself) weighing them on his scales and finding them wanting. Even as he had finally and regretfully (or so he told himself) been forced to do in the case of Belle Larabee, the woman he knew well and who knew him well.

Because he knew her, he had been more forbearing than with any of the others. Because she had exhausted his forbearance, willfully throwing away each new chance she was given, his ultimate attitude toward her was unusually severe. She had a good husband. (None of the other victims had been married.) So it was only just that she should suffer some of the torture he had suffered before she was struck down.

Hence, his deliberate delay in meeting her—a delay that would be a fearsome, worry-filled eternity for her. Thus, his demand for a sum that she could not possibly pay—something which had to be done, yet could not be, and must agonizingly tear her apart as her husband had been torn.

She would come tonight, of course, to beg. He, the Killer would take her back to one of his cabins and there tell her the price she was to pay. And the dope would be working on her by then, and while she could listen and understand, that would be all she could do. Only listen in paralyzed horror as he pronounced sentence and carried it out:

The loss of the loveliness that she had misused. The loss, insofar as possible, of everything that identified her as a woman. So that she would go to her deserved death as something so hideous that even the sharks would pause before—

The Skeleton jerked fantastically, as it made a sudden start. Part of the bones of its left arm disappeared, as the sleeve of the shroud was pulled up.

A watch glowed in the darkness. The Killer looked at it, grunted in dismayed surprise. Could he have been wrong? Would Belle Larabee fail to come and beg?

No—the Skeleton head moved in a firm negative. No, that couldn't be. He knew Belle too well, knew exactly how she would think and act. She would come, all right. In fact, she would have had to be here by now. And that being the case—

· The Killer yanked down his sleeve. Angrily, he strode across the patio, stepped through the rear door of the place. His table was obscured by a mass of masqueraders. But he saw the Witch and the rail-thin Demon. Almost at the same time, the Demon saw him and he interrupted the Witch's pleading with an urgent nudge—a hasty nod toward the rear door.

The Witch turned around, stood fear-frozen for a moment. Then, at a faltering but anxious pace, she hurried up to the Killer.

"Got her," she mumbled. "Fixed her good, just like you said."

"Did you?" said the Killer. "How long ago?"

"Well, I . . . not very long. Honest, not very long."

"What does that mean?" the Killer asked. "Ten minutes, fifteen, thirty?"

"N-not very long, h-honest. H-honest, n-not v-v-very—"

The Killer looked at her. His hand closed over her arm in a steely grip. "Come," he said coldly. "Come."

Pulling her along with him, he started toward his table, the masqueraders almost frantically falling back to make way for him. At last the were out of the throng, the Killer and the Witch, and into a relatively open space. And there they stopped short. The Witch looking fearfully up at the Killer. The Killer staring incredulously at Eve Whitfield.

This woman? Not the woman who was to die. What in the—

Never mind! *Never mind!* The Killer, the Deity, was just. Always, always just. In punishing the wicked he was —was he not?—protecting the righteous. Only with this knowledge, this rationalization, could he go about his self-appointed duties. Only thus—and only by permitting, admitting no error. For the hand of the Deity must always be sure, and an erring Deity is no Deity at all.

"You!" he told the Witch. "You get her out of here. *Now!*

"B-but—but—"

"Say that her party can't see her! Tell her anything! Just get her out!"

The Witch nodded numbly, but she didn't move. She was bewildered, terrified by something in his tone. Incapable of speech or movement.

"Didn't you hear me? If I have to—"

There was a soft thud, the clatter of shattering glass. The Killer's eyes swerved toward the table.

Eve had pitched forward in her chair. Her face half-turned toward him, her arms limply outspread, she lay crumpled across the smeared top of the table.

The Witch had found her voice at last. What was wrong she didn't know, but she knew the Killer, knew that he did not tolerate wrong. And mumbling incoherently, she pleaded for mercy. And almost sobbed with relief at the evidence of his forgiveness.

He wasn't sore at her, thank God. He couldn't be. For here in her hand was proof positive.

A small white disk. A precious cap, whose crystalline whiteness testified to its purity.

"Have it now," the Killer said gently. "You deserve it."

This World, Then the Fireworks

1-MINUS

I remember the night well. It was our fourth birthday, Carol's and mine. We'd had a small cake and a half-pint of ice cream with our dinner. Mom was putting us to bed when we heard the blast of the shotgun.

She stood staring down at us, her eyes getting wider, and then—I think she must have suspected Dad's highjinks—she tore out of the house and across the street. Carol and I got up and followed her.

We were pretty scared. We paused on our front porch, wondering if we dared proceed further in our nightclothes. Then, we heard a second blast and what sounded like a scream from Mom, and we were too scared to stay where we were.

It was early summer. The air was balmy, sweet with the smell of newly budded trees, and the horizon still glowed with the golden pastels of the late-setting sun. We crossed the street, hand in hand, walking in great beauty.

We crossed the lawn of the other house, the grass kissing and caressing our bare feet. We went up the steps and peered through the open door.

Mom had caught part of the second blast as she burst into the house. She wasn't seriously injured, merely branded for life. We didn't know she'd been injured at all, despite the spurting pinpricks on her face. So meager was our knowledge of life, of good and bad; and Mom was laughing so loudly.

She screamed, yelled with laughter, spraying the blood that trickled down into her mouth. Carol and I gripped hands tightly, and slowly stared at one another. We were twins, as I've indicated, and our resemblance was indeed strong at that age. We not only looked alike, but our thoughts were very nearly identical.

So we stared at each other. And as my eyes misted doubtfully, so did hers. And her lips trembled as mine trembled. And as she—I laughed—

We burst into laughter simultaneously. It was so funny, you see. It was funnier even than Charlie Chaplin in the movies, or Krazy Kat in the funny papers.

The man on the floor didn't have any head, hardly any head at all. And that was funny, wasn't it? And it was funny the way Mom was laughing, spraying out pink stuff and making shiny red bubbles with her mouth. But the funniest thing, what we laughed loudest about, was Dad and the woman. The woman who was the wife of the man without any head. The wife of the man Dad had killed to keep from getting killed.

Dad and the woman. Dad who went to the electric chair, and the woman who committed suicide. Standing there naked.

We laughed and laughed, Carol and I. We were still laughing occasionally—shrieking and screaming—weeks later. It was so funny. It seemed so funny, I remember.

And I remember the night well.

1

Most of the city lay below the railway station.

My taxi took me down through the business section, sparkling and scrubbed-looking at this early hour, and on down a wide palm-bordered hill overlooking the ocean. Carol and Mom's house did not front on the water, as the best homes did, but it was still very nice, considering. After all, Mom had no income, and Carol's alimony was a mere two hundred and fifty a month.

My cab fare came to ninety-five cents. I had a total of two dollars. I would have had much more, but at the last moment I'd literally turned out my pockets to Ellen. It had to be done, I felt, her folks being the type they were. They wouldn't bar their doors to her, of course. But they doubtless would be very difficult—extraordinarily so—if she and the two kids could not pay a good share of their upkeep.

I can't understand people like that, can you? I mean, people who would extend adult conflict into the defenseless world of children. I don't condemn them, mind you; everyone is as he is for sound reasons, because circumstance has so formed him. Still, I cannot understand such people, and they make me a little ill at my stomach.

I gave the cab driver my two dollars. I started up the walk to the house, broke but happier than I had been in years. It did not matter about being broke—Carol, dear child, had usually been very expert at obtaining money, and she was obviously in good form now. Anyway, broke or not, money or not, it didn't and wouldn't matter. We were together again. After three long years, the longest we had ever been separated, Carol and I were at last together. And nothing else seemed to matter.

Mom had heard the cab arrive and was waiting at the door for me. She drew me inside, smiling with strained warmth, murmuring banal words of welcome.

I set down my suitcases and returned the kiss she'd given me. She stepped back and stared up into my face. Gazed at me with a kind of awed wonder, wonder that was at once worried and unwillingly proud.

"I just can't believe it, Marty." She shook her head. "You're even handsomer than you used to be."

"Oh, now," I laughed. "You'll make me blush, Mom."

"You and Carol. You get better-looking all the time. You never seem to grow a day older."

I said that she didn't look a bit older either, but of course she did. I had the impression, in fact, that she had aged about ten years since I stepped through the door of the house. There was a haunted, sickish look in her eyes. The only brightness in the sallow flesh of her face were the bluish pocks of that long-ago shotgun blast.

I remember how she got those pocks. I remember it well. It was our fourth birthday, Carol's and mine, and—

"Where's Carol?" I asked. "Where's that red-headed sis of mine?"

"You eat your breakfast," Mom said. "I have it all ready."

"She's still in bed?" I said. "Which is her room?"

"Come and eat your breakfast, Marty, I know you must be tired and hungry, and—"

"Mom. MOM!" I said.

Her eyes wavered nervously. She sighed and turned away toward the kitchen. "At the head of the stairs, next to the bath. And Marty . . ."

"Yes?"—I was already at the stairs.

"You and Carol—you won't get into any trouble this time?"

"Get into trouble?" I said. "Why, that's pretty unfair, Mom. When were we ever in any trouble?"

"Please, Marty. I j-just—I don't think I can take any more. Get yourself a job right away, son. You can do it. There's three newspapers here in town, and with your talent and experience and looks—"

"Now, Mom," I laughed. "You're making me blush again."

"Bring your family out right away. Set up your own household. I know how hard it must be on you to be around someone like Ellen, but you did marry her—"

"Better stop right there. Right there," I said.

"You'll do it, won't you? You won't stay here a bit longer than you have to?"

"Why, Mom," I said. "I know you don't mean it that way, but you almost sound as though I wasn't welcome."

I looked at her sorrowfully, with genuine sorrow. For it is rather sad, you know, when one's own mother fears and even dislikes him. It was almost unbearable, and I say this as one who has done a great deal of bearing.

"This saddens me, Mom," I said. "I quote you from Section B, Commandment One-minus: If thy son be birthed with teeth in his tail, kick him not thereon. For this is but injury upon injury, and thou may loseth a foot."

A faint flush tinged her sallowness. She turned abruptly and entered the kitchen.

I went up the stairs.

I eased open the door to Carol's room, tiptoed across the floor and sat down on the edge of her bed.

2

We are only fraternal twins, fortunately, since it would be a shame if she were as big as I. As it is, she is approximately a foot shorter—five feet to my six—and about eighty pounds lighter; and our physical similarities are largely a matter of coloring, skin texture, bone structure and contour.

I looked at her silently, thinking that I could look forever and never tire.

I am confident that she was awake. But knowing how much I like to see her awaken, she played 'possum for two or three minutes. Then, at last, she slowly opened her eyes —my eyes—revealing their startling blueness to me.

And her lips curled softly, revealing the perfect white teeth.

"Mr. Martin Lakewood," she said.

"Mrs. Carol Lakewood Wharton," I said.

"Sister," we said. "You wonderful, darling redhead!"

"Brother!"

And for the next few minutes we had no time nor breath for talk.

Finally, I got her robe for her and accompanied her into the bathroom. I sat on the edge of the tub while she washed and primped before the mirror.

"Darling—Marty." She touched a lipstick to her mouth. "How did that—uh—matter turn out in Chicago? I know you couldn't write me about it, and I was a little worried."

I didn't answer her immediately; I was only vaguely conscious of hearing the question. I was looking at her, you see, and now, so soon after our reunion, it was difficult to look at her and think of anything else.

"Mmm, darling?" she said. "You know the matter I mean. It was right afterwards that Mom went on her rampage, and dragged me out here."

I blinked and came out of my trance. I said that certainly I remembered. "Well, that worked out pretty well, darling. The cops had a guy on ice for a couple of other mur-matters. He was indubitably guilty of them, understand? So they braced him that one, and he obligingly confessed."

"Oh, how sweet of him! But of course, he had nothing to lose, did he?"

"Well, he was really a very nice guy," I said. "It's hard to repay a favor like that, but I did the little that I could. Always took him cigarettes or some little gift whenever I interviewed him for the paper."

She turned her head for a moment, gave me a fondly tender smile. "That's like you, Marty! You always were so thoughtful."

"It was nothing," I said. "I was only glad that I could make his last days a little happier."

Mom called up the stairway to us. Carol kicked the door shut and picked up her eyebrow pencil.

"Goddamn her, anyway," she murmured. "I'll go down and slap the hell out of her in a minute. Well, I will, Marty! I'll—"

"I'm sorry," I laughed. "I'm not laughing at you, darling. It's just that it always seems so incongruous to me, the things you say and the way you look. Such words from such a tiny sweet-faced doll!"

I had reason to know that her words, her threats, were not idle ones. But still I was amused. She laughed with me, good sport that she was, but it was patently an effort.

"I guess I'm losing my sense of humor," she sighed. "I don't like to complain, but honestly, I never saw such a town! Things have really been very difficult, Marty. I can't remember when I've seen a hundred-dollar bill."

"Oh? I thought it was supposed to be quite a lively place."

"Well, it may be. It may be just my luck."

"It'll change now," I said. "Things will be a lot better from now on."

"I'm sure they will be. I certainly hope so. I think if I go to bed with one more sailor I'll start saluting. Well"—she finished her primping and turned around facing me. "Now, what about you, darling? What was this little, uh, misunderstanding you were involved in?"

I said it was nothing at all, really. More a problem of semantics than ethics. The paper called it blackmail and extortion. I considered it a personally profitable public service.

"Uh-huh. But just what did you do, Marty?"

"Well, I was on the city hall beat, you know, and I had the good fortune to feret out some smelly figurative bodies and to identify the office-holders responsible for them . . ." I took out my cigarettes and lighted two for us. I dragged the smoke in deeply, exhaled and went on. "Now, the paper's attitude was that I should have reported the story, but I couldn't see it that way. I couldn't and I still can't, Carol."

"Mmm-hmm. Yes, darling?"

"It would have simply meant the ousting of one bunch of crooks and the election of another. They'd either be crooked, the second bunch, or too stupid to be; incompetents, in other words. So . . . so I did the best possible thing, as I saw it. I made a deal with a friend of mine, an insurance salesman, and he had some confidential talks with the malefactors in question. They all bought nice policies. They seemed to feel pretty much as I did—that they were paying a just penalty for their malfeasance, and that I was no more than justly rewarded for a civic duty."

Carol laughed delightedly. "But how did you happen to get caught, Marty? You're always so clever about these things."

How? Why? I wasn't sure of the answer to that question. Or perhaps, rather, I was more sure than I cared to be . . . I'd wanted to be caught? I'd subconsciously brought about my own downfall? I was tired, fed up, sick of the whole mess and life in general?

I wasn't conscious of feeling that way. I didn't want to believe that I did. For if I did, then I and, inevitably, she were lost. Time was already in the process of taking care of us. Of course, if we could accept the truth, see the danger and completely alter our way of life—But how could we? We would have to, but how? Where the compromise between the imperative and the impossible?

On either side, the possible truth showed the same hideous face. It could neither be accepted nor denied, and so I did neither. At any rate, I did my incoherent best to warn Carol, to put her on guard, without alarming her.

"That question," I said. "I'm a little wary of it, baby. I may have simply bungled or had some bad luck. Or it may have been another way. I could give you an explanation, and it would be completely believable. And it might even be true. But whether it actually was or not . . ." I shook my head, tossed my cigarette butt into the toilet. "As I say, I'm a little afraid of this one. It's too basic, the implications are too grave. At some point, you know—at *some* point— you'd better look squarely at the truth or look square away from it. You can't risk rationalizations. There is the danger that the rationalization may become the truth to you, and when you have arrived at this certain point—"

I broke off abruptly. It had struck me with startling suddenness that this might be that certain point and this, the words I was speaking, a rationalization.

I sat stunned, unseeing, my eyes turned inward. For a terrifying moment, I raced myself about a swiftly narrowing circle. Faster and faster and—and never fast enough.

And then Carol was down on her knees in front of me. Hugging my knees. Her voice at once hate-filled and loving, her face an angel's and a fiend's.

"Shall I kill her, darling? Would you like sister to kill her?" The words were blurred together, smeared with tenderness and fury. "I don't mind. Brother would always do anything for sister, always, anything, so s-sister will j-just—"

"What?" I said. "What?"

"She was mean to you, wasn't she? She got you upset, and—a-and I'll kill her for you, Marty! She deserves to die, the old scar-faced hag! I ought to have killed her long ago, and now—"

"Don't!" I said. "DON'T CAROL!"

"B-but, darling she—"

"It's too basic, understand? We can't think of such things. We can't use words like deserve and ought."

"Well . . ." The glaze went out of her eyes, and for a few seconds there was no expression in them at all. They were merely empty blue pools, blue and white pools. Blue emptiness and empty crystalline whiteness.

Then, I smiled, and instantly she smiled. We laughed, uncomfortably . . . And lightly.

"Now, didn't I sound silly!" she said. "I don't know what got into me."

"Forget it," I said. "Just put it out of your mind."

I boosted her to her feet, and she helped me to mine. We went down to breakfast.

3

I was prepared for Mom to be discomfiting, but she was not particularly so. Not nearly to the extent, at least, that she was capable of. I suspect that she was still a little cowed by Carol's outburst. Moreover, so soon after my arrival, she was unwilling—I might say, unable—to toss her weight around. To be annoying, a mild nuisance, was all the prosaic instincts would permit.

She was sure, she said, that Ellen and the kids would love this city. As for herself, an older person, she was beginning to feel that it might not be very healthy. It was too damp, you know, but for Ellen and the kids . . .

Did Ellen's folks still feel as they had? she said. Did they feel they had been unconscionably imposed upon, and were Ellen and the kids made to feel the brunt of their attitude?

She said—well, that is about all she said. Her most annoying remarks.

I said virtually nothing, being busy with my breakfast.

Carol and I left the house soon after breakfast. We walked toward town a few blocks, then sat down on a bench in a small wayside park. Carol was very much concerned about the children. She was concerned for Ellen, too, of course—she and Ellen have always been fond of each other. But Ellen was an adult. She was able to absorb things that children could not and should not.

"Do you remember that time at Uncle Andrew's house, Marty? Uncle Frank had put us out because everyone in town was talking about us, and . . ."

I remembered. Uncle Andrew's three big boys had dragged Carol behind the barn, and when I took a club to them—I'd gotten the life half-beaten out of me. By Uncle Andrew, with Mom helplessly looking on. I'd lied, you see. It was the boys' word against Carol's and mine, and our word was worthless.

"I remember," I laughed, "but you know how we look on those things, Carol. They were normal, just what they should have been, broadly speaking. We weren't discriminated against, mistreated. What we endured was simply the norm; for us, for those particular times and situations."

"Yes, I know. But—but—"

But there could be no buts about this. You may be wrong, and exist comfortably in a world of righteousness. But you may not be right and live in a world of error, the kind of world we had once *seemed* to live in. It is impossible. Believe me, it is. The growing weight of injustice becomes impossible to bear.

"The norm is constantly changing," I said. "It is different with every person, every time, every situation. One person's advantage may be the disadvantage of another, but the position of both is always normal."

"Uh-huh. Of course, Marty," said Carol. "But, anyway..."

She took a roll of bills from her purse and thumbed through them rapidly. She pulled off a few of them for herself, probably a total of forty dollars, and pressed the others into my hand.

"You take this, Marty. I insist, now, darling! Keep what you need—I imagine you're broke, aren't you—and send the rest to Ellen. Wire it to her so she'll get it right away."

I counted the money. I looked up from it suddenly, with deliberate suddenness, and I saw something in her face I didn't like. I couldn't analyze the expression, say why it troubled me. And that in itself was alarming. We were so much alike, you know, we thought so much alike, that it was as though my brain and body had separated and I had lost contact with my own thoughts.

"You said things had been tough," I said. "But there's more than three hundred dollars here . . ."

"So?" She laughed nervously. "Three hundred dollars is *money?*"

"Your alimony would just about pay your rent," I went on slowly. "And you said Mom's doctor bills ran very high. So with your other living expenses, your clothes, groceries, household bills, personal expense—"

She laughed again, laying one of her beautifully delicate hands on my knee. "Marty! Stop making like an auditor, will you? I've never heard such a fuss over a little bit of money."

"It's not a little bit, under the circumstances. It's around four hundred dollars with what you've kept. What's the answer, Carol?"

"Well . . ." She hesitated. "Well, you see, Marty, I was—I was saving this for something. I've saved it a few dollars at a time, and I knew that if you knew I needed—wanted—it for myself, you wouldn't want to—"

"Oh," I said, and I could feel my face clearing. "What was it you wanted, baby?"

"A—a mink. A cape stole. But I don't have to have it, darling. Anyway, now that you're here, we'll be rolling in money pretty soon."

I shoved the bills into my pocket. I hated to deprive her of anything, but since it was only temporary and not of vital importance . . .

She didn't have the clothes, the accessories, she'd used to have. I'd noticed that in glancing around her room that morning. She had sufficient to be very smartly turned out, mind you, but it was little by her standards. She had no jewelry at all. Even her wedding ring was gone—pawned, I supposed.

"Well, darling?" She smiled at me, her head cocked on one side. "Are you satisfied, now?"

I nodded. I had no reason to be anything else. Only a vague feeling of disquiet.

"Satisfied," I said.

We walked into town. It was a quiet walk, being largely uphill. But we had had so little time together, and the walking gave us a chance to talk.

As I had imagined was the case, knowing her independent nature, she was carrying on on her own. The local vice syndicate was a laughable outfit. They had no real stand-in with the police, and their hoods were spineless oafs. Once, shortly after she had come here, they had tried to take Carol in tow, but they had left her strictly alone since then.

"Two of them came to the house, Marty. I gave them

some money, and then I fixed them both a nice big drink. And can you imagine, darling?—they gulped it down like lambs. I do believe they'd never heard of chloral hydrate! Well, fortunately, I had a car at the time, so . . ."

So when the stupes had awakened, they were out in the middle of the desert, sans clothes and everything else they owned. It was almost a week before the highway patrol found them. One of them died a few months later, and the other had to be committed to an insane asylum.

"That's my sister," I murmured. "That's my sweet little sis . . . Mom didn't know about the deal?"

"We-el, she didn't *know.* She was out somewhere that evening. But you know her. She always seemed to sort of feel it when—when something's happened, and she was fussing around, nagging at me, for days. It was simply terrible, Marty! I almost went out and got a job just to shut her up."

"A *job?*" I said. "She wnted you to tke a *job?*"

"Isn't it incredible?" Carol shook her head. "But what about you, Marty? You won't let her hound you into going to work, will you?"

I said that I wouldn't let anyone force me to do anything: my norm period for being forced had expired. Still, I probably would go to work. For a while, and when the notion struck me. A job could be amusing and often very useful.

"I suppose," Carol nodded. "I guess it wouldn't hurt to work a *little* bit." She gave my hand a squeeze, smiled up at me sunnily. "I'll have to leave you here, darling. Have a nice day, and be sure to wire the money to Ellen."

She started toward the entrance of a swank cocktail lounge, her principal base of operations. Then, she paused and turned around again.

"Send a telegram with it too, will you, Marty? To the kids. Tell them Aunt Carol loves them more and more every day, and she wants them to be real good for their mother."

4

I went to work the following day on the first paper I applied to. I had no difficulty about it. Not since I was a child—and a very small child—have I had any difficulty in getting work. It would be very strange if I did. Personably and in intelligence, I am a generous cut above average; I must admit to this, immodest as it seems. Also, and when I choose to, I can be exceedingly irritating. Then, there is my experience in job-getting—my childhood training by earnest teachers. One gets work readily when the penalty for failure is a clubbing. Well-clubbed—a minor fracture or so always helps—he learns not to take no for an answer.

Carol did not get this valuable training. Being sorely undernourished and frequently raped, she had little energy and time for other endeavors.

However, as I was saying . . .

It was the best and biggest paper in town, which is not to say, of course, that it was either very good or very big. Most of the staffers were fair, about average, I suppose. They had been getting by nicely until I came along. Then, well, there I was, a *real* newspaper man, a towering beacon of ability. And by comparison, these average people looked like submoronic dolts.

The publisher no longer made his face to shine upon them. He griped at everyone—except me. No one—except me—could do anything to suit him.

Whenever I've cared to, when I've had an amusing objective in mind, I've always advanced in my work. But I set an all-time record on that paper. I was assistant city editor at the end of that week. Two weeks later, I was made city editor. And at the end of the month—Correction. It was the beginning of my fifth week . . .

By this time, the city room was in a mess. All the

staffers were jumpy—almost to the point of total incompetence. The news editor had resigned. The copy-desk chief had reverted to acloholism. The Newspaper Guild was raising hell. The—Well, as I say, it was a mess. Exactly the situation I had wanted. If it wasn't straightened out fast, the paper would be on the skids.

Now, the managing editor *was* a pretty good man. So much so that given a little time, and even with me around, he could have righted things. But the publisher was in no mood to give him time. The m.e. was a bum, he declared —in so many words. He was at the root of all the trouble, he would have to go. And his replacement should be you-know-who.

I held the job for two days, just long enough to make sure that the previous incumbent had left town. Then, I resigned. Needless to say, the publisher was shocked silly.

I couldn't do it! he sputtered. I simply couldn't do it! And when I pointed out that I had just done it, he virtually went down on his knees to me . . . Why was I doing it? he pleaded. What did I want from him?

I told him I already had what I wanted, and I was doing it because he was a wicked old man. He had violated Commandment One-minus, the commandment that had never been written, since even a god-damned fool could be expected to know it.

"Yea, verily," I said. "It is the pointed moral of all happening from the beginning of creation; to wit: Take not advantage of thy neighbor with his pants down, for to each man there comes this season and in my house there are many mansions, and in the mansions are many bastards longer-donged than thyself."

He didn't argue with me any more. He was afraid to, I imagine, believing me insane and himself in actual physical danger.

I collected my pay from the cashier and walked out.

It was now around three in the afternoon—my normal quitting time, since most of the work on afternoon papers is done in the morning. I had a couple drinks in a nearby bar. Then, feeling rather at loose ends, I wandered on down the street to the public square.

It was in the approximate center of the business district, a departure and arrival point for most of the city's bus lines. I found an unoccupied bench near the psuedo-Moorish fountain and sat down. Letting my mind wander comfortably. Pleased with myself. A little amazed, as I sometimes am, that I could have risen so relatively high.

I had almost no formal education, no more than a few months of grammar school. I had learned to read from the newspapers—from the newspapers I had hustled. And squeezing past this first barricade, leaping over it, rather, I had raced up the casually tortuous trail of the newspapers. Street sales. Wholesale street. Circulation slugger. Copy boy. Cub reporter . . . The newspapers were grade school, high school and college. They were broad education, practically applied. And they never asked but one question, they were interested in only one thing. Could you do your job? I always could. I always had to.

Now, rather for some years past, I no longer had to. My norm for having to had expired; I had expired it, if you forgive the verb. And for the future, the present—

I was quite pleased with myself. At the same time, the abrupt cessation of intense activity left me with a hanging-in-the-air-feeling—restless and mildly ill at ease. And while what I had done was entirely logical and fitting, I was afraid I might have acted a trifle selfishly.

Carol wouldn't think so, of course. She would appreciate the joke as much as I. But still, her luck was running very bad—there was still no prize chump in the offing, no one like that character in Chicago. And since she'd insisted on sending most of my salary to Ellen—

Well, what the hell? I thought. We were bound to get a break before long. She'd latch onto some well-heeled boob, set him up where I could safely get at him, and that would be the end of him, and the end of our financial troubles.

I yawned and leaned back against the bench. Then, I sat up again; casually, oh so very casually, but very much alert. I got up, went down the flagstoned pathway and stopped squarely in the middle of the sidewalk.

She smacked right into me. She'd been trying to look at me and not look at me for the past ten minutes, so we piled right together.

I had to catch her by the shoulders to keep her from going over backwards. I continued to hold onto her, smiling down into her face.

It was what you might call a well-organized face, one that would have been pretty except for its primness and the severity of her brushed-back, skinned-back hairdo. Not that I place any emphasis on prettiness, understand. My wife Ellen is the ugliest woman I have ever seen.

She, this one, wore glasses, a white blouse and a blue suit and hat. The blouse was nicely top-heavy, and the suit was curved in a way its maker had never intended.

"Well," I said, "if it isn't Alice Blueclothes! Boo, pretty Alice."

She was trying to look stern, but she just wasn't up to it. Under my hands, I could feel her flesh trembling. I could feel it burn.

"L-Let—let go of me!" she gasped. "I'm warning you, Mister, let go of me, instantly—"

"Not 'instantly'" I said. "Marty. You're thinking about my brother, Alice. He has pretty red hair, too."

"You l-let—I'll fix you!—"

"But, Alice," I said. "We haven't had our waltz yet—or would you rather make it a square dance? I'm sure these smiling bystanders would be glad to join in."

She tore herself free. Red-faced, acutely conscious of the aforesaid bystanders, she thrust a hand into her purse, came out with a leather-backed badge.

"P-Police officer," she said. "You're under arrest!"

5

I went along willingly, as the saying is. I had been sure from the beginning that she was a cop. She had a firm grip on my arm as we left the square, a grip strong with fury. But it rapidly grew weaker and weaker, and as we turned into a side street she let go entirely. She stopped. I stopped. I glanced at the plain black car at the curb, noted the absence of official insignia.

"All right, Mister," she said, trying to look very stern, to sound very harsh. "I should take you in, but I'm off duty and—"

"Is this your car, Alice?" I said. "It matches your shoes, doesn't it?"

"Shut up! If you don't behave yourself, p-promise to behave, I'll—"

"Yes, it's an exact match," I said. "It matches your hair too. Are you brunette all over, Alice, or just where it shows?"

Her face went white. White, then red again, about three shades redder than it had been. She turned away from me suddenly, jerked open the door of the car and literally stumbled inside. I slid into the seat with her.

"G-Go away," she whispered. "Please, go 'way. . ."

"I will," I said. "You say it like you mean it, and I will."

She hesitated. Then, she turned toward me, faced me, her chin thrust out. And her lips formed the words. But she did not speak them. I have played this same scene a hundred times, five hundred times, and never have I heard the words spoken.

Her eyes wavered helplessly. She looked down into her lap, shamefaced, her fingers twisting and untwisting the strap of her purse.

"W-We could . . ." She hesitated, went on in a barely audible whisper. "We c-could . . . go some place for a drink?"

"I wouldn't think of it!" I shook my head firmly. "I know something of your city, you see, and I know that cops in uniform may not drink."

"But—"

"I know something else, too. Local lady cops must be single; marriage is grounds for immediate dismissal. And one would also be dismissed, naturally—promptly—if her conduct were anything less than circumspect. She can't sleep around as other women might. A very small breath of scandal, and she'd be out. So—so what is our lady to do, anyway? What is she to do, say, if her womanly desires are somewhat stronger than normal ones, if she is highly sexed, loaded with equipment which screams for action? What—yes, dear? You'll have to speak a little louder."

She wasn't blushing any more. *Yet* is the word. I had to bend over to hear what she said.

"Well," I nodded, "that's fine. I'd like to go to your house. I always hate to take a woman to a hotel."

"No! I m-mean we could have dinner. We c-could talk. We—it's on the beach. We could swim, if you like and—"

I told her that of course, we could—and we would, if she still wanted to. We'd get right in bed first, and if she wasn't too tired afterwards . . .

I paused, looking at her inquiringly. I put a hand on the door latch.

"It's entirely up to you, dear. Don't consider me at all. I can walk a city block and pick up a half-dozen women."

"I k-know . . ." she muttered humbly. "I know you could. But—"

"Well?"

"I—*c-can't*! You'd think I was awful! It would be bad enough, if we were acquainted and—"

"Don't apologize." I swung the door open. "It's quite all right."

"Wait—C-could I call you somewhere? If-if I th-thought about it and decided t-to—"

"But suppose I decided not to?" I pointed out. "No, I think we'd better forget it."

"B-But—" She was almost crying. "I c-couldn't respect myself! You wouldn't respect me! You'd t-think I was terrible, and—Wait! *Wait!*"

I smiled at her. I got out and slammed the door and started up the street.

I really didn't care, you know. At least, I cared very little. She was a cop, of course, and it was a cop that Dad had killed. But I wasn't sure that I cared to do anything about that or her, to take care of that by taking care of her. I just didn't know. The situation seemed to offer possibilities, but I just didn't know. Whether I wanted to do anything about it and her. Whether there was anything suitable to do if I did want.

She called after me. She called louder, more desperately. I kept going.

I heard the car door open. Slam. She called once more. Then, she was silent, she was running after me, a fiercely silent animal racing after an escaping prey.

She caught up with me. Her fingers sank into my arm, half yanked me around. And her face was dead white now, even her lips were white. And her eyes were blazing.

"D-Don't you go 'way!" she panted. "Don't you dare go 'way! You come with me! Come right now, you hear? *N-Now!* Now now now NOW or I'll—"

"But you won't respect me," I said. "You'll think I'm terrible."

"You better! You j-just better! You don't, I'll—*I'll do it here!*"

. . . It was the latter part of February, but it can be warm there in February and it was this night. Not hot-warm, but cool-warm. Balmy. The kind of night when bedclothes are unnecessary and naked bodies warm each other comfortably.

I raised up on one elbow, reached across her to the ashtray. I held the cigarette over her a moment, letting its glow fall upon her body, moving the glow slowly downward from her breasts. Then, I crushed it out in the tray, and lay back down again.

"Very pretty," I said. "A very lovely bush. Not as extensive as my wife's, but then you don't have her area."

"Crazy!" She snuggled against me. "You and your four-hundred-pound wife!"

"She probably weighs more than that now. She gets bigger all the time, you know. Elephantiasis. It's not fat, but growth. I imagine her head alone weighs as much as you do."

"I'll bet!" she snickered. "I can see you marrying a wife like that!"

"But who else would have married her? And wasn't she entitled to marriage, to everything that could possibly be given her? It would have been better, of course, if she had been put to sleep at birth, as our first three children were—"

"Un-huh. Oh, sure!"

"It's done. What kinder thing can you do for three hopeless Mongoloids? One you might take care of, but three of them—triplets—"

"Mmmm-hmm?" She yawned drowsily. "And what's wrong with the other two, the two you have now? They don't have all their parts, I suppose?"

"Well," I said, "They're my children. So, no, I don't suppose they do. Something is certain to be missing . . ."

A balmy gust of wind puffed through the partially open window, swirling the curtains, sucking them back against the screen. They rustled there, scratchily, flattening themselves. Trying to push out into the moonlight. Then, they gave up limply, came creeping back over the sill. And slid down into the darkness.

I closed my eyes. I drew her into my arms and pulled her tightly against me.

She shivered. Her lips moved hungrily over my face, burning, pressing harder and harder. Whispering in ecstatic abandon. *"Marty . . . Oh Marty, Marty, Marty! Y-You—you know what I'm going to d-do to you?"*

I had a pretty good idea, but I didn't say. She probably thought it was something original—her own invention—and there was no point in playing the kill-sport.

What I said was that that was beside the point. "It isn't what you're going to do to me, lady. It's what I'm going to do to you."

6

It was very late when I reached home. Mom was asleep—the doctor had come and given her a sedative. Carol let me in the door and we swapped news briefly. Then, since both of us were tired and didn't want Mom waking up on us, we turned in.

I had trouble getting to sleep—I don't think I'd slept more than an hour or so when my alarm sounded off. But I got up anyway, promptly at seven. Mom didn't know I'd quit my job. The longer she could be kept in ignorance the better.

I left the house and had breakfast in a drugstore. Afterwards, I sauntered down to that little park I've mentioned and sat down to wait for Carol. We hadn't had a chance to talk much last night. She'd indicated that she had things to tell me, and I of course had things to tell her.

I yawned, blinking my eyes against the warm morning sunlight. I yawned again and put on my sunglasses. Thinking about last night, about my lady cop. Putting together the bits of personal data I'd been able to get out of her.

Her name was Archer, Lois Archer. She was about twenty-eight years old. (My guess—she hadn't told me.) She'd been with the police department for five years. She'd worked as a secretary for three years, then there'd been an opening on the force so she'd shifted over to that. The pay was considerably higher. The work had promised to be much more interesting. She'd detested the job almost from the beginning—she simply wasn't the cop type. But she'd felt that she had to stick with it. Good jobs, even reasonably good jobs, were hard to get out there. So many people came here for the climate and were willing to work for next-to-nothing to remain.

She had a brother overseas in the army. He and she owned the house jointly. She—well, that was about the size of things. The sum total of what I knew about her, and probably all it was important to know.

I saw Carol approaching. I stood up and waved to her. I'd been so busy that I'd hardly gotten a good look at her for weeks. And I noticed now that she seemed to have put on a little weight. It was hard to spot on anyone as small-boned as she; doubtless no one but I would have spotted it. I thought it made her even more attractive than she had been, and I told her so.

She laughed, making a face at me. "Now, that's a nice thing to say to a girl! You say that to your cop, and she'll probably pinch you."

"Well, turnabout," I shrugged, "Turnabout. I think she'll wish she could, incidentally, when she goes to sit down."

I filled her in on Lois, on the setup as a whole. I said that it looked quite promising.

"The house is on the outer outskirts of town; the nearest neighbor is blocks away. Of course, that's not all to the good. It would be worth a lot more if it was closer in."

"Uh-huh," Carol nodded. "But it's a nice place, you said, and it's on the waterfront."

"Yes. So, well, I'd say about fifteen thousand. That's at a forced sale—a fast sale—which naturally it would have to be. Now, this brother angle presents a bit of a problem. She'll have to get his okay, and I got the impression he might be a pretty tough customer. She seemed rather uncomfortable whenever she mentioned him. But . . ."

I paused, remembering the way she'd acted. After a moment, I went on again . . . She'd been uncomfortable, conscience-stricken, about the whole situation, hadn't she? Afraid I wouldn't respect her, that I'd think she was awful and so on.

"I think it can be worked out," I said. "Say the house is worth fifteen thousand at the outside. She cables him she has on offer for twenty, and he'll leap at it."

"Will it take very long, Marty?"

"I don't think so. She's already got the going-away notion—you know, just the two of us going off somewhere together. Possibly, probably I can swing it in a month."

"Oh," said Carol slowly. "Well, I suppose if"—she saw my expression, gave me a quick smile. "Now, don't you worry about me, darling. We'll get by all right. I'm a little behind on some of the bills, but my alimony is due next week and—well, something will turn up."

"I don't see how I can do it much faster," I said. "Not the main deal. But I might be able to promote a few hundred. Her brother is pretty certain to be half-owner of the car and furniture, but there's quite a bit of pawnable stuff around, hunting and fishing gear that belongs to him, and—"

I broke off. It wasn't a good idea. In reaching for a few hundred, I might blow the main chance.

Carol said I shouldn't do it. She studied my face searchingly, so intently that I wanted to look away.

"Marty . . . You like her, don't you?"

"I like everyone," I said. "Except, possibly, for one William Wharton the Third—your ex-husband, in case you've been able to forget."

"You know how I feel about Ellen, Marty, and it's not out of pity. When a person thinks you're wonderful, knowing just about everything there is to know—well, I just about have to feel as I do. But . . . but I've thought a lot about it, Marty, and I think sometimes you really did it for me. You couldn't do anything about my marriage, but you could make yourself as miserable as I was."

"I didn't do it for you," I said. "I would have done it for you, of course—that, or anything else. But I didn't. Don't you remember, Carol? I did what I said I was going to do, back when we were kids. What we both said we were going to do."

"I know, darling, but—"

"Someone that no one else wanted. Someone scorned and shamed and cast aside. Someone who had never known real love, or even simple kindness, and would never know unless we—"

Her hand closed over mine. She smiled at me mistily, winking back the tears in her sky-blue eyes.

I felt sick all over. I felt like my guts were being ripped out of me, and for a moment I wished they had been.

"Don't," I said. "For God's sake, don't cry, darling! I don't know how I could have been so stupid as to—"

"I-it's all right, Marty." She made the tears go away. "You didn't do it. I just happened to think of something, something that Mom said to me one night, and—"

"What! What was it?"

"Nothing. I mean, she didn't actually say it. She started to, and then she—she just shut up. Let's forget it, hmmm?" She patted my hand, cocking her head on one side. "I'm probably wrong about it. She probably didn't intend to say anything at all like I thought she did."

"Well," I said, "I don't know what she could say that she hasn't said already."

"She didn't. She really didn't say anything, darling. Lend me your handkerchief, will you?"

I gave it to her, and she blew her nose. She opened her purse, took out her compact and studied herself in the mirror.

"About afterwards, Marty. Will you have to dispose of her—Lois?"

"I don't know," I said. "I don't think I'd have to—I imagine she'd be too ashamed to squawk. But that still leaves the question of whether I should. It would seem kind of fitting, you know, something virtually required."

"Yes?" said Carol. "Well, perhaps. It seems that it would be, but on the other hand . . ." She shook her head thoughtfully, returning the compact to her purse. "Whatever you think, Marty, whatever you want. I just don't want you to feel you have to do it on my account."

"I won't," I promised. "For that matter . . . well. Skip it. I have a feeling that it should be done, that it must, but—"

"Yes?"

"I don't know," I said. "I just don't know."

7

We walked into town together, and I left her at the cocktail lounge. I had a light second breakfast and settled down in the public square. Except for a very vague sense of uneasiness, of something left undone, I felt quite happy. I had Carol; we were brought together again. I had Lois—at least, I would have her for a while. Life was back in balance, then, poised perfectly on the two essential kinds of love. And there was little more to be asked of it. There was much to be grateful for, to feel happy about.

I lolled back on my bench, basking in the sunlight. Warm inwardly and outwardly. Deciding that I should be able to send for the family in a few weeks. This would be a beautiful place for Ellen to die, I thought. And, of course, she was dying. I had been temporarily unable to go on watching the process—and I had felt that her folks should be forced to do so. But in a few weeks, as soon as my emotional resources were replenished, and theirs, if they had any, depleted . . .

I would give her a beautiful death. It would make up for many things.

As for the present . . .

I got up quickly and went out to the sidewalk.

The cocktail lounge was about a block away. Carol and a young navy officer had just emerged from it and started up the street. And a man who had been loitering near the entrance had followed them.

I ran across the intersection. I ran partway up the block, then slowed to a walk as they, and subsequently he, rounded the corner. I reached the corner myself and crossed to the other side of the street. I stood there, my back half-turned, ostensibly looking into a shop window.

They turned in at the entrance of one of those small, lobbyless hotels. He glanced up at its neon signs, consulting his watch and took out a notebook. He wrote in it briefly, looking again at his watch. Then, he returned it to his pocket and walked on down the street.

I followed him at a discreet distance.

Some four blocks away, he entered a small office building.

It was a shabby place, a diseases-of-men, rubber novelties, massage-parlor kind of building. At the foot of the steps, immediately inside the door, was a white-lettered office directory. It was divided into five sections, one for each story. Since the building was a walk-up, tenants became fewer and fewer after the second floor. And on the fifth there was only one.

He was all alone up there. J.Krutz, Private Investigations, "Divorce Cases a Specialty," was all alone.

I pulled my hat down low, readjusted my sunglasses and started up the steps.

There was a small lavatory, a chipped-enamel sink, in one corner of his office. He was bent over it, his back turned to the door, when I arrived, and I stood back from the threshold for a moment, giving him time to dry his hands and face. Then, I strode in brusquely, curtly introduced myself and sat down without waiting for an invitation.

He was a flabby-looking, owl-faced fellow. Obviously wounded by my manner—servilely hostile, if you know what I mean—he sat down across from me—at a scarred, untidy desk; memos to himself on a paper spike and an ashtray probably appropriated from a hotel overflowed with cigarette butts.

He was cert'n'ly glad, he said, to meet Mr. Wharton's West Coast representative. But wasn't we kind of rushing things? After all, he'd only been on the job four days; yessir, it was just four days since he'd got Mr. Wharton's wire from New York, and he'd already sent in two reports.

He paused, giving me a wounded look.

I ripped out a handsome curse.

"That Wharton"—I shook my head. "Always driving someone. Always trying to put on the squeeze. Why, he gave me the impression you'd been on the case for weeks!"

"Well," he hesitated cautiously. "I'm not criticizing, y'understand. But . . ."

"You should," I said firmly. "You have every right to, Mr. Krutz. Doubtless he can't help it, I bear him not the slightest ill-will, but the man is a bastard. This case itself is proof of the fact."

"Well . . ." He hesitated again. Then he leaned forward eagerly, an oily grin on his owl's face. "Ain't it the truth?" he said. "Yessir, you really got something there, Mr. Allen. I know all about the case, even if there wasn't much of it got on the papers. Why, the guy was just as lowdown as they get—washed-up, worn-out punk, pimping for a living. He was nothin', know what I mean, ten times lower than nothing. So somehow this swell little dish decides to marry him—I never will be able to figure that one out— and she starts getting him back on his feet. There's nothing he's any good at, so she supports 'em both. What time she ain't knocking herself out on the job, she's working to build him up. Nursing him, waiting on him hand and foot, actually making somethin' out of nothing, y'know, and she does so good at it that his family decides to take him back. Then . . ."

Then he'd given her a big fat dose of syphilis and divorced her for having it. She was very young, then. She was too dazed to fight. Probably she didn't care to fight.

"I see you know all the facts, Mr. Krutz," I said. "You're thoroughly grounded in the case."

"Sure. That's my business, know what I mean? . . . What's the matter with the guy, Mr. Allen? I'm tickled to have the job naturally, but why does he want it done? How can he do a thing like this just to save himself a few bucks?"

"I wonder," I said. "How can you do it to make yourself a few bucks?"

"Me? Well, uh"—he laughed uncertainly. "I mean, what the hell, anyway? That's my job. If I didn't do it, someone else would. I—Say ain't I seen you somewhere be—"

"Would they do it?" I said. "How can you be sure they would, Mr. Krutz? Have you ever thought about the potentials in a crusade for not doing the things that someone else would do if you didn't?"

"Say n-now," he stammered. "Now, l-looky here, Mister—"

"I'm afraid you have sinned," I said. "You have violated Section A of Commandment One-minus. Yea, verily, Krutz—"

"Now, l-looky. Y-you—you—" He stood shakily. "You c-can't blame me f-for—"

"Yea, verily, sayeth the Lord Lakewood, better the blind man who pisseth through a window than the knowing servant who raises it for him."

I smiled and thrust out my hand. He took it automatically.

I jerked him forward—and down. He came down hard on his desk, on its sharp steel paper spike. It went through his open mouth and poked out the back of his head.

I left.

It just about had to be done that way, to look like an accident. But still I was not at all pleased with myself. It was too simple, a stingy complement to the complex process of birth, and there is already far too much of such studied and stupid simplicity in life. Catchword simplicity —"wisdom." Idiot ideology. Drop-a-bomb-on-Moscow, the poor-are-terribly-happy thinking. Men are forced to live with this nonsense, this simplicity, and they should have something better in death.

That is and was my feeling, at least, and Carol shared it.

"The poor man," she said. "I wish I could have had him in bed with me. They're always so happy that way."

She did not, of course, receive her alimony check.

8

I went to work the following week and quit at the end of it. Although I felt uncomfortable in doing so, I sent most of the money to Ellen at Carol's insistence. Mom was very cross that night, the eve of my resignation. She had learned, meanwhile, of my quitting the first job. And this seemed to be a little more than she could take.

"You just don't want to amount to anything!" she said furiously. "Neither of you do—you do your best not to! Well, all I have to say is . . ."

We were eating dinner at the time. Carol had been eating very little, and now she was beginning to look ill. I held up my hand, cutting off all that Mom had to say, which was obviously interminable.

"Before you go any further," I said. "Before you say anything more, perhaps you should establish your qualifications for saying it."

"What—how do you mean?"

"I don't know how to make it any plainer. Not without being much more pointed than I care to."

She didn't understand for a moment; she was too absorbed in her tirade against us. Then, she understood, and her face sagged and her eyes went sick. Mouth working, she stared down dully at her plate.

"I . . . I couldn't help it," she mumbled. "I—I did the best I could."

I said I was sure of it. Carol and I didn't blame her at all. "Now, why don't we finish our dinners and forget all about it?"

"I—I don't feel like eating." She pushed back her plate and stood up. "I think I'd better lie—" She staggered.

I jumped up and caught her by the arm, and Carol and I helped her up the stairs to bed. We fixed her some of the sleeping potion. She drank it down, looked up at us from her pillow; eyes dragging shut, face a crumpled, blue-dotted parchment.

"Just don't," she whispered. "Just don't do anything else."

And she fell asleep.

I was seeing Lois that night. Carol was also going out, having had poor luck that day; and she stood at the curb with me for a few minutes, while I waited for Lois to come by.

"Now, don't you worry about me, Marty," she smiled. "I feel fine, and—and, well, after all, it's really the only way we can do anything very profitable."

"I know," I said. "But . . ." But it *was* the only way. If she was to pick up, or rather be picked up by, a prize chump, there could be no witnesses to the act. It must be done unobserved, and night offered the least chance of observation.

"Well. Don't wear yourself out," I said. "It's not necessary. I should be able to swing this other matter very soon."

"Don't you wear *yourself* out," she said. "Don't do anything at all, if you don't want to."

I promised I wouldn't. I added that I still hadn't decided what Lois' final disposition should be.

"It's an odd thing," I said, "but I have a feeling that it isn't necessary for me to decide. The fitting thing will be done, but I will have nothing to do with it."

Carol left as Lois drove up. We rode out to her house, and she was pouting and peevish throughout the trip. She just didn't see *why*, she kept exclaiming. My sister had money. She just had to have, the way she dressed and living in that big house—and everything! So why—

"She'd die if she didn't live that way," I said. "She lived too long another way."

"Oh, stop talking nonsense! Tell me why, Marty. Just tell me why I should be expected to give up everything when you could just as well ask that fine sister of yours to—"

We had stopped in front of her house, in the driveway, rather. I turned suddenly and slapped her across the mouth.

Her eyes flashed. Her hand lashed out in instant, angry reaction—then stopped, just short of my jaw.

"Well?" I said. "Well, Lois, my peevish bluecoat?"

She bit her lip helplessly, trying to smile, to pass it off as a joke.

"Well, how about *this?*" I said, and I swung my hand again—I kept swinging it. "And this and this and—"

"P-please, Marty!" She tried to cover her face. "It'll s-show—I have to work, and—"

"All right," I said. "All right, my inky-haired incontinent, my sloe-eyed slut, my copulating cop. How about this?"

I caught my hand into the front of her blouse, her brassiere. I yanked, and her naked breasts bloomed out through the torn cloth. And . . . and she flung herself forward, crushing them against me.

"H-harder, dearest! Oh, Marty, I—I—"

"I'm trying to do you a favor," I said. "I love you, Lois, and I'm trying to—"

"D-don't talk darling. J-just—Marty! Where are you going?"

"Home," I said. "I'm walking up to the highway and catching a cab."

"*No!* D-don't you dare! You just t-try to, and—"

I did try to, after certain preliminaries. But I didn't make it. Got as far as the highway, three blocks; then I gave up and went back. Carrying her in my arms. Carrying her as I'd left her in the car. With every stitch of her clothes ripped off.

9

I stayed there that night. The next morning she phoned in to the department, reported herself sick and was given the day off. So I kept on staying.

It was a pretty wild day, a sweetly wild day. A perfect commingling of sweetness and wildness. We had breakfast. We took a bath together. We had a half-dozen drinks.

Then, we stripped every damned picture in the house from the walls, dug up a couple of her brother's rifles and lugged the lot down to the beach.

They were the most hideous kind of crap, those pictures. Cute stuff—dime-store junk. Pictures of kewpie-doll babies with their pants falling off and dogs smoking pipes and cats rolling a ball of yarn. Her brother liked such junk, it seemed; he also liked to have his own way. So we carried it down to the beach, and we blasted it to pieces. Taking turns at it. One of us tossing an item into the air for the other to shoot at.

It was noon by that time. We went back to the house, ate and drank some more and took another bath. We rested, dozed in each other's arms. We got up and went on another romp.

Her brother belonged to some half-assed lodge—one of those dress-up outfits. She got out his uniform hat, pulled the plumes off of it and made herself into a peacock.

She was a very lovely peacock. She crawled around on the floor, wiggling her bottom and making the plumes sway. I crawled around after her, snapping at them, barking and yipping like a dog. I caught up with her. We rolled around on the floor, locked together, working up static electricity from the carpet. We rolled into the living room —laughing, yelling and jerking with jolts of electricity. We knocked over the tables and chairs and lamps, making a mess of the place. And then I grabbed a bottle of whiskey and we rolled back into the bedroom and under the bed.

We came out finally. We took our third bath, washing away the dirt and lint and climbed into bed again. It was night. The balmy, cool-warm breeze of the night was drifting through the window. My back was to it, and she was afraid I might catch cold. She bent over me, shaking out her soft, black, waist-length hair; she tucked it over and under my shoulders, her face pressed tightly to my chest, drawing herself against me with her hair. And we wrapped together.

We had said nothing about money all day; we were

afraid of spoiling that sweet wildness. We were afraid of spoiling this now, this gentle sweetness, so we still did not speak of money. We ignored that chasm and placed ourselves in the wonderland beyond, the green pastures of accomplished fact.

"Huh-uh, Marty . . . " she murmured. "I don't want you on any old newspapers. I want us to be all alone, away off somewhere by ourselves."

"Well, let's see then," I said. "We might run a dairy. None of this mechanized stuff, mind you. I would operate it by hand, and you, my lamb, or I should say—"

"Now, Marty!" she snickered. "That's dirty."

"Well, I could write my book," I said, "my treatise on taxation. 'Cornucopia of Constipation, or the Martin Lakewood Bowel Movement Single Tax.'"

"Crazy! You—*ha, ha*—you crazy sweet thing!"

"I would do away with all taxes on food and other necessities," I said, "and the only levy would be on bowel movements. It's really a very sensible plan, Lois. The most just, most equitable plan ever invented. The less money a man has, the less he eats, the less are his taxes."

"Uh-hmmm, and suppose he didn't have any money at all. What would he do then?"

"What does he do now?" I said.

"Oh, Marty! *Ha, ha, ha* . . ."

"What's so funny about it?" I said. "If it's right to let a man starve then it's right it let him die of constipation. It's more right, goddammit! At least we give him a choice, a little control over his own destiny. We can deny him food, but we can't keep him from holding in his bowels. If he can hold in long enough—What's so funny? Goddammit, what are you laughing about?"

"Why, Marty!" She laughed nervously. "We're just talking, joking. There's nothing to be angry about."

"But"—I caught myself. "Yeah, sure," I said. "It's all a joke, and a pretty bad one; not even original. Just about the oldest joke there is."

We lay silent for a time. The curtains scratched restlessly

against the screen, and far in the distance somewhere there was the faint howling of a dog.

"Marty..." She pressed in on me at the hips. "Love me, Marty? Love me very much?"

"Yes," I said. "I'm afraid I do."

"More than anyone else?"

We had been on this line before. I imagine every man has, and has been as frustrated by it as I.

"Do you, Marty? Love me more than you do your sister?"

"I've told you," I said. "It's two different things; entirely different kinds of love. The two aren't comparable."

"But you have to love one of us more than the other. You *have* to, Marty."

I said that, goddammit, I didn't have to, and no one out of his infancy would say that I did. It was a milk-and-highball proposition. Both were satisfying, but each in its own way. "Take your brother, now. As a brother, you love him more than—"

"I do not! I only love you, and I love you more than anyone else in the world!"

"Well," I said helplessly. "Well—"

The phone rang. She murmured to let it go, and I let it go. And after the second ring it stopped.

It was Carol's signal. I waited tensely for her to call back, and Lois waited for something else. She nudged me again, pressed forward with her thighs. The phone rang.

I turned suddenly and grabbed for it. Lois let out with an angry "*Ouch!*" and sat up glaring at me, rubbing her scalp.

"What's the matter with you? You knew my hair was—"

"Please," I said. "Be quiet a minute!"

It was Carol. She spoke rapidly, her voice pitched just above a whisper.

"... understand, Marty? A hunting lodge ... take the left turn at the crossroad, and ..."

"Of course, I understand," I said. "I'll start right away, Carol. As soon as mother gets to feeling better, I can come back."

We hung up. I gave Lois a kiss and apologized for yanking her hair.

"I'll have to leave for a while now, baby. My mother's taken ill—nothing serious, but Carol thinks I ought to be there, and—"

"Oh, she does, huh?" She pushed me away from her. "Well, go on then, and call yourself a cab! You're not going to use my car to rush home to her!"

I started dressing. If I had to—and I was sure I wouldn't have to—I could get along without her car. It would take extra time; I'd have to go into town and rent one there. But I could do it.

"You and your darling Carol! I've seen the way you act around each other. You know what I think about you?"

"Something nasty, I'm sure," I said. "Something very naughty. Otherwise, you wouldn't be wearing that pretty blush."

She told me what she thought. Rather, she yelled it. And I laughed and kissed her again. Because she didn't actually think it, of course. She didn't mean it; it was meaningless. It was mere words, said not out of hate but love.

She was crying, apologizing, as soon as they were spoken.

"I'm s-sorry, darling. I just l-love you so much, and—"

"It's all right," I said. "I have to run now, baby."

I took the car, naturally. She insisted on it.

10

The lodge was about thirty miles up in the mountains, about a mile off the main mountain road. It was heavily wooded country up there. I shut off the car lights as soon as I left the road and weaved my way through the trees by moonlight. I drove very slowly, holding the motor to a quiet purr. After a few minutes of this creeping, I stopped and got out.

I was on the edge of a clearing. The lodge was about fifty yards. It was a low, log-and-frame structure with a lean-to at one end. Inside the lean-to was a black sports coupe.

I glanced up at the sky, watched the moon drift behind a mass of clouds. In the brief darkness, as it vanished from view, I raced stooping across the clearing. I stopped in the sheltering alcove of the door, getting my wind back, reconstructing the interior of the place from the description Carol had given me.

This, immediately beyond the door, was the living room. The kitchen was straight on through. There was a bedroom on the right—of the living room, that is—and another at its left extreme. They were supposed to be in the one to the right.

Pressed gently down on the latch. I pushed against the door, ever so easily, and it moved silently open. I stepped inside.

A small lamp was burning on the fireplace mantel. I looked swiftly around the room, then crossed it and glanced into the kitchen. I couldn't see very well, but I could see enough. A wood stove with a row of implements above it. I lifted down one of them, a heavy meat cleaver, and reentered the living room.

It was an old place, and the floors were not what they had been. Several times, as I went toward the bedroom, there were dangerously loud squeaks. And just as I reached the door there was a *pop* like that of an exploding firecracker.

I stopped dead still in my tracks. Holding my breath. Listening.

There was no sound for a moment. Then, I heard the rattle of bedsprings, the rustle of bedclothes thrown back. The quiet but unmistakable sound of feet touching the floor. And crossing it.

I stepped to one side of the door. I raised the cleaver. I stood on tiptoe as the latch clicked softly, then clicked back into place. From the other side of the panels, there came a nervous whisper:

"M-Marty . . . ?"

"Carol!" I laughed out loud with relief. "Are you all right, darling?"

"Fine"—she didn't sound exactly fine. "He let me fix him a drink, and—well, it's all over, Marty. I'll be out as soon as I dress."

I wiped the cleaver off and returned it to the kitchen. I sat down on a cowhide-covered lounge, and after a few minutes she came out. She sat down next to me, running a comb through her thick red hair, touching up the make-up on her innocent child's face.

There'd be no trouble, she said. There was no danger of future trouble. The guy had picked her up on a dark street and they'd come directly to this place. Being unmarried and on a vacation, it might be days before inquiries were made about him.

"So it's all right—*that* part's all right." Carol smiled tiredly. "But look at this, Marty."

She opened her purse and handed it to me, a thick sheaf of bills with a rubber band around each end. I riffled it and silently handed it back. It was a Kansas City roll, big bills, a couple of fifties on the outside; the inside, little stuff, ones and fives and a few tens.

"Five hundred dollars. Just about five hundred." Carol looked down at it, her blue eyes dull and empty. "And Marty, he apologized for it. He gave it to me—afterwards, when it was already done and there was nothing I could . . ."

I shook my head silently. It hardly seemed the time for words. I did a little wiping up with my handkerchief and then we left.

She was sick once on the way back to town. I had to stop the car and let her out by the roadside. We drove on again, she huddling against me, shivering with the cold mountain air. I talked to her—to myself. I talked to both of us, and for both of us. And if it was rationalization, so be it. Perhaps the power to rationalize is the power to remain sane. Perhaps the insane are so because they cannot escape the truth.

We were culpable, I said, only to the degree that all life, all society, was culpable. We were no more than the pointed instruments of that life, activated symbols in an allegory whose authors were untold billions. And only they, acting in concert, could alter a line of its text. And the alterations could best be impelled by remaining what we were. Innocence outraged, the sacred defiled, the useful made useless. For in universal horror there could be universal hope, in ultimate bestiality the ultimate in beauty and good. The blind should be made to see—so it was written. *They should be made to see!* And, lo, the Lord World was an agonized god, and he looked not kindly upon the bandaging of his belly whilst his innards writhed with cancer.

"Yea, verily," I said. "If thy neighbor's ass pains him, do thou not divert him with bullshit, but rather kick him soundly thereon. Yea, even though it maketh him thine enemy. For it is better that he should howl for a doctor than to drown in dung."

We had reached the house. Carol sat up, blinking her eyes sleepily.

"Don't worry about the money," she said as she got out of the car. "It'll be a big help, more than I need, really."

I drove on out to Lois's house. I went inside just long enough to give her an ultimatum. She was to cable her brother immediately or at least the first thing in the morning. Otherwise, we were washed up.

She was too startled, too furious to speak for a moment. When she did it was to tell me to go to hell, that she would neither cable him in the morning nor any other time.

I got away fast—pleased, saddened. Glad that I had tried, but knowing that I had changed nothing. She was certain to relent. She had to. For she was a symbol also, one more character in the allegory of unalterable lines.

I don't know why I had been so long in identifying her

and seeing the part she had to play. Certainly, I should have seen it long before.

I got home and went quietly to bed. A few minutes later my bedroom door opened, and silently closed again. I sat up. I held out my hands in the darkness, and Carol found them, and I drew her down into the bed. I stroked her hair, whispered to her softly.

"Bad?" I said. "Is it bad, little sister?"

"B-bad . . ." She shuddered violently. "Oh, M-Marty, I keep—"

"Don't," I said. "Don't think, don't remember. It was the way it had to be. It was the best way, and you'll see that it was."

She shuddered again. And again. I drew her closer, whispering, and gradually the shaking subsided.

"It—the Things will go away in the morning, Marty? They'll go far away?"

"Yes. Just like they used to, remember? When day came, the night Things went away, and when night came the day Things went—"

"Y-yes," she said. "Yes! Tell me a story, Marty."

I hesitated. I had told her so many stories, and I was not sure of the kind she wanted.

"Well . . ." I said. "Well, once upon a time there were three billion bastards who lived in a jungle. They ate dirt, these bastards, of which there was more than enough for all. A total of six sextillion, four hundred and fifty quintillion short tons, to be exact. But being bastards, they were not content with—"

"Marty."

"Another one? A different kind?"

The other one, Marty. You know."

I knew. I remembered. How could I help but remember?

"Once upon a time," I said. "Once upon a time, there was a little boy and a little girl, and the little boy was her father and the little girl was his mother. They—"

The door banged open. The light went on.

Mom stood staring at us, her chest rising and falling. Her eyes gleaming with a kind of evil triumph.

I sat up. Carol and I both sat up. One of her breasts had slipped out of her nightgown, and I tucked it back inside.

"Yes, Mom?" I said. "I hope we didn't wake you up."

"I'll bet you do! I'll just bet you do!"

"But"—I frowned, puzzled. "Of course, I hope so. We tried to be as quiet as we could. Carol had a little trouble sleeping, so I was just—"

"I know what you were doing! The same thing you've been doing for years! Scum, filth—no wonder everyone hated you! They saw through you all right, you didn't fool them any. They should have beaten you to death, starved you to death, you r-rotten . . ."

She believed it. She had made herself believe it. It was justification; it excused everything, the moral cowardice, the silence in the face of wrong, the years of all-absorbing, blindly selfish self-pity. She had hoped for this—what she believed this was. Doubtless, she had hoped for it right from the beginning. That abysmal degradation had been her hope for her children. And who knew, who was to say, how much that hope had been expressed in our lives?

I wanted to say something, do something to comfort Carol. I could not.

I lay back down on the pillow and covered my face with my hands. Carol laid one of her hands over mine.

She spoke very quietly, but somehow her voice rose above the tirade.

"You made Marty cry," she said. "You made my brother cry."

"I'll—I'll do worse than that!" Mom panted. "I'll—"

"There is nothing worse than that. Go to your room."

"Now-now, see here," Mom faltered. "Don't you tell me to—"

"Go to your room."

There was silence, complete suspension of movement, for a moment. Then, Carol threw back the covers—I felt her throw them back. She climbed out of bed and pointed —I could see her pointing.

"N-no!" It was Mom, but it was not her voice. "NO, Carol! I'm sorry! I d-didn't mean it! I—"

"You meant it. I mean it. Go to your room."

"No! You can't! I'm your mother. Y-you—"

"Are you? Were you?"—she was moving away from the bed, and Mom was moving out of the door. Backing away as Carol advanced. "Go on. Go. You have to go to sleep."

"No!"

"Yes."

Their voices grew fainter and fainter. Then, right at the last, they rose again. Not strident but clear. A little tired but peaceful.

"That's right. Drink it all down. Now, you'll be a lot better."

"Thank you. Thank you, very much, Carol . . ."

11

Figuratively, at least, most people do die of oversedation; fumbling about fearfully, blindly, they grasp the sweet-smelling potions handed them with never a look at the label, and suddenly they are dead. They died "natural" deaths, then. As she died. At any rate, the doctor chose to call it natural—heart failure—and we could not, of course, dispute his word.

He, the doctor, left after a period of condoling with us. The undertaker came to supervise the removal of the body and remained to discuss funeral arrangements. He thought something very nice could be done for about twelve hundred dollars, something that our loved one would have loved. The price fell gradually, his falling with it, until he was down to the rock bottom of "adequacy" which bore a price tag of four hundred and fifty.

Carol paid him. The funeral was set for the following

afternoon. It was a little after he left us, with a barely pleasant good morning, that Lois called.

"I've just got one thing to say to you," she began. "If you think for one minute that you can—Marty! Marty, darling! What's the matter?"

I couldn't answer her. How did I know what the matter was? Carol took the phone out of my hand and talked to her.

They talked for several minutes, and I could hear her weeping as Carol hung up. An hour or so later, as Carol was getting ready to go to town, she called back. I still couldn't talk, so Carol took a message for me.

Would I please, please call her as soon as I could? She didn't want to disturb me, felling as I must, so—would I, please? It was important. It concerned something that I wanted.

I lay down. I hadn't felt at all sleepy, but I fell asleep instantly, and night had come when I awakened.

I called out to Carol. I got up and ran into her room, and there was a note pinned to her pillow:

> **Marty darling:**
> I storied to you about what I was going to do today. I knew you'd be worried, and there's really no need to because I'm going to be perfectly all right. I'll be with you as soon as I can, but I won't be able to be there for the funeral. Don't you go either, if it bothers you. And tell me a story tonight, darling. I'll be listening for it.

The signature was mixed up, jumbled. The initial letter was both *M* and *C* and the second letter was both *o* and *a*.

I fixed a bite of dinner. I shaved and started out to look for her, and then I remembered that this was tonight, so I came back. I went up to her room. I stretched out on her bed and took her into my arms. And I told her a story, I told it all through the night. She was so frightened. She was trembling and shaking constantly. So I talked on and on, on and on through the night, holding her tightly against me.

Day came, at last.

At last, she slipped quietly out of my arms.

At last, she was asleep.

I lay watching her for a time, selfishly hoping that she would awaken. Because I had always loved to watch that awakening, the coming to life of purity and beauty, reborn by night and as yet untarnished by day. I waited and watched, but she did not awaken. She did not come to life. And finally I fell asleep at her side.

When I awoke, she was gone. I was anxious about her, naturally—I wondered where she had gone. I sat for a long time wondering, about her and the others who went. Then it was almost time for the funeral, and I had to leave.

I went to the funeral, but I did not stay. I strolled away from the graveside and off toward the bus line, meandering casually through the hummocked greensward, the marble-and copper-bordered streets of The City of Wonderful People. It was a crowded city; neighbor elbowed against neighbor. Yet no one felt the need for more room. They dwelt peacefully side by side, content with what they had. No one needing more than what he had, nor wanting more than he needed. Because they were so wonderful, you see. They were all so wonderful.

There was Annie, for example, devoted wife of Samuel. And there was William, faithful husband of Nora. There was Henry, dutiful son, and Mabel, loving daughter, and Father and Mother, who were not only devoted, faithful, dutiful and loving, but God-fearing to boot. One had to look closely to see that they were all these things, their gravestones being only slightly larger than a cigarette package. But one always does have to look closely to see virtue, and as in this case, it is always worth the trouble.

Yes, hell. Yes, oh, God, yes it was a wonderful place, The City of Wonderful People. Everyone in it was everything that everyone should be. Some had a little more on the ball, of course, than others; there was one guy, for instance, who was only humble. But think of that! Think of its possiblilities! Think of what you could do with a guy like that on a world tour. Or if war prevented, as it indubitably would, you could put him on television. A nationwide hookup. You could go to the network and say, Look, I've got something different here. Something unique. I've got a guy that's—No, he doesn't do card tricks, he's not a singer or dancer. Well, he does have a sense of humor, but he doesn't tell—No, I'm afraid he doesn't have big tits, and his ass looks just like yours and mine. What he's got is something different. Something there's a hell of a need for. And if you'll just give him a chance . . .

They'd never go for it.

You'd have to nail him to a cross first.

Only here, only in the City of the Wonderful People, was the wonderful wonderful.

12

The phone was ringing. Ringing again or still.

I let it.

It would only be Lois, weeping and apologizing and commiserating with me. Telling me she'd sent the cable. Begging to see me. Telling me she quit her job, that she was giving up everything for me, so wouldn't I—couldn't I—come out for just a little while?

Yes, it would only be Lois. And, of course, I would go to see her—I had to. But it was not time yet. She had sent the cable to Japan four days ago. Even in a suspicious world, where days were hours and miles were feet, it was not yet time.

So I let the phone ring, even when it rang with that flat finality which phones assume when ringing for the last time. I did not want to talk. Carol would not want to talk. Carol was asleep and must not be disturbed, and—

It wasn't Lois calling. Lois was answering it. The front door was open, and she was speaking into the phone. Frowning, stammering, her face slowly turning gray. She mumbled something that sounded like, "J-just a minute, doctor"—which made no sense at all, naturally. She looked at me concernedly.

"Can you talk, Marty? It's some doctor down in Mexico. Just across the border. He says—it's about Carol, darling —h-he says that . . . Oh, Marty, I'm so s-sorry—he says th-that—"

I took the phone away from her. It couldn't be about Carol, but she was obviously in no condition to talk.

It was a poor connection, and his English was poor. I had to keep asking him to repeat things, and even then he was almost impossible to understand.

"You must be mistaken," I said. "Five months pregnant? What the hell kind of doctor would abort a five-month pregnancy?"

"But I do not know, señor. She tell me is barely three months, and it do not show mooch, you know. She is so small, an'—"

But he'd know, dammit. Any kind of doctor would. If he wasn't completely stupid, willing to run any risk to pick up a few dollars . . .

"I am so sorry señor. I do my ver' best. It is not mooch, perhaps—but for twenty-five dollars, what would you? Soch as I am, as leetle as I know, I—"

"Well, it doesn't matter," I said. "It's all a mistake. You've got the wrong party."

"No! Wait, señor!"

"Well?" I said.

"What should I do? What do you wish done? I am poor man, and you must know—"

"I'll tell you what I know," I said. "You're trying to work some kind of racket, and if you bother me again I'll sic the authorities on you."

"*Señor!* Please"—he was almost crying. "I mus'—you mus' do something! Almost four days it had been, an' the weather she is so hot, an'—What shall I do?"

I laughed. I imagined it must be a hell of a mess.

"What the hell do I care what you do?" I said. "Throw it in the ocean. Throw it on the garbage dump. Throw it out in the alley for the dogs to piss on."

"But she is—"

"Don't lie to me! I know where my sister is!"

I slammed up the phone.

Lois wet her lips. She came toward me hesitantly, wanting to protest, to take charge, to do what her essential primness and ingrained propriety demanded. She want to say, You'd better go, Marty. You must or I'll do it. But she did not say that; she could not say it, I suppose. Her instincts had not changed during these past few weeks, but she was no longer sure of them. She no longer relished and took pride in them. They were something to be scorned, ignored, pushed out of the path of desire.

"Let's go out to my house, Marty. You need to get away from here."

"I think so, too," I said. "It's about time that I did."

13

I needed to be diverted. I needed to forget. I needed to make merry. I did. She said I did. And who does not? So there was the sweet wildness again. Then, wildness without sweetness. Wilder and wilder wildness. Babel.

There was the lewd peacock, the weird, waggling, wiggling mutation of woman and bird. There was the breastless woman, the woman with three faces, with two bedaubed grinning faces for breasts. There was the serpent woman, the frog woman, the woman who was man. There was the man who looked like a dog, the man horse, the man who was woman, the man who was not man. There were the shrieks, the fierce grunts and growls, the howls and snarls, the clucking, groanings, whinings, barkings, yippings, moanings. There was the rolling and crawling, the laughter and the prayers, the talk in unknown tongues. There was Babel.

And there was peace.

And there was night, and I was wrapped in Circe's hair.

". . . don't think I'm awful, do you, Marty? He's just, well, nothing. And he doesn't want to be anything. Just a big, stupid, hateful boor. He's lucky I didn't do something like this long ago!"

"You should have," I said. "You should have split up with him and gone your own way."

"Sweet"—she brushed her lips against my face. "You do think I'm right, then, don't you, Marty? He deserves to lose every last penny he's got! Every penny he put into this place."

"Why didn't you split with him?" I asked. "Why didn't you get married? Of course, there was your job, the department's single-woman policy. But couldn't you have kept it a secret?"

She hesitated. Her body moved in a small shrug. "I suppose, but you know how it is. I guess I just got in a rut, and, well, I guess there wasn't any one I cared about marrying."

I reached over and lit a cigarette. We smoked it, taking turns, and I crushed it out in the ashtray. I turned a little on my side, looked out into the quiet night. It was early summer now. The air was sweet with the smell of budding trees, and the horizon still glowed with the golden pastels of the late-setting sun.

Lois laughed venomously; she could just see her brother, she said, when he received her cable. "He's always been so slow and stodgy, but I'll bet he moves fast for once. I told him I'd been offered thirty thousand dollars for the house."

I laughed with her. Thirty thousand dollars for *this* place! Yes, that would make him move all right.

"You don't think I'm awful, do you, Marty? About

everything, I mean. You don't think I'm cheap and trashy and—and—"

"I want to tell you something," I said. "I want to tell you about my dad."

"But what's he—No, huh-uh, Marty. Don't tell me any of those crazy stories about—"

"Well, we'll say it's just a story," I said. "It isn't true, we'll say, but just a story."

"Well"—she squirmed uncomfortably. "Oh, all right! I suppose, if you simply *have* to."

"I've often wondered about him, Lois. He wasn't any genius, but he had at least average good sense. He must have known that fooling around with another man's wife— and a cop's wife, at that—was certain to cost him a lot more than it was worth. It was a continuing relationship, you see. Not just a one-night stand. She wasn't that kind of woman, and he wouldn't have been interested in her if she had been that kind. So I kept asking myself, why did he do it? Why did he carry on an affair that could only end in one way? And why did she, a woman of excellent reputation, ostensibly a model of womanly virtue—"

"Marty." She put her fingers over my mouth. "Please don't. Let's just talk about us, mmm?"

"We will." I pushed her hand away. "The woman killed herself that night, the same night Dad killed her husband. She didn't live long enough to explain, and Dad never chose to. It wouldn't have helped him any, and there was no point in looking like a bigger fool than he did already. So . . . so, Lois, I was left with a riddle. One that's nagged me for an answer for almost thirty years. And yet the answer's been before me all the time. In people. In hypocrisy and deception and self-deception. In walling ourselves up in our own little worlds.

"There was the husband, for example, a real cold fish. He minded his own business—was sufficient unto himself. We were his neighbors, but only geographically. So far as social contact went, we might just as well have been on another planet . . . It was a bad attitude. Inevitably, as it always does, it got him killed."

"*K-killed!* . . . Marty, please don't talk any—"

"It was a factor, certainly. If he'd been a little more sociable, friendly, talkative . . . But let's leave him there, and take up his wife. She was what you call a nice woman, as I say. Very proper. At the same time, she resented her husband. She might have gone to work on him, talked things out with him, reformed him into a reasonable facsimile of the man she'd loved and married. But that would have been a lot of trouble, and she'd convinced herself that it wasn't worthwhile. It was easier to pick up another man —Dad. And there was a way she could do it and still cling to a few shreds of propriety. He was married, of course, and that was bad. But she could believe that it was his badness, rather than hers. If he thought, if he was willing to think that she—" I paused, stroking her hair gently. "Don't cry, Lois. It can't be changed. There are not enough tears for this sorrow."

"M-Marty! Oh, Marty, Marty! H-how you must hate me!"

She wept uncontrollably. The tears were hot against my chest, and her flesh was icy.

"I've never hated anyone," I said. "Never anyone."

The lawn was bright in the moonlight. Soon a little girl would come trudging across the grass, it seemed that I could see her coming now, and she would be frightened because she was alone. And then she would not be alone . . .

"I love you, Lois," I said. "We're going to go away together. We'll all go away together."

A cab stopped in front of the house.

A man in uniform got out.

And, of course, it wasn't her brother.

Sources and Dates

Prologue: A Road and a Memory, Prairie Schooner, 1930; also *Cap and Gown: A Collection of College Verse,* edited by R.L. Paget, Paget Publishing, 1931.

1. Exactly What Happened, Ellery Queen's Mystery Magazine, 1967.
2. The Threesome in Four-C, Alfred Hitchcock's Mystery Magazine, 1956.
3. The Dark Stair, Master Detective, 1946.
4. Forever After, Shock, 1960.
5. The Cellini Chalice, Alfred Hitchcock's Mystery Magazine, 1956.
6. The Frightening Frammis, Alfred Hitchcock's Mystery Magazine, 1957.
7. Pay as You Exit, unpublished.
8. The Flaw in the System, Ellery Queen's Mystery Magazine, 1956.
9. Sunrise at Midnight, unpublished.
10. "Hell" — chapters 20, 24, and 25 from *Ironside*, Popular Library, 1967.

11. This World, Then the Fireworks, previously published with editorial amendation by Max Allan Collins in JIM THOMPSON: THE KILLERS INSIDE HIM and THE BLACK LIZARD ANTHOLOGY OF CRIME FICTION. The version published here retains Thompson's original ending.

MORE MYSTERIOUS PLEASURES

ROBERT CAMPBELL
IN LA-LA LAND WE TRUST   #508 $3.95

RAYMOND CHANDLER
RAYMOND CHANDLER'S UNKNOWN THRILLER:
   THE SCREENPLAY OF "PLAYBACK"   #703 $9.95

GEORGE C. CHESBRO
The Veil Kendry suspense series
VEIL   #509 $3.95
JUNGLE OF STEEL AND STONE   #606 $3.95

EDWARD CLINE
FIRST PRIZE   #804 $4.95

K.C. CONSTANTINE
The Mario Balzic mystery series
JOEY'S CASE   #805 $4.50

MATTHEW HEALD COOPER
DOG EATS DOG   #607 $4.95

CARROLL JOHN DALY
THE ADVENTURES OF SATAN HALL   #704 $8.95
THE ADVENTURES OF RACE WILLIAMS #723 $9.95

NORBERT DAVIS
THE ADVENTURES OF MAX LATIN   #705 $8.95

MARK DAWIDZIAK
THE COLUMBO PHILE: A CASEBOOK   #726 $14.95

WILLIAM L. DeANDREA
The Cronus espionage series
SNARK   #510 $3.95
AZRAEL   #608 $4.50
The Matt Cobb mystery series
KILLED IN THE ACT   #511 $3.50
KILLED WITH A PASSION   #512 $3.50
KILLED ON THE ICE   #513 $3.50
KILLED IN PARADISE   #806 $3.95

LEN DEIGHTON
ONLY WHEN I LAUGH   #609 $4.95

AARON ELKINS
The Professor Gideon Oliver mystery series
OLD BONES   #610 $3.95

JAMES ELLROY
THE BLACK DAHLIA	#611	$4.95
THE BIG NOWHERE	#807	$4.95
SUICIDE HILL	#514	$4.50

PAUL ENGLEMAN
The Mark Renzler mystery series
CATCH A FALLEN ANGEL	#515	$3.50
MURDER-IN-LAW	#612	$3.95

LOREN D. ESTLEMAN
The Peter Macklin suspense series
ROSES ARE DEAD	#516	$3.95
ANY MAN'S DEATH	#517	$3.95

ANNE FINE
THE KILLJOY	#613	$3.95

DICK FRANCIS
THE SPORT OF QUEENS	#410	$4.95

JOHN GARDNER
THE GARDEN OF WEAPONS	#103	$4.50

BRIAN GARFIELD
DEATH WISH	#301	$3.95
DEATH SENTENCE	#302	$3.95
TRIPWIRE	#303	$3.95
FEAR IN A HANDFUL OF DUST	#304	$3.95

THOMAS GODFREY, ED.
MURDER FOR CHRISTMAS	#614	$3.95
MURDER FOR CHRISTMAS II	#615	$3.95

JOE GORES
COME MORNING	#518	$3.95

JOSEPH HANSEN
The Dave Brandstetter mystery series
EARLY GRAVES	#643	$3.95
OBEDIENCE	#809	$4.95

NAT HENTOFF
THE MAN FROM INTERNAL AFFAIRS	#409	$3.95

PATRICIA HIGHSMITH
THE ANIMAL-LOVER'S BOOK OF BEASTLY MURDER	#706	$8.95
LITTLE TALES OF MISOGYNY	#707	$8.95
SLOWLY, SLOWLY IN THE WIND	#708	$8.95
THE BLACK HOUSE	#724	$9.95

DOUG HORNIG
WATERMAN #616 $3.95
The Loren Swift mystery series
THE DARK SIDE #519 $3.95
DEEP DIVE #810 $4.50

JANE HORNING
THE MYSTERY LOVERS' BOOK
OF QUOTATIONS #709 $12.95

PETER ISRAEL
The Charles Camelot mystery series
I'LL CRY WHEN I KILL YOU #811 $3.95

P.D. JAMES/T.A. CRITCHLEY
THE MAUL AND THE PEAR TREE #520 $3.95

STUART M. KAMINSKY
The Toby Peters mystery series
HE DONE HER WRONG #105 $3.95
HIGH MIDNIGHT #106 $3.95
NEVER CROSS A VAMPIRE #107 $3.95
BULLET FOR A STAR #308 $3.95
THE FALA FACTOR #309 $3.95

JOSEPH KOENIG
FLOATER #521 $3.50

ELMORE LEONARD
THE HUNTED #401 $3.95
MR. MAJESTYK #402 $3.95
THE BIG BOUNCE #403 $3.95

ELSA LEWIN
I, ANNA #522 $3.50

PETER LOVESEY
ROUGH CIDER #617 $3.95
BUTCHERS AND OTHER STORIES OF CRIME #710 $9.95
BERTIE AND THE TINMAN #812 $3.95

JOHN LUTZ
SHADOWTOWN #813 $3.95

ARTHUR LYONS
SATAN WANTS YOU: THE CULT OF
DEVIL WORSHIP #814 $4.50
The Jacob Asch mystery series
FAST FADE #618 $3.95

BILL PRONZINI
GUN IN CHEEK   #714 $8.95
SON OF GUN IN CHEEK   #715 $9.95

BILL PRONZINI AND JOHN LUTZ
THE EYE   #408 $3.95

ROBERT J. RANDISI, ED.
THE EYES HAVE IT: THE FIRST PRIVATE EYE
   WRITERS OF AMERICA ANTHOLOGY   #716 $8.95
MEAN STREETS: THE SECOND PRIVATE EYE
   WRITERS OF AMERICA ANTHOLOGY   #717 $8.95
AN EYE FOR JUSTICE: THE THIRD PRIVATE EYE
   WRITERS OF AMERICA ANTHOLOGY   #729 $9.95

PATRICK RUELL
RED CHRISTMAS   #531 $3.50
DEATH TAKES THE LOW ROAD   #532 $3.50
DEATH OF A DORMOUSE   #636 $3.95

HANK SEARLS
THE ADVENTURES OF MIKE BLAIR   #718 $8.95

DELL SHANNON
The Lt. Luis Mendoza mystery series
CASE PENDING   #211 $3.95
THE ACE OF SPADES   #212 $3.95
EXTRA KILL   #213 $3.95
KNAVE OF HEARTS   #214 $3.95
DEATH OF A BUSYBODY   #315 $3.95
DOUBLE BLUFF   #316 $3.95
MARK OF MURDER   #417 $3.95
ROOT OF ALL EVIL   #418 $3.95

RALPH B. SIPPER, ED.
ROSS MACDONALD'S INWARD JOURNEY   #719 $8.95

JULIE SMITH
The Paul McDonald mystery series
TRUE-LIFE ADVENTURE   #407 $3.95
HUCKLEBERRY FIEND   #637 $3.95
The Rebecca Schwartz mystery series
TOURIST TRAP   #533 $3.95

ROSS H. SPENCER
THE MISSING BISHOP   #416 $3.50
MONASTERY NIGHTMARE   #534 $3.50

VINCENT STARRETT
THE PRIVATE LIFE OF SHERLOCK HOLMES   #720 $8.95

DAVID STOUT
CAROLINA SKELETONS — #829 $4.95

REX STOUT
UNDER THE ANDES — #419 $3.50

REMAR SUTTON
LONG LINES — #830 $3.95

JULIAN SYMONS
CONAN DOYLE: PORTRAIT OF AN ARTIST — #721 $9.95

ROSS THOMAS
CAST A YELLOW SHADOW — #535 $3.95
THE SINGAPORE WINK — #536 $3.95
THE FOOLS IN TOWN ARE
   ON OUR SIDE — #537 $3.95
CHINAMAN'S CHANCE — #638 $4.50
THE EIGHTH DWARF — #639 $4.50
OUT ON THE RIM — #640 $4.95

JIM THOMPSON
THE KILL-OFF — #538 $3.95
THE NOTHING MAN — #641 $3.95
BAD BOY — #642 $3.95
ROUGHNECK — #643 $3.95
THE GOLDEN GIZMO — #831 $3.95
THE RIP-OFF — #832 $3.95
FIREWORKS: THE LOST WRITINGS — #833 $4.50

COLIN WATSON
SNOBBERY WITH VIOLENCE: CRIME
   STORIES AND THEIR AUDIENCES — #722 $8.95

DONALD E. WESTLAKE
THE BUSY BODY — #541 $3.95
THE SPY IN THE OINTMENT — #542 $3.95
GOD SAVE THE MARK — #543 $3.95
DANCING AZTECS — #834 $4.95
TWO MUCH! — #835 $4.95
HELP I AM BEING HELD PRISONER — #836 $4.50
TRUST ME ON THIS — #837 $4.50
The Dortmunder caper series
THE HOT ROCK — #539 $3.95
BANK SHOT — #540 $3.95
JIMMY THE KID — #838 $3.95
NOBODY'S PERFECT — #839 $3.95